MW00775263

A SEASON OF LIGHT

ALSO BY JULIE IROMUANYA

Mr. and Mrs. Doctor

A SEASON OF LIGHT

A NOVEL

JULIE IROMUANYA

ALGONQUIN BOOKS
OF CHAPEL HILL 2025

Published by
ALGONQUIN BOOKS OF CHAPEL HILL
an imprint of Little, Brown and Company
a division of Hachette Book Group, Inc.
1290 Avenue of the Americas
New York, NY 10104

Printed in the United States of America.

Design by Steve Godwin.

ISBN 9781643755519

For all
who have lived
in the house of War

A SEASON OF LIGHT

I

ONE

FIDELIS

Everyone in Econlockhatchee always said Mr. Kostyk was a little cracked. When the Ewerikes arrived, everyone said the same about Fidelis Ewerike. One night 276 schoolgirls were taken from the Government Girls Secondary School in the town of Chibok in Borno State, Nigeria, and he was never the same again. Even in America, far from his homeland, his dreams became a menace. In daylight, he could be less afraid. To prove it, he would playact merriment—shrill laughter, song, dance—at such a frenzied pitch that there was a thrill in senility; by night he would walk.

Like all men, he had been taught that girls are trouble. For some, trouble leads to desire. And so, in a way, he did not quite blame the men for the attack. He blamed the girls, but not for their beauty or innocence or their just-budded breasts. In the photographs, he looked past their uniformity—their youth, the dusk and navy cloths draped from head to toe—and into their faces. Each night as he walked, it was the complicated stillness of these nameless girls' expressions that haunted him.

Looking at them looking at him—in the photograph, on the television, on the websites, and, at last, in his nightmares—was like his past, his present, and his future had aligned, and here he was caught unawares in its flush light. When she had first seen the girls in the news, his wife, Adaobi, had wept, pulling their daughter, Amarachi, into her embrace; his son, Chukwudiegwu, had only sighed. Fidelis walked.

He did not feel pity, not exactly, not even empathy, for the schoolgirls; instead, there was something useless and angry inside him that urged him to pluck them from a part of the world that he had once, long ago, called home, and place them within his protection. He did not yet know that one can confuse protection with possession.

Perhaps it was all for his sister, Ugochi—she, a child, having slipped from his grasp, when he, a boy, was off doing man things. War belonged to men, but he had been just a child then. Wasn't it a privilege, in a way, to arm and flatter boys instead of men, speak of the great feats their might could achieve—boys with their hardy and infinite innocence? Now he was only a man of holes. He had grown old overnight.

Fidelis hardly remembered Ugochi's face, hadn't looked at her photo in many years, but after the kidnapping of the Chibok girls, suddenly, he was in the attic, in a panic, pulling down that box, and looking at her photo every moment of every day. Rather than seeing her face, he began to see his daughter, Amarachi, just her age—no, just their age, the Chibok schoolgirls, just their shade of brown, just her shade of brown, with that damned burdened expression.

Despite her aversion to him and her teenage affection for her mother as of late, he had always found Amarachi wholesome, complete, even endearing. No, she did not adore him, but then for a man whose first child had been born after forty, to desire such a thing would only be vanity.

On the whole, he had always found his daughter competent and unobjectionable. She talked back, but only under her breath and mostly when his back was turned; she kept high marks, in the subjects that mattered; she was modest, but not too modest as to be misused; she was also content, but not so easily contented as to be duped. She was tender, not so brash as other girls. Nor would she be bullied or bent. But, he cautioned himself, she was inflexible. When pushed or pulled, something so unyielding was bound to break. Girls like her were not so durable. Look at his Ugochi. She had been a wild, unbridled thing. And look where that had gotten her. What would the world do with a daughter broken to pieces?

And then one day, not long after the Chibok girls were taken, through the sliver in the bathroom door, he spied Amarachi applying her mother's lipstick. Suddenly, she, with that red smear of a mouth, became so alien and nonsensical to him that he hated her. His hate was so whole, so consuming, that it could only be equaled by his shame. What he understood, perhaps only by instinct, was that she was no longer his.

So, he crushed the lipstick in his fist. He cut holes into her leggings and miniskirts, poured bleach on her spaghetti strap camisoles. He threw her cell phone out of the window, and he put a lock on her bedroom door.

Later that day, when Amarachi's mother returned home from work, in bewilderment, she struggled to pry the lock free. On one side, the daughter wailed and pounded at the door, calling out to her mother, begging her to liberate her from her jail. On the other side, the mother boxed her husband until, exhausted, she collapsed into a deep yet fitful slumber; he, like a madman, slumped next to her, his chest tight, breath ragged, having plunged into a dream.

TWO

ADAOBI

Agatha Adaobi Ewerike had spent the night in an uneasy dream.

A forest of mahogany timbers had enclosed her, and above, a canopy of leaves so impressive that one could not perceive the turn of the stars. Only rain, a slight touch, percolated the seams of the shade. And she, a child, so reckless, having wandered far from her mother's watch, wailed until, spent, she groaned.

Every fairy tale begins with a maiden whose beauty cannot be paralleled, who is then joined by a warrior of immensity and wisdom. But in Adaobi's dream, a comely warrior led her deep into the forest only to desert her. And when her wits had failed her, it was a maiden of infinite might and extraordinary perception who found her.

The maiden promised to return Adaobi to her mother, but she did not have room on her back, so she opened her womb and cleared her insides, creating a deep, dark cellar that smelled of earth. Adaobi climbed comfortably inside. But then she dropped, soundlessly, as if in an enormous sack.

A kick, and then another.

Of a sudden, Adaobi understood her fate. She, like the girls before her, had been stolen.

Had her strange dream of stolen girls been prophetic? Would her future and her family's be stolen, as theirs had? Adaobi could accept the facts of her family's present condition, but she could not abide its permanence. Since the kidnapping of the Chibok schoolgirls, her husband had undergone a swift decline until he was asked to take an indefinite leave from the firm, and they had been forced to relocate from their comfortable Winter Park residence to this hell. Econlockhatchee was an almost-town named for the "Rivers of Mounds." It was the season of fires. All spring, control fires had blurred the wilting sweet gum and cyprus trees dotting the central Florida preserves, and now ash filled the air with a gray blush. Termite-eaten HUD houses, trailers, and the Calumet Row housing development populated the hamlet, where marathon domino games were played on dimly lit porch stoops, clouded by the smoke of Black & Milds, and late-night basketball games on rimless backboards soundtracked their melody.

Every family has its secrets. Adaobi's was that her husband was going mad. Fidelis had barred their daughter in her bedroom under his watchful eye. There was the excuse of war, a defense that she had leaned on for so many years, she almost believed it. But she had known him long before war, when he was just a schoolboy whose junior sister, Adaobi's house daughter at her school, had introduced them, acting as Cupid by surreptitiously slipping Fidelis's adoring poetry into Adaobi's schoolbooks only for him to stubbornly deny his intentions when cornered. He had always exhibited a strangeness that, in the eyes of a lovelorn young woman, felt like desire, a something oft mistaken for that mercurial temper of select men, of depthless vision and largesse—exemplified as he filled her pockets with a bounty of persimmons and nectarines from his well-tended garden—followed by interludes of cruel aloofness.

From afar, the mechanics of madness can be indistinguishable from sanity—they share a symmetry. Upon closer inspection, the telltale signs of lunacy emerge. In Fidelis, the patterns were conclusive. He believed that if his sister, Ugochi, could be stolen, could disappear into thin air, then the same fate could befall his daughter. Never mind that this was America, not Nigeria. Never mind that the year was 2014, not 1969. Never mind that he was a man in his sixties, not sixteen. Never mind that the offenders weren't enemy combatants or even aid workers, rather, they were terrorists, thugs. After retrieving his daughter and declaring that she would be barred in her room for all eternity, he abruptly returned to composed normalcy. He sipped his coffee and invited Adaobi to take tea at midday. He scanned the headlines of the morning paper, groaning and whistling at the state of the world.

He resumed his work, reviewing contracts, revising the language, sewing up financial agreements. Piles of papers—neatly arranged into quarterly reports, mergers and acquisitions, and a table of disputes—surrounded him. With his head bent under the arc of lamplight in concentration, a monocle at his eye, issuing the occasional mutter, he seemed rather studious and unassuming, except for the fact of his situation: a sturdy yet rotting tabletop, a flimsy patio chair, and a rusted desk lamp from the attic now formed a makeshift study in the narrow corridor outside of Amara's bedroom.

He hadn't addressed his battle with his wife the other night. He didn't acknowledge that their daughter remained alone behind her bedroom door. Instead, he dragged out his old Hewlett-Packard, a jumble of wires snaking down the hall to an outlet. He knelt so close to the speakers that the tip of his nose just barely grazed the screen of the chunky monitor. His body arced as each word trembled in the air. Of late, he had taken to listening to the Radio Biafra revivalist network. Snatches of a rambling voice raved across the flimsy connection:

"I want to speak and take the opportunity to talk about what is happening in Biafraland," a man's voice bellowed through the static. "They are going against the will of God. God Almighty has made it so that Biafra will be in this region and the Northerners will be in their region."

Since the abduction of the schoolgirls, Fidelis had developed a renewed interest in the sovereignty of the Biafran nation. His nights of wandering began as he recalled the brutal 1966 campaign against Igbos living in the northern region. Thousands had died, among them his cheerful uncle Charles, whose body, riddled with bullet wounds, had only been discovered when one escapee of the pogrom described its location to Fidelis's father. If such miscreants could kidnap schoolgirls in the north, what was to stop them from brutalizing Igbos? Fidelis had contacted a man from FOB—Fathers of Biafra—an assemblage of aged veterans who planned to one day lead a battalion to the capitol and demand the emancipation of Biafra. Now he sat listening to a man raving on the Internet.

What was this but a ploy to do it all over, to be the sixteen-year-old boy called up to fight for a cause on its last leg, the year he had been stripped from Adaobi's embrace. Imagining the Fathers of Biafra, Adaobi shuddered. They were only an assembly of balding and overweight men in their sixties hobbling toward liberation on canes in a clumsy formation. How could her aging husband lead any battalion? He, with his potbelly, his dusty files filling shelves and drawers; he, with his particular tastes: three cubes of sugar, two tablespoons of evaporated milk, and one teaspoon of cinnamon to flavor his tea.

That night had passed under a cloud. But now surely, they could put away this nonsense. By the time Adaobi had finished dressing for work, Fidelis had been at it for what seemed hours, slouched in front of old, yellowed newspapers, urgent voices booming from the computer speakers. Adaobi approached him, looking in his face for those precious signs of lucidity. Surely this charade would end, and like any other morning, Adaobi could drop the children at school on her way to work. Their fight could be put aside like a bad dream.

"Fidé," she said, "keys, biko."

"Proverbs chapter twenty-three: 'Do not remove the ancient landmark!'" the voice on the radio shrilled. "The Redeemer is mightier. You have to remember that God Almighty is seeing what you're doing against the Biafrans. Taking the oil from Biafraland. They have come to steal!"

Eyes fixed on the screen, Fidelis nodded furiously. Adaobi took that as a yes.

"Remember, the Word of God has said it," the man on the radio boomed. "You shall not go unpunished. Remove your hand from the land of Biafra. You must surely fall into the pit. God must surely judge you!"

Squeezing past him, Adaobi took the keys from the table, and she turned toward her daughter's bedroom door. As she began to unlock it, she could already hear Amara rustling behind it.

Fidelis spun around. "What are you doing?"

"Di m, my husband, darling, the children will be late for school."

His large shadow suddenly loomed over her. He yanked the doorknob, snapping the door shut. "Remove your hand!" Just as swiftly, he retrieved the keys and locked the door.

"What is this?" she asked. "Amarachi is a good girl. Is she not? Does she find trouble in the streets? Does she cock her nyash like the Americans?"

"I am promising you," he said, "if you do not leave this door at once, this house will fall today."

"Don't delay us," she said, an uncertain coax to her voice. "Amarachi has an exam."

"Bring her assignments here," he said amiably.

Heat rose to Adaobi's temple. She was losing her patience. "Stop this!"

Fidelis's eyes narrowed. "You want to find trouble today, abi?"

"Tufia! Today we will put two legs in one basket," Adaobi retorted, meeting his glare.

"Mommy?"

She glanced up. Her son, Chuk, looked wide-eyed and fearful.

"Mom." Another voice, muted by the thickness of the door, chorused his. It was Amara.

On one side, her daughter; on the other, her son. Adaobi swayed.

"Leave us in peace, foolish boy," Fidelis said.

Finding Chuk wild and unrestrained, Fidelis had always been harsh with the boy, launching abuses of frustrated sighs and disapproving grunts. That was why Adaobi had always heaped their son with extra praise and tenderness. After all, a marriage was a song. As consummate partner, the wife's duty was to make up for what her husband lacked, and he hers, and so in every way that Fidelis was intemperate, Adaobi found her strength in producing his countermelody.

"Are we going to school?" Chuk asked. He now wore his collared school uniform, his book bag slung over his shoulder. Only then did Adaobi realize that Fidelis had prepared breakfast. But there was only one dish. For their daughter. Was Chuk hungry, too? Had he eaten? While his mother and father had argued, their poor menace of a boy had dressed, combed his hair, and moisturized his face and scalp. He had even ironed his uniform without her pursuing him. In his own desperate way, he was trying to restore peace in the household.

Adaobi couldn't abide her children witnessing their parents' marital discord. Not like the other night. As a youth, she had vowed that her own children would not be raised among the shouts and jeers that she had endured in her childhood, but in serenity. In those days past, when all she had were her dreams, there were two wars, the one at home and the one that consumed the nation. So, Adaobi had made carefully calculated choices: she studied music so soothing arias could mask the trill of bullets and the boom of bombs. She allowed herself to be courted by the humble, sensitive poet who bumbled his way through a proposal, not the boastful boxer. She had married the bespectacled loner, not the leader of the pack. She had defied her father, had run away to join her poet and begin life anew.

What had they become? The other night, in front of their own son, she had boxed her husband like a boar. She stared at her bruised palms. No, Fidelis didn't have the appearance of the tattered, dreadlocked, dada-haired onye ara that she remembered from her childhood trawling the streets and shouting at passing cars, whispering and cackling to invisible fiends. Rather, Fidelis had hardly resisted her, absorbing each blow without blinking. Had he, in a fury, pummeled her to the floor, even that would have made sense. Striking back at an assailant was human. Looking at someone—no, looking through someone, well, that was unnatural. How could you defend yourself against something unnatural? How could you reason with something not quite human?

"O di egwu." In a daze, Adaobi tilted her head to the side, speaking to no one in particular. "My son, you've forgotten your lips again. Let me see your elbows." She grasped them. "What will your teachers think of you, eh? What will they say about your family? You want them to say 'starving African'? Come."

He looked at her strangely.

Giving him the once-over, she added, "You want them to call you 'dis nigga from da ghetto'? Chai! You want them to say you're a boy without a father? Bring me Vaseline."

"We do live in the ghetto though, don't we?" Chuk asked timidly.

"Ekwensu! It is Satan! This boy, he will kill me!" She looked up, intending to meet the eyes of her Maker, but all she found was the popcorn ceiling. "You are not one of them. Understand? Ngwa, hurry. Osiso!"

Chuk scurried off and returned with the Vaseline. Adaobi plucked off the blue cap and gently, lovingly, spread an excessive layer on her son's lips and both elbows. His glossy lips parted with uncertainty. Adaobi smiled anyway. Now her son would be protected from the elements. He'd never be harmed. Anyone could see that her child was well brought up, not some fatherless street rat or a gangster loitering about.

While this small-small mess was sorted at home, the Ewerikes mustn't rouse nonsense gossip.

Adaobi sat in the driver's seat of the family's Volkswagen station wagon and snapped on her seat belt. As she waited impatiently for her son, she glanced into the mirror and swatted flyaways from her halo braids. A neighbor was laughing too early and too loud for the day. As not to meet his eye, Adaobi ducked. She felt hot and damp and was certain that she was already stinking of sweat. She wanted desperately to be back in their stately home in Winter Park, where her neighbors' absent hellos greeted her on her way to work each morning. Not this shithole.

If not for its stink, Econlockhatchee was just another sleepy not-quite-somewhere, an unincorporated community made up of Orlando's castoffs. It wasn't exactly a smell. Rather, it was the way of its being. Instead of tranquility, there was stillness; instead of peril, dolor. Adaobi feared its gloom would swallow her family up whole. In better times, the Calumet Rows temporarily sheltered seasonal migrants who came for the harvest of the vast orange groves and tobacco plantations. Only the sanctuary had outgrown its use. When she rose each morning to prepare for work, Adaobi often turned her eyes askance at the view outside her window. A place so saturated with decay could only beget the death of dreams. Such a setting could only cloak its residents with despair or, worse, indifference. Would such a fate befall her family? Mba!

Chuk reluctantly dropped into the passenger seat. He and Amara had fought over who would sit in the front until an eight-year-old Amara had devised a contract of markers and crayons, *Negotiations of Occupancy*. Her daughter would be a barrister like her father, though the silly girl didn't know it yet. Her ideals would be tempered when the realities of adulthood were upon her. Fondly, Adaobi smiled.

And their Chuks? Well, she had often bemoaned her mischief-making son. They'd planned on a medical doctor, perhaps a surgeon, but she had to admit that he was much too unruly and undisciplined for such a destiny. His greatest joy in life was to provoke the ire of those around him, especially his sister, but perhaps his argumentative spirit destined that *he* be the lawyer, while his sister became the doctor.

Adaobi sighed. She yearned for those innocuous feuds that she refereed most mornings. The sullenness with which her son entered the car unsettled her.

"Put on your seat belt," she said.

Frowning, he slouched forward in his seat, staring at his hands.

"Biko," she begged.

"How come Amara can't come to school today?"

Adaobi dug into her handbag and retrieved a tube of lip balm. She squeezed it onto her fingertip. Before he could resist, she spread it on her son's already glowing lips. With an old brush she kept in the glove compartment, she busied herself with scraping at the tight curls on his head. Oh, she abhorred this mohawk nonsense.

"Stop touching me!" He shrugged her away. "Answer my question. Why isn't Amara coming to school?"

"Because your father would like her to stay home."

"She's grounded?"

"Not exactly."

"If she doesn't have to go to school, then I don't have to."

"You have to," Adaobi said.

"Why? It's not fair."

"Because you have an important task."

He looked up, meeting her eyes.

"Chukwudiegwu, you are my okpara, my first-born son, is that not so?" she asked, seizing his gaze. "You are my rock. I have an important task for you, a job befitting the inheritor of his father's name, his legacy, understand?"

He nodded.

"I will call school today to tell the secretary your sister is sick. You will go to all her teachers and obtain her assignments, understand?"

He stared down at his hands again, his voice a whisper. "Why won't Daddy let her come out of her room?"

A hard knot formed in Adaobi's throat as she lied. "Your sister did something very bad."

THREE

AMARA

The world went on in spite of its prisoners. Somewhere schoolgirls were led deep into a pitch-black forest on the backs of trucks, but in Econlockhatchee, Florida, from the window of a unit in the Calumet Graveyard, Amara Ewerike watched in agony as day turned to night. A steady thudding echoed in the distance. A boy's outline was highlighted on the setting sun as he pounded out a series of combinations on a punching bag. Between the lights and shadows, he seemed electrified. Amara wanted to call out to him.

During the first hour of her confinement, she had slammed her palms and fists at the locked door, imploring her father's ear until her protests shrank to whimpers. She knew nothing of the girls who menaced him in his sleeping and walking hours. She only knew that he was unfair and, frankly, a fascist. That's what

Sahara would call him. Amara hadn't done anything wrong. Not yet anyway. The plan to skip the spring formal and hitchhike to Cocoa Beach as they launched firecrackers hadn't belonged to her. That, too, was Sahara. And it was Lois who had suggested the weed and wine coolers. Amara's contribution had been singular. She had devised the plan for the trio, wearing matching sequined halter-top dresses, to shoot and share Vines of their misadventures that would humiliate those unfortunate enough to attend the silly dance.

Now, as darkness eroded daylight and the nighttime din swelled outside her window, she gravely inspected the torn straps of the dress. In despair, she tossed it aside, its glittery sequins seeming to pop and sparkle among the damaged tops and skirts. Only sturdy blue jeans and ratty band T-shirts had been spared her father's wrath, clothes tucked away in the bottom of her dresser drawer, having long gone unworn since she had turned sixteen and been inaugurated into makeup, false lashes, acrylic nails, and, to her mother's chagrin, hair extensions.

Before turning sixteen, Amara would squat between her mother's knees for hours, letting her hair be twisted into neat concentric cornrows or thin, sinewy box braids, the hairstyles her mother said were practical for a schoolgirl. But with Amara's sixteenth year, a new beginning commenced. Sahara and Lois, seniors in her art period, had glimpsed her sketchbook and been so impressed that they'd taken her under their wing. Now, once every month, while her mother shopped and ran errands, Amara sat very still in a chair at a salon on Alafaya Trail, and for two hours a hairdresser pulled, plaited, and crocheted sleek, colorful wefts into place. Another such appointment had been scheduled for the day, in anticipation of their secret spring fete. Did her father find out about the plan? Her brother. Somehow Chuk had found out and snitched. Amara glared. And then her face softened. Until now, she had always been the favorite.

In a flash, Amara had a memory of a time when she, just a girl, lay nested in her father's lap, putting together puzzles as they listened to King Sunny Adé, Fela, Femi. When she was small, he'd scoop her into his lap, and she would curl there for hours listening to the rumble of his heart, timing her own breaths with the soft collapse of his lungs each time he sighed and flicked the pages of the book or newspaper in his hands. He read poetry, stocks, or the funnies. He told her about what was growing in his beloved garden. He never shouted. And when she engaged in mischief, he only capitulated with a chuckle.

Amara sank to the floor, the dress puddling around her feet. Suddenly, something cracked and rolled free. "We didn't do anything wrong," she pleaded to the sole survivor of the purge, a renegade tube of red lipstick.

Then, with the edge of her pinkie finger, she began to spread the varnish on her lips.

Gazing in her dresser mirror, she blew her reflection a kiss.

She felt armored. One way or another, she decided, she would find her way to the beach.

Forget the dress. Heart hammering in her chest, Amara fiddled with the window of her room until it finally opened. Then she yanked at the screen until it disengaged. Beads of sweat freckled her face. Damp and oppressive air hung like a veil, but in triumph, she paused for a deep in-suck of cleansing breath before dropping to the ground, landing on her feet. How easily it could be done once she put her fear aside, the business of chasing down her freedom.

If she hurried, she could catch the Lynx bus to Sahara's place. Ignoring the feel of the blades of grass, gravel, and something sharp that suddenly pierced her shin, she sprinted across the overgrown lot. Nothing mattered but getting out of that stinking room, away from her father and his unfairness. All she wanted was sky and air.

Not until she had reached the end of the complex's border, where ribbons ensconced a column of pine trees and a flag announced CALUMET ROWS, did Amara notice something like a speck on the remnants of the setting sun. She squinted. Was that her father? Veiled by his bathrobe, he staggered, his body leading and his head following. He wasn't wearing shoes. In a drag-step, he stumbled toward Old State Road 50. Light filled the road as a car whooshed past him; he didn't even flinch.

Her throat clenched. "Daddy," she hissed, but it was futile. He was too far away. Twin bright lights punctured the pitch sky. Wind caught in her throat. Her heart seized as a white van bore down on him.

She hated herself for what she was about to do; she'd end up jailed again. Now she'd never make it to the beach. She took off in a sprint.

Just as she met him, a pair of bleary eyes blinded her. A blink. The world blurred. Everything moved at a gelatinous pace. Amara turned to look for the Calumet Graveyard, but for some reason, it was gone. What was happening? It was as if the darkness of her father's anomalous vision had swallowed everything up, for all she could see was him. His body still, head cocked to the right, unblinking eyes glared at her—through her—at the dusky night, at a specter so far in the distance no one else could see it.

Eyes static, Amara's father hummed. Gradually, his features fell into place and a mystified smile creased his lips. "Ugochi," he said softly.

Light was so far away, it was a pinpoint, yet Amara wanted to stay there, standing before her father until the end of her days, listening to him speak with such familiarity, like when she was a little girl, so she answered, "Yes?"

"Are you afraid?" he asked.

Afraid? Afraid, she supposed, that she'd lose this sense of serenity; that she'd lose him in the depths of this deep, dark recess. Or worse, that she'd never find her way back. Amara held on to the delicate thread of light, but she could feel it slipping from her grip. Still she felt like she had slipped into a skin stretched out for each contour in her body. This was a body that was more hers than the skin she wore at school. And Amara wondered if she and her aunt were one.

"Daddy?" she asked.

Suddenly, lights swung toward them as a van veered off the road and into a tree. A cry leaving the taste of blood in her throat escaped her mouth. The loudest crash she had ever heard filled her ears, a sound that was all gravel, screeching tires, and a combustion. The horn's wail splintered the night so thoroughly that lights came on in the apartments up and down the two stretches of buildings of Calumet Rows. It looked like a burning graveyard.

"Papa," a boy's voice wheezed into the dark. It was the boy she'd seen from her window. "Tato," he called. Save for the deep gash in his forehead that sent pearls of blood trickling down his face, he seemed okay. He had pried himself free of the passenger seat. "For fuck's sake, help me!"

Amara's arms enfolded her father's body and held him tightly as she pulled him from the road, steadying him. She caught her breath on the back of his bathrobe. She breathed in and out until the shaking of her fingers subsided. It was the first time that she had touched him in a long time. Only then did she face him, wiping the smear of saliva from her mouth with the back of her hand.

"What is this?" he asked, his voice thick.

Murmurs. Foamy lights cut through darkness. The van was smashed, accordionlike. Now someone was trying to figure out what to do about it. By then, the boy had dragged his father from the van. The older man's face was so pooled with blood that Amara could no longer see the bleary eyes that had met her own before veering away and hitting the tree. His leg jerked.

Two boys who had been dribbling a basketball up the street helped lift the boy's father to a distance safe enough from the scorched and smoking hood. Everyone waited until the sounds of an ambulance overtook the horn's blare.

Before long, two EMTs were carrying the man to a stretcher and transporting him to a waiting ambulance that filled the pitch sky with a loop of red lights.

When the EMTs revived him, the boy's father howled.

"Calm down," the EMT said. "What's his name?" he called to the boy.

The boy told them.

"Mr. Kostyk, we are taking you to the hospital," the EMT shouted into his face.

"No!" he bellowed. "You kill me first."

"Everything will be fine, Mr. Kostyk."

"Free me."

"Tato," the boy pleaded.

That only made Mr. Kostyk more ferocious. "My Maksym, my

boy." He wrestled the EMTs with such vigor that they had to strap him to the stretcher. When the doors of the ambulance began to close, he was still howling "Maksym" in a loop of cursive-sounding Eastern European syllables. "Where is my son?"

The doors slammed shut. It was eerily quiet.

Hands clasping a clipboard, an officer approached Maksym. As Amara led her father from the scene, another officer flagged them to stop. She swallowed. Her father was the cause of the accident. That much was certain. He had been sleepwalking, and Mr. Kostyk had swerved and hit the tree to avoid him.

"Excuse me," the officer said, "can you tell me what happened here?"

Her father stood helplessly, his bare toes dusty from the gravel lot. Amara moved her lips to answer, but no words came. She didn't know what to say. Where was her mother? Where was Chuk? She couldn't say her father had been out for a walk, not without shoes on. They'd think he was stoned. Was he?

"It's fine," called the officer with Maksym. "Got what we need." He shook his head at Maksym. "You think twice, son. Coulda killed someone."

Maksym grunted in answer. He had lied. Taken the blame for his father. In turn, he had taken the blame for Amara's father. Told them he was behind the wheel, not his father. Hadn't even mentioned her father. And since he was a white boy, a Florida backwoods boy, there would be no arrest, no juvie *this time*. He'd simply be turned over to his old man with a shake of the finger. After all, nothing had been destroyed but his own property.

Amara let out a sigh of relief as the officers drove off, still shaking their heads. By then, her father had turned and started for the house.

Amara stopped Maksym. She wanted to thank him, but how? Instead, she sputtered, "You!"

He waited expectantly.

"I mean, what about your dad, your van?"

He shrugged. "He'll be okay."

"I should have stopped him. I was right there."

"I'm telling you," he said tartly, "he will fucking be okay."

Her expression hardened.

Regretful, he shrugged again. "Look, whatever happens to my old man, he probably has coming to him anyway." He glanced over at Amara. "You should clean that." A pool of blood had settled along her ankle.

"It's fine."

"Don't need stitches, but it's pretty bad," he said.

"It's fine."

"Come on," he said. "I've got some stuff."

Amara was certain she didn't like this boy, but when she gazed back at her father, she could only see his stony face just before he had slammed her bedroom door shut. No way would she go back. She'd face whatever consequences came later, but only after she caught up with her friends. Maksym was already up ahead waiting. She was sixteen-going-on-seventeen that year. Eighteen was just around the corner. Soon the world would be hers. Only her father stood blocking the way, and now she had grown wild with impatience.

Maksym and his father lived in a trailer at the bottom of the hill on a slope bordered by the Hal Buckman Preserve. His father was the handyman for the complex. A sign in front of the trailer proclaimed MISHA KOSTYK YOUR FIXER-UPPER, yet one look around the housing complex and anyone could see that Mr. Kostyk wasn't much of a repairman. Amara had seen the father and son many times, Mr. Kostyk smoking cigars or chucking cans of pilsner on the green while Maksym shadowboxed under the thin awning of the trailer when he wasn't running the mower.

Stacks of dishes, paper, and boxes filled the dank, dark trailer. In the kitchen, Maksym pointed to a stool. Amara sat while he rummaged in drawers until he came up with a bottle of iodine, a square of cloth, some tape, and a bandage. With surprising dexterity, he cleaned her wound and wrapped it. Once he'd finished, he dressed the gash on his own forehead. They stared wordlessly at one another.

"Thanks," she said at last.

He shrugged. "It's no trouble."

"Are you a medic?"

"No. My tato taught me. He's always had a survivalist mindset, what I call a moribund survivalist." He laughed at his own joke. "It's what happens when survival and death are the same."

"Our dads should go bowling together."

"Let's drink to that," he said.

Before she could answer, Maksym was already fishing two glasses out of the sink and rinsing them. He flung the cabinets open, revealing an assortment of bottles, nearly all of them empty. It became abundantly clear to her that the alcohol had been hastily dumped into the sink. He disappeared into another room, then reappeared, glaring through the shiny, dangling beads that separated the kitchen from the living room. He held up an unopened bottle of vodka triumphantly, then broke the seal with his teeth. "Taaka," he said, grinning. "Goes down like rubbing alcohol, but it'll do the job." He filled their glasses, held up his own, and shouted, "Budmo!"

Maybe this was her cue to leave. She'd likely missed the bus, but she could walk the shoulder until the next one came.

"Hey," she said, uncomfortably.

"That's right," he said, cackling with outrage. "That's what we say." Suddenly, he was laughing so hysterically that his eyes were electric with tears.

Shifting awkwardly, she said, "Your dad, I'm sure he'll be okay."

"That's not fucking it!" he blurted out, slamming his glass against the countertop.

Amara flinched.

"That fucking accident was the best fucking thing that could happen to him. Let him stay there. Let him dry out. And when he comes back, I'm gone!"

Amara fixed her eyes on a framed photograph of a man, presumably Mr. Kostyk, in his youth; anywhere was better than looking into Maksym's red-rimmed eyes. In the photo, Mr. Kostyk was slim with chiseled arms. He struck a boxer's pose, shorts arced just above the muscular ridge of his hip flexors, fists knotted and ready. In another photo, Mr. Kostyk's shoulders were squared. He wore a pressed and well-decorated military uniform.

"My dad was a soldier, too," she offered, "in Nigeria. He wasn't always like this. He used to be a lawyer. And he'd go to work wearing ties and carrying a briefcase before—" She felt herself choking up. To prevent tears from spilling, she went silent.

Maksym nodded in recognition and sat heavily into his own stool, losing the stiffness of his rage. Then he told her about his father, and Amara told him about hers. That night, she discovered that they were both unlikely members of their own clan, Children of Prisoners of War. Amara's father had fought in the Nigerian Civil War; Mr. Kostyk had fought somewhere in the USSR. "At first, he was one of the bad guys, too stupid to figure out he was just a pawn, so when they got their chance, the people did to him what they couldn't do to anyone else of his rank," Maksym said. "Because he dared to look his captors in the face, he was starved and left overnight in a forest, in the dead of winter, without shoes, as his penalty."

He never forgave them for that, even after the Soviet Army discharged him from military service. Now, in America, he was excluded from two worlds, a Ukraine that didn't want him and a Russia that didn't need him, so he lived his life in a fury. For Maksym's dad, America meant sitting alone with the curtains drawn and a shot glass next to a flipped bottle of Taaka, cursing and spitting at the *World News*. When Tiananmen broke out in protests, when the Berlin Wall came down, when the Movement joined hands in their human chain across Ukraine, he drank and wept in misery at the insult of democracy.

"Sometimes," Maksym continued, "I wake up to my old man standing over me, beet red and drunk from his nightmares, with a 2B-A-40 to my head. I look into his eyes, look really hard, to see if I can find my tato there. Sometimes I find him, sometimes I don't."

All Amara knew of her father's past was that he had been conscripted to fight for Biafra when he had not yet turned seventeen. It was impossible to believe that the potbellied man with a slightly British accent from his years in England after the war—the man who had always been so pompous about keeping tea at certain hours—had been in any war. A poet, a gardener, a lawyer, he had never had the muscled appearance of a fighter.

"The one time he answered my questions was when I was seven or eight years old," she said. "We were putting together a giant jigsaw puzzle. It was all spread out in front of us. When he moved, I could see the knots on the backs of his thighs. I asked him about the bike accident I'd figured caused the scars because I had marks on my own legs from a fall on my purple Huffy." Amara moved to show Maksym the scars but stopped herself.

"He laughed and said he lost his youth to war," she continued. That was all. So, the scars in his body told the story for him: a string of keloids, a cluster of hard, inflated pimples along the backs of each thigh. And his silence. After he had spoken that day, he fell into a gloom. "Now there are times when you can't tell if he's awake or if he's dreaming."

In Amara's mind, she swapped the stories of their fathers: Mr. Kostyk was the one sitting in the dark room, and the blinding light of a winter snow surrounded her father. While her father writhed with Mr. Kostyk's fury, Mr. Kostyk sat still, calcifying with her father's rage. They sat so long in the darkness or in the lightness that the start and end of each day meant nothing to them, until eventually all time and space collapsed in on itself: now it was all one unending eve.

"Some rooms are filled with darkness and some rooms are filled with light," Maksym said, draining another glass of vodka, "and these rooms can calcify your heart."

Now she saw both: the dead of winter in Ukraine and a dirty Harmattan sunset in Nigeria where light shot through dust in brittle shocks of brightness. Again, Amara thought of that eerie moment out on the street. It was as if she and her father had been completely alone. But were they? He had called out to Ugochi. She hadn't heard that name in years. His younger sister hadn't been seen since the war. That was all Amara knew. Perhaps she had run away or stayed behind when others had left. But it hadn't made much of an impression. After all, she and her brother had always been instructed to refer to their parents' friends as Aunt *this* or Uncle *that*. And there were no family gatherings with this Ugochi like there were with the women from her mother's women's council or the men from her father's firm. But why had he asked if Ugochi was afraid? Was it just a dream?

With a start, Amara remembered Sahara and Lois. Were they at the beach setting off firecrackers and smoking blunts? Or had they ended up at the dance like everyone else, or were they a block away from the gymnasium smoking cigarettes, too cool to go inside, but not cool enough to stay away? Their plans, like everything else, ash.

FOUR

FIDELIS

Armed with a shotgun, Fidelis went looking for his daughter. Neighbors stood on porch stoops and overgrown strips of lawn watching with relish. Everybody's family had been a spectacle at one time or another. Some families, once a week—a drunk shouting obscenities at his kid for a failing grade, a girlfriend rushing out the door with a pot of hot grits to dump on her philandering boyfriend, a schizophrenic nephew singing off-key into a bent spoon, and once, a pit bull howling, howling, howling at the moon inconsolably until his festering agony was cut short by the single report of a revolver. This time, it was the Ewerike family's turn.

It had only just begun to rain. Whispers of water would turn to shrieking showers by midday, and a brooding sky castigated by lightning would fill them with wonder. But for now, the neighbors were blind to any distraction, focusing instead on the powerful descent of a father who believed that some man had carried his daughter off to some place where sisters and daughters could never be found.

Fidelis had only gone halfway down the hill when he spotted Amara on the horizon, alone, partially shaded by a tree. It was a lovely sight. He laughed with relief, but when he neared, she had an inexplicable expression on her face. Had she sat there, so still, all alone through the night?

Looking fearful, as if she had eaten the last piece of goat meat set aside for him after a long day of work, she ran to him. As he had when she was a small girl, he wanted to playfully chide her. He wanted to groan and bellyache about his hunger. But then he recalled her eyes when they had met in the middle of the road the night before; he felt grave.

At that instant, he loved her so completely that he believed his heart would burst, for she had saved him; now he must do the same for her.

As she wept, he sheltered her in his arms, told her it was a strange, sad world.

"Ada m, my daughter, you will never be alone again, you hear?" he promised. "You will never be without my protection."

That afternoon, Fidelis reinforced Amara's bedroom window with a padlock and secured her door with his presence.

FIVE

AMARA

Two large buckets were now lined up adjacent to the bedroom door. After her brief escape, Amara's father had brought the buckets in early that morning, while she slept. One bucket was filled with water. Behind it, her toothbrush, a tube of toothpaste, a bar of soap, a washcloth, and a hand towel were neatly laid out. The other bucket was empty; behind it, a roll of toilet paper.

At first, she had refused to use the makeshift chamber pot, then, with her abdomen eddying under the weight of her bladder, she had been induced to squat over the bucket to relieve herself. Afterward, she shook with humiliation.

Thrice daily, for the past forty-eight hours, he had returned to her door, mute and morose, to empty the buckets and deliver her meals. For all her noise that first day banging on the door and bellowing at him, she had been too afraid to speak when he stood face-to-face with her those early hours of the morning after her escape. Now she couldn't do anything but cower under her covers, averting her sullen gaze even from the tattered clothing still scattered around the room.

But when Monday morning arrived, Amara had risen, dutifully brushing her teeth, scrubbing her face, and bathing her body with the towels and bar soap her father had provided. She reluctantly slipped into a fresh pair of underpants and jeans. In resignation, she pulled on a ratty old band T-shirt. At last, mortified, she stared at her boyish reflection in the mirror. And then, remembering the renegade tube of red lipstick, she had spread a tiny bit over her lips.

Watching the clock, Amara had stood before the door, awaiting the turn of the lock. Minutes passed, and then what seemed hours, and then there were household stirrings of muted voices, clinking silverware, and at last the sound of the front door slamming shut as her mother and brother left for the day. Heart pounding, Amara sank to the floor. Life had gone on without her.

When the door opened that evening, for the first time since her ordeal had begun, Amara's mother stood balancing a tray in her hands, a large knapsack over her shoulder. Mother and daughter silently regarded one another. Her mother set the tray and bag down. Suddenly, they grasped for one another. Tears beading their eyelashes, they held one another like they hadn't in years.

Theirs had always been a tenuous relationship, mother and daughter forever in the midst of some battle. Her mother would often try to enlist her father's support, but he would only be flummoxed and flustered by all the attention. Eventually, he would take Amara's side, asking her mother to give ada anyi another chance or to reconsider from her position. Bitter and aggrieved, Amara's mother would complain, "You give in too easily to her manipulations!" But today she enfolded Amara in her bosom.

"Never let me go," Amara said.

Her mother peered down into her face. "Nne," she said softly, "have you eaten?"

"I can't," Amara said.

"But you must."

"Mom, it's not fair."

"Your father isn't himself today," her mother said. "Don't worry yourself. Just eat. I'll speak to him."

"But this isn't fair."

"Please, eat." She motioned at the tray: macaroni and cheese, fried plantains, greens, and a grape soda. "Look, your favorites."

With a protracted growl, Amara's stomach admonished her stubborn refusal. Mother and daughter laughed. Finally, Amara sat on the edge of her bed with the tray on her lap. While her mother watched, Amara dug in. One bite of the macaroni and cheese revealed bits of pickles. She groaned. "Dad made this?"

"Yes." Her mother chuckled. "It's not so bad, is it?"

Amara made a face. "Pickles don't belong in mac and cheese." There was always a surprise when her father prepared a meal, and it depended entirely on what was growing in his garden. He was convinced that he was an undiscovered talent, a chemist on the brink of some great discovery in the kitchen, yet his meals were often barely digestible. Once he had even sent out an audition tape to *Cooking Wars*, a reality TV show. Though he was summarily rejected, he had insisted that the judges would apologize to him once they learned of their grave error.

Setting aside the pickles, Amara picked her way through the

macaroni and cheese. Then she chased down too-greasy fried plantains and greens with grape soda.

"One more thing," her mother said, motioning to a rolled napkin that Amara, in her haste, had overlooked. Inside was a red-foil-wrapped morsel with a decadent red bow fastened to it. Amara unwrapped it, revealing a chocolate bar.

"Do you remember that time we went to the boutique in Winter Park, and you begged your father for the famous chocolate from Belgium?"

How could she forget? Amara pictured that day, her parents embarrassing her with their unrestrained shouts—*Chineke! What is this?*—when they had looked at the price tag. At thirteen, all she had wanted was to know what fine European chocolate tasted like. Instead, her parents had humiliated her in front of a clucking white lady donning a furry stole and designer shades.

"I'm not eating chocolate anymore," Amara said, setting it back on the tray. "No one is."

"You can enjoy it just this one time."

"No," Amara said.

"Fine. More for me." Her mother took the chocolate bar, opened it, and made a show of savoring a bite.

Amara snatched the bar back and bit into it herself. It was damn good.

In triumph, her mother smiled. "He knew you'd be pleased."

Mid-bite, Amara set the bar down again and folded her arms across her chest. "Tell me, Mom, what did I do?"

Her mother's smile grew unsteady as she began to gather the items on the tray. "I can't explain. You won't understand."

"I will."

"No. It isn't that." She placed her hands in her lap, her gaze at Amara unbroken. "You won't understand because I don't know how to explain."

"Try," Amara said. "Please."

"Amarachi, do you know how lucky you are?"

"Lucky?" Amara asked. "Are you kidding?"

"Silly girl, open your eyes." Her voice cracked. "Your father, he loves you so much. Look at this chocolate he bought you. Look at this grape soda. I told him you like Fanta, he said, 'No, my daughter likes Crush.' He knows you best. Can't you see? He loves you too much. You're such a lucky girl. There are schoolgirls just like you who didn't make it home last night. Instead of an angry army, you have the love of your father. You have a fortress. Miss America, you are a queen lounging in your bed eating chocolate and drinking soda instead of doing chores or going to school. Your mother and father are your servants. Your father cooks meals specially for you with vegetables grown from his own hands. Aren't you a lucky girl to be so cherished? What more could a girl ask for?

"You are so lucky," her mother continued. "When I was a girl, when I was your age, sef, nothing, not even a new day, was promised." Amara opened her mouth to protest, but her mother lifted her hand to silence her. "I will speak to your father. Allow me time. Finish your schoolwork, study for your exam." She motioned at the bag. "By tomorrow this trifle will be resolved, and you will cry when I send you to school. For now, behave. Don't upset your father. Clean this room." She gestured at Amara's scattered belongings.

"This isn't fair." Tears streamed down Amara's face, yet she felt the urge to cling to her mother once more. What if something happened to her on the way to work? What if Amara never saw her again? Would she be locked in her room forever? "Wait. Don't go. Please, Mom, don't leave me."

"Nne, stop this. I said stop this." But her mother stilled. "Do you remember the stories I used to tell you?"

Amara nodded. Those were the days when her mother would spend Saturday mornings preparing Amara's hair for the following week. Amara would squat low while her mother plaited her hair. The only way to keep still was to hear a story.

Her mother dropped back onto the bed next to Amara. "When you were a baby," she began, "Chukwu planted mkpuru in your obi." She stabbed a finger in Amara's chest. "Do you remember what *mkpuru* means?"

"A seed," Amara said.

"I fed you my milk each time you cried, and it fertilized the seed until it bloomed into a marvelous flower in the shape of a heart." She ran her fingers along the length of Amara's rib cage. "Nne oma, this heart of yours has a stem and roots that connect to all your body," she said, "and if you are still, and if you are quiet, you can feel the flower dance in the breeze."

Like she had when she was a girl, Amara played along. Careful not to twitch a single muscle, she held still until her lids grew heavy and dark descended upon her.

That night, Amara woke with a start from a nightmare. In the dream, she stood out in the middle of a field sawed by a breeze that rippled the grass like the waves of a foamy green sea. On the horizon, a sky all orange. It was the fires. Somewhere there, in that distance, the top of a man's hat. She felt such angst and frustration. She squinted. She fanned her face. She could not make out his face. Who could it be?

Amara sat up in bed and went to the window. She stared out at the pitch sky. In the distance, the howl of a triggered car alarm descending and looping; the scattered pings of BB gun pellets ricocheting off tin cans, somewhere. And in the glow at the rise of the hill, just outside of a trailer, leaned a boy. He was with some girl. Amara couldn't make out her face or even his, but she saw the small of the girl's back, the pale ridge where her miniskirt was hiked up, where his hand disappeared. Their bodies wriggled against the tin side of the trailer.

It was fast. They came separately, a desperate quickening of movements and the sudden quaking of their backs, singularly, as if they weren't joined together in passion. Suddenly, he stopped moving and spun around, looking. She caught her breath. It was that boy, Maksym. He was the one in the compromised position, yet it was Amara's breath that had stalled. The hair on her arms stood straight up. Something yawned inside her. But she couldn't move, she couldn't hide, she couldn't even look away. Every bone in her body had gone taut.

He turned back to the girl; Amara exhaled.

She thought about their strange first meeting. He had said he was running away, yet he was still here, stuck in the Graveyard. Like her. And for some reason, this was a comfort.

She thought of them as the Clan of Children of Prisoners of War, and although she hadn't known him for long, in a way, she felt she could see all parts of him. She knew that he was seventeen, and lonely, like her, and that he ached for his mother and despised his father, while secretly loving him. She knew that when he slung around foul words, it was a way to keep the fear at bay. And she knew that the longer she watched him, the more certain she was that she wasn't completely alone.

By morning, the buckets had been emptied and her dinner tray had been removed, even the tiny metal foil and red bow from her chocolate had disappeared. In protest of her condition, she had refused to crack open her schoolbooks over the weekend, but now, as her mother had prescribed, she dutifully sat solving algebraic equations and beginning an analysis of *Paradise Lost* for her AP Language and Literature course.

Her mother would speak to her father, let him know he was being an asshole. But she'd say the words in Igbo, the language where decisions were made. Except for basic greetings, commands, and reprimands, Amara and Chuk hadn't been taught their parents' native tongue, so it had always been a de facto parental code in which decisions, debates, and arguments were settled. She would be patient.

SIX

ADAOBI

Early morning, and already evangelicals, cloaked in dark frocks, had descended on their neighborhood. Crowded together on the porch stoop now, they looked like a murder of crows. Heads bowed, their lips bucked with the occasional "Hallelujah!"

The poor expected such visits—Witnesses, Mormons, or Hare Krishnas whose backs were bent by the burden of their ecstatic devotion, coming to offer pity, prayer, and the promise of libations in exchange for fellowship. But not the Ewerikes. Adaobi had the mind to curse and slam the door at such vultures who had been sent to scavenge her sorrow. Regardless of their circumstances, her family, the indomitable Ewerikes, could never be called indigent.

Instead, voice clipped, Adaobi greeted the evangelicals, "Good morning." She wondered if Gertrude Afolabi, who prepared lazy salted beans for Christmas and Easter every year while complaining loudly about another's more ambitious Ofe Akwu or Egusi, had somehow gotten wind of the Ewerikes' troubles. Despite Adaobi's efforts to maintain their status, surely Gertrude must have noticed the lacking finishes on her at functions—the repeated wardrobe, the diamonds and pendants replaced with rhinestone necklaces and simple studs. That woman had two tongues, one for a greeting and the other for a lie. Gertrude Afolabi, an Anambra woman who had married a Yoruba man from the west and had often boasted of inheriting his name—"born into wealth, high status"—when she brought bland English dishes to association events, was just the sort who would arrange such a visit to their house to malign Adaobi's character.

Dispatching lunatics who quivered and moaned, enraptured by the Call, was indecent. Adaobi didn't consider herself an atheist, but if a bullet should lodge into your lungs, you still bled out, no matter how loudly you prayed. Only out of propriety would a tall, upright priest or pastor who prayed and preached at the same decibel level be summoned for her social events. It added an air of dignity.

But this? To scorn her family so publicly! True, Fidelis had been suspended from the firm, but, Adaobi reasoned, it was a temporary leave. Once rested, he would rise again. True, her family had been banished to this hellscape *affectionately* referred to as the Calumet Graveyard; with prescribed fires at a negligible distance, each of the units, set in identical rows, looked like tatty tombstones.

Still, it was only temporary; their situation had changed, but only for a time. To hush the whispered canard, she had kept up appearances in Winter Park, maintaining her social calendar of brunches and teas, feigning a diet or a fast to explain her sparse plate, until that dreaded night when Fidelis and two sturdy movers had stuffed a truck with as many belongings as they could wrest, leaving the rest to be auctioned off and put toward debts.

Since moving to Econlockhatchee, Adaobi preferred not to answer her phone, regarding the callers as molesters of peace. All the social calls were a nuisance, anyway. That was what she told her children. Really, this was a repose, an oasis. Adaobi's throat tightened, thinking of Gertrude Afolabi licking her lips when she prepared to tell another lie. It was because of her envy.

Gertrude Afolabi's eyes twinged with jealousy when she used to visit the Ewerikes' former home in Winter Park. Her compliments were just as two-faced as her nature. At the same time that she bestowed unreserved praise of Adaobi's refined sensibility, Gertrude rolled her eyes at the exquisitely glass-cut chandeliers in the dining room and the vast wardrobes in the European style. Gertrude chuckled at the frothing fountains enshrined by doves, at the balustrade that resembled the Corinthian columns Adaobi had once studied in textbooks. But then months later, at whose house should Adaobi see Doric columns, and not doves, but parakeets? That Gertrude Afolabi had too much money for such small-small taste!

The Ewerikes, on the contrary, could settle for nothing less than the best. Adaobi wanted nothing of the gauche American style. Her children would grow up in a household that resembled a French chateau so that they could fancy themselves victors. Yes, even if the formidable central Florida real estate market could only supply a Spanish-style fixer-upper with a little spot of land for her Fidelis to grow his vegetables.

What Gertrude would never understand was that Adaobi and Fidelis had built their lives from the ashes of ruins. No, she and

Fidelis were not "born into wealth, high status." She had married a delicate man, a poet, a dreamer who had been summoned to fight in a futile war. Even in the end, when their defeat was imminent, her cousin—not yet thirteen—and her old grandfather had suited up, their dues paid with their lives.

So, yes, if Adaobi and her Fidelis had chewed more than their throat could swallow, it was only because she and her husband were adherents of the bible of the American dream. Their home, their life, had been a declaration of their triumph. He, a barrister, she, an educator. Two who had once starved had grown fat! If they should make it here in the land of the white man, they could make it anywhere!

Yet, after all that, Agatha Adaobi Ewerike had stood on the curb, weeping as her Steinway upright piano jostled against the cracks in the walkway on its way to a waiting truck, weeping as Fidelis and the movers packed a van with their belongings, noticing for the first time how obtuse she seemed in her lavish home with all its Parisian embellishments on a densely populated suburban cul-de-sac. She, reckoning for the first time that she and Gertrude Afolabi were more alike than she had ever realized. And now, all she could imagine was Gertrude Afolabi, with a smug superior pucker of her lips, pityingly suggesting that the evangelicals visit the Ewerikes.

Apart from a proud smile, Adaobi was too distressed to arrange herself, so her bonnet and bathrobe remained scattered. But then one of the flock, a tall man, raised his head and the wide brim of his dark hat fell away, revealing pale tufts of cottony hair, a round blanched face, and a white collar at his neck. He was a clergyman. And he was so badly sunburnt that the edges of his face were clumped with angry peeling red knots and sores. Adaobi had the sudden desperate urge to caress his face in the manner of a mother to a child. She could sense that his had been a life of woe far greater than hers, and she felt baffled at her self-pity.

She reached a hand to him.

Suddenly, his mouth jerked as he joined the chorused "Hallelujah!"

Her hand fell away in astonishment.

She might've been afraid. She might've called him cursed, the way affliction had been regarded throughout her childhood. The lame, the dumb, the imbecile, all were beheld with suspicion if not outright derision and fear. A babe afflicted with albinism, like he, might have once been considered not a sin but an omen. His suffering was so complete that Adaobi felt his closeness to God, and she was overwhelmed by its beauty. She had the sudden conviction that this strange, unlucky man, tall and white as a bolt of lightning with the stubborn head of a ram, had inherited his looks from Amadioha, god of thunder and lightning, the great diviner of justice. With fondness, she conjured the halt of her old grandfather's breath as he told her stories about a time before the human race. Long before the nuns taught her it was wicked to believe such things, her grandfather's stories kept her watchful at night: stories about a time when turtles talked, crocodiles laughed, pythons danced, and thunder spoke. At once, Adaobi had the confidence that a great storm would adjudicate in her favor.

Their eyes met. In that moment, Adaobi felt she had confessed all her troubles. Then, deeming it an insult to look such a messenger in the eye, she shied away. Something squeezed into her palm, but when she looked up, she was alone. The evangelicals had moved on to another neighbor, insensible to her shaken pride as they raised their ecstatic hallelujahs. Adaobi stumbled out the door after them, remembering herself naked under her robe only as she reached the edge of the stoop. She clutched at the robe's lapel, gawking, her throat too parched and hoarse to speak. They moved on to yet another neighbor.

In her bruised palm was the colorful handbill the man had passed to her, covered with the faces of ecstatic parishioners and the name of their order, the Kingdom of the Second Coming of the Marvelous Creator and Holy Redeemer. Her heart sank. Such a fanciful name. A hyperbolic ladder of words. She felt ridiculed. Amadioha? No. Just a man, like any other, an itinerant preacher of an order with an indulgent name to delight the imagination of the lowly masses. She crumpled the handbill and squished it into her pocket. What a simpleton she had been. She laughed. *Imagine that! Amadioha, god of thunder and lightning, standing on* my *doorstep, come to save us.* Adaobi laughed.

And laughed again.

And then she was suddenly quiet as if eyes were upon her.

The urgent voice of First Lady Michelle Obama spoke. Adaobi straightened up, swung the screen door open, and crossed the threshold into her home. There, she followed the sound of Obama's voice to the television. Chuk was flopped on the couch, and he flipped the remote control to BET. Adaobi yanked the remote out of his hand.

"Off the TV! Go dress for school, lazy boy," she said, ignoring his protest as she shooed him out of the room.

Anxiously, she flipped through the channels until she found the First Lady again. Elegant, composed, regal, FLOTUS gazed sorrowfully from the television, hands gripping a placard proclaiming #BringBackOurGirls. At first, the First Lady's melancholy had seemed mute and unimpressive, useless, but after noticing the tweets shared around the world, the agitation and protests, Adaobi realized that if anyone could save the girls, it was First Lady Michelle Obama, the most powerful woman in the world—after Oprah—whose sorrow was so complete, so devastating, that Earth stood still on its axis. Michelle Obama, a barrister, her head full of polysyllabic verbiage, phrases of complicated syntax, knew that in this odd moment, a wordless expression of maternal mourning was her most powerful weapon. At the end of the segment, Adaobi was kneeling in front of the television, her body quivering.

First Lady Michelle Obama had not forgotten all the mothers of the disappeared girls, mothers who had labored to birth each daughter. Why should Adaobi?

In that instant, she understood that the elements of her dream were indeed prophetic. Her daughter, Amarachi, sequestered in her room without reprieve, would languish without intervention if she did not go mad first. Like Michelle Obama, Adaobi would act. Having failed at force and reason, she had only one recourse left.

As her son disappeared into the clot of students at his school's entrance that morning, Adaobi sat shaking in her car. Nothing could provide refuge from her disquietude. Her key was in the ignition, yet her hands were trembling too fast for her to grip the gearshift. She would be late to her school if she didn't leave soon; still, she couldn't steady herself enough to drive, though there were scales to be practiced and wiggling first graders to herd together, so they could sing a silly song about spring for the upcoming May Day festival.

Adaobi was overcome, first by fear, then a simple comfort. She remembered a time before war when she'd attended the village school where her uncle was headmaster. A tall reed-thin American woman had taught English at her boarding school during one term. She was the youngest of three Peace Corps volunteers, so she had been assigned to the lower levels. Every morning, she rode in on a bicycle the headmaster had loaned her. It was a strange, loud contraption announcing her arrival with shrieks and groans. But it gave the pupils enough warning to stand in formation outside of the school, giggling and ready to greet her.

When she saw them standing in formation each morning, their voices raised simultaneously to chant, "Good morning, Teacher," she seemed embarrassed by the attention. Talking through her nose, her face reddened as she pushed her hair away and reminded them, "Just Sally." Only one child, doltish enough to do so, was promptly flogged by Headmaster when he learned of her over-familiarity with their guest.

At the start of every class, Teacher would announce the lesson for the day on the chalkboard—*nouns*, *verbs*, or *adjectives*. Each of the girls would mimic her, writing on their slates in the same big, loopy hand. Even though they had already learned these lessons the year prior from Mrs. Okwuma, the girls suspected that Headmaster had assigned Teacher to their level, the second form, not by accident, but to impress their guest. Instead of the standing stories and songs, with the call-and-response that Mrs. Okwuma had used to color each lesson, Teacher read aloud from an English grammar textbook in a trembling voice that the girls mimicked to sound American.

They were so impressed by their unusual guest and her odd accent that it had never occurred to them that she might believe they were teasing her. Face reddened, Teacher would stand before the loudest imitator and call out a name from the roster, any name, in a voice much too exotic to sound like a reprimand. In answer, the class would erupt in bashful giggles. The lucky one who had earned Teacher's attention that day would win the honor of playing her during afternoon recess. There, in the school courtyard, as they lunched on jollof rice, they imitated the way Teacher sat, legs crossed, smoking a cigarette while she sipped from the Coca-Colas she purchased from town and picked at the English-style fish-and-chips that the cook, an old man who had served overseas during World War II, insisted would remind her of home.

One day, a day like any other, the girls imitated Teacher as she read from her book, but this time, she suddenly flung her textbook across the room. All the girls stopped, gawking as the book fell to the ground. Everyone knew books were for the wizened, not for children to mess about, so they sat frozen in admiration. Teacher must have mastered the subject, memorizing the words on every page, as to deem the printed page insulting!

Before any of the other girls could move, Adaobi—who was Agatha at school—picked up the book and returned it to Teacher, setting it on the desk before scurrying back to her seat, praying Teacher would take notice of her just this once, say her name.

Lips quivering, Teacher began to read again. This time, she did not raise her voice, or even her face, when the girls imitated her. That afternoon, they watched as she rode her bicycle over the slope to return to her sleeping quarters. The next day, she did not return. Nor the next day, and the girls waited, hopeful, but they never saw her again.

Because her departure had preceded the end of the term, and teachers and headmasters did not answer to the inquiries of busybody schoolgirls, naturally, there were rumors. One was that

Teacher fell pregnant and ran away with the postman, a handsome young man who delivered the mail once a fortnight; another was about her bicycle breaking down, leaving her stranded in the middle of some strange town, where she was captured by Fulani bandits and made a concubine in their harem; and still another, the one that Adaobi suddenly realized was the true one: the one about a shy young girl far away from her friends and family, in a strange new land with different ways; a girl who had an anxious disposition; a girl who, upon her return to her homeland, had been taken to a hospital where ailments of the mind, not the body, were healed. Perhaps such a place could cure Adaobi's husband.

At Orlando General Hospital, large plexiglass doors opened onto a breezeway that led into a bright open hall. Ascending circular open-air floors were crowned by skylights that filled the room with stipples of gray light. Adaobi stopped short and tilted her head back in awe. Was it possible to leave someone you loved in a place such as this, a place so large and unfeeling? Did she really have it in her heart to call the hospital and report her husband? Would they drag him here in handcuffs, like a thief? Would they strap him to a stretcher in a straitjacket, like in the movies?

When a hand clasped her elbow, she flinched, shocked to find none other than Gertrude Afolabi, whom Adaobi, with enough notice, would normally avoid. But this time, there was no tasteful exit. In her anxiousness to explain her presence at the hospital, Adaobi began to stumble through a long-winded defense. "My husband . . . his allergic rhinitis . . ." she began, waiting for the usual greeting, "Hey, hippopotamus!" In loathing, Adaobi would always suck her teeth in reply: "*Mschwww.*" True, Adaobi was larger than Gertrude. But at least she was stacked neatly. Not like

Pear-o-Mango Gertrude, a woman with ample, uneven breasts. Even so, each time Gertrude uttered the ill-mannered salutation, Adaobi's retort would come off sounding like a babe's wounded protest, which Gertrude would gleefully deflect: "What a compliment to have your bakkasi commended so publicly, sha."

But without warning, Gertrude swallowed Adaobi in her large, throbbing arms. She heaved against Adaobi. A silent cry rose to a whisper in her ear. "Abiala, dear friend," she greeted in Adaobi's dialect. "You are the first to come." Gertrude freed Adaobi's face, only to grasp her hand. "Come. He is this way."

Adaobi had the good sense not to say a word. Instead, she allowed Gertrude to drag her past the reception desk at the center of the hall, where a tired-looking woman wearing a security uniform sat with a phone balanced against her ear. As they neared the guard, Gertrude called out, "My sister has come."

The guard exchanged little more than a nod. Adaobi followed her friend down an endless series of hallways and elevators until they rose three floors and stood outside a room.

Just as they reached the door, Gertrude stopped. Gertrude Afolabi, who had never been at a loss for words for a single second in her entire life, stood motionless. Eyes large in alarm, she turned to Adaobi.

"We don't have to enter yet," Adaobi said. And so, they didn't.

They sat silently for several long moments before Gertrude spoke. "They say he'll make it," she said. "But he won't be the same." Her words were a whisper. "I don't know what I'm going to do."

Adaobi opened her mouth to speak but found no words. All she could think of was the two women switching places, Adaobi sitting outside of some room waiting to hear news of her Fidelis.

For a long time, they sat in silence. When an orderly came to speak to them, Gertrude was still clutching Adaobi's hand, and the facts of the situation quickly became apparent. Then a doctor arrived to update Gertrude, leaving Adaobi alone for the first time, and she had a chance to sneak away. And she did, rushing down the hallway and then stopping, breathless, unable to push the elevator button. She took out her phone and dialed the front office at the school. As the phone rang, she felt relief, realizing that, for the first time in a long time, she had forgotten her own worries. How easily one's own sorrows could be displaced by the mishap and mayhem of another's.

In the moments before Sally Hall, the administrative assistant, answered, Adaobi imagined her first graders, whispering in glee right this moment as the flummoxed school resource officer or the principal, Randy Jansen, tried to soothe them by handing out coloring books and crayons. It was too late for Adaobi to make up any excuse, so she told Sally the truth. "It's an emergency," she said. "My friend's husband has had a stroke. He will make it. But surgery is imminent. I cannot leave her side."

Violence and reason had failed to persuade Fidelis that Amara's internment was unwarranted, but love had yet to be tested, so Adaobi resorted to means only available to mothers and wives. As Gertrude Afolabi's family began to arrive at the hospital, Adaobi had slipped away. Then, while Fidelis remained glued to his computer, Adaobi spent the rest of the day preparing fufu, egusi soup, okra soup, and ogbono soup—what the children referred to as "Obama soup" in jest. She was determined to love her family whole.

That evening, she watched as Fidelis gulped back hefty, satisfied swallows that he chased down with mugs of thick Guinness. Late in the night, her teasing laugh and flirtatious wink were successful at luring him back to the bedroom, but after that final blissful sigh, rather than toss his head back in surrender as he had done in his youth, Fidelis reknotted his wrapper at his waist and returned to his post outside Amara's door.

Adaobi remembered First Lady Michelle Obama. One simply cannot stand by! Adaobi threw on her bathrobe and rushed to the living room. She would dial 911. The police would arrive before another hour passed. An officer would unlock the door, haul Fidelis away, put him in a cell overnight, and then perhaps he would wake up with a sober and remorseful outlook. In the morning, he would return home, and there would be peace. Gertrude Afolabi's husband would never return home the same again. He would be mute or lame or incontinent, cheerless or prematurely doddered. But Adaobi's husband would laugh again, marvel over his garden, chuckle at Adaobi's stories, hold his offspring close. Phone in her lap, she sank onto the living room sofa.

But how could she call the police on her own husband, sef? In Nigeria, the police would laugh in her face. In fact, they would applaud Fidelis for performing his rightful duty as patriarch. Daughters needed extra protection. If Adaobi were to make such a report against her own husband, as if *he* were the criminal, they would label *her* a menace. They'd drag her off to jail for wasting their time. But this was America. She must phone the police.

Maybe she was overreacting. Like Chuk had said, Amara was just grounded. Fidelis was only a strict father, like her own, a disciplinarian. At home, they called it a strong hand. Here in America, when a child was locked up for misbehaving in school, Americans referred to it as "ISS" (in-school suspension), "detention," though, lately, the slip that came home with her Chuk said "safe seat" and "safe space." No matter the appellation, it was all the same to Adaobi: isolation, seclusion, and sequestration begat repentance. But for what must Amara repent?

When she reached to dial the numbers, Adaobi could not see Fidelis, but she felt his body suddenly behind hers. Tenderly, he cradled her in a warm, clammy embrace. "Nke m," mine, he began affectionately, "I am grateful to you. God has blessed me!" He burrowed his face into her neck. His whisper tickled her ear. "We have been through so much, abi? Yet we are still here. Some of ours didn't make it."

Adaobi's heart went still.

"I know you, nwunye m," my wife, Fidelis continued. "If you had been there with Ugochi, you wouldn't have allowed anything to happen to her. You would not have allowed them to take her."

"Don't say her name," Adaobi whispered. "What's the use? She's gone."

"But our Amarachi is here," he said.

"But our Amarachi is not *her*," Adaobi protested.

"I know you may not understand my ways," he said. "But what would you do if you knew what I know?"

Adaobi sat numb in foreboding.

"You may think me daft," he continued. "Go ahead. But it happened once. Did it not? I was a buffoon then. I didn't listen to my head, but I will not be a laggard again. I cannot allow it to happen again." His voice rose with righteousness. "I will die to protect my daughter."

How could it be a crime to love one's child endlessly?

Could love ever be too powerful?

"Fidé, if I may, let me tell you a story," she began. "When

I was a small-small girl, I used to visit my grandmother's compound for the holidays. There, I befriended a rare red bird that sang such a triumphant song every morning from one of the frangipani trees in the courtyard. I loved the bird so completely that once, when it landed on my hand, I brought it to my chest and hugged it, squeezing it with all the fondness of my heart. When I pulled away to look into its face, it was no longer moving. That was my first lesson on love, understand? You cannot hold on too long or too hard to anything. If you leave no room for air, love will suffocate."

Waiting for her husband to release her from his hold, Adaobi closed her palm over the phone. Fidelis drew her nearer. "You are wise," he said. "Iron Lady!" He cupped her body with his, forming an upright spoon. They hadn't made love in months, not really. What they had done earlier that night was only spectacle. But suddenly, with urgency, they were backing into the bedroom once more, feverishly unwinding their faded-print wrappers. Adaobi was surprised to feel her flesh's ready response, an answer to his body's every question.

Their passion, a sudden swift tempest, at last receded, betraying Adaobi and Fidelis as deflated balloons, middle-aged fogies rutting on their matrimonial bed, attempting a sorry pantomime of their youth. Damp with sweat, Adaobi sneezed. Fidelis breathed hard next to her. She retightened her wrapper. What a relief that the telephone should suddenly call to her.

"Never mind it," Fidelis said. "They will leave a message."

She went to the living room anyway, wondering if it was Gertrude, but when she answered the phone, there was a quick intake of breath and then the caller hung up. The dial tone rang in her ear. Should she call the police? Adaobi lingered before the phone.

But memories took over—of Fidelis's sister, her dear friend Ugochi, and all they had once been. And all they should have been. And the scars. They had all been through too much. The world could never understand. Their children would never understand. No one could ever understand the choices they had made, even the ones for which they might never atone. War is a cruel wit.

Fidelis dropped down on the couch, flexed his ankles, and crossed his legs. He flipped through the channels on the television. Adaobi swallowed. While she had made love to her husband, their daughter could barely breathe. Remorse filled Adaobi. What kind of woman can't contain her man? What kind of mother can't protect her children?

He had settled on the eleven o'clock news. A reporter with steely bleached-blond hair was reporting about that boy again—what was his name?—a teenage boy, not much older than their own Chukwudiegwu, wearing a baggy hood, like the one she forbade her son from wearing ever again, a boy beaten and abused and then shot dead outside of his own papa's home.

O di egwu. Adaobi shuddered. A son's death before his father's was an abomination. Yet so many sons had died before their fathers in wartime. Now this Florida boy's family was left only to inherit the indignity of loss, as they had, the brave Biafrans. On the news, the anchorwoman was saying the boy's killer, a man calling himself Neighborhood Watchpolice, had been found not guilty of murder. Now he was patrolling the streets again. Here was the boy's mother sounding sure, despite her pain, that on behalf of her son, justice would eventually be served.

"They are wasting their time," Fidelis proclaimed.

Was he right? Would the wicked man, unpunished, murder another Black boy?

Would this man massacre their own Chukwudiegwu next?

In America, police shot first and asked questions last. Was this land so different from Nigeria? A brave Biafran had been arrested and jailed without charge, but everyone knew it was because of how Radio Biafra had broadcast the latest movement of his comrades. Was the Sanford Police Department so different from the Special Anti-Robbery Squad? All over social media, Adaobi had seen the pictures of those bloody and beaten, merely suspects.

Well, the only real difference was that in America Black skin, not wealth or lack thereof, enraged police. Amara had been a toddling child, Chuk an infant, when the African man in New York City was shot to death outside of his own home. Forty bullets. They had shot him with forty bullets to make sure he was dead before asking why. His murderers went home to their wives' milk and banana bread and slept well.

No, Adaobi would not be her husband's executioner, not after they had survived so much. War had wounded his flesh, and a prison had wounded his psyche. Anything more would be an assassination. A woman's greatest might was not her ability to contain her husband; it was her ability to protect him from himself.

It was all quite simple. A man needed to puff his chest, swagger into a room, and swing his phallus about when the world had defied his order. Once Fidelis had sated his bruised ego, her calm and even-tempered husband would reemerge. For his outsized reaction, he'd offer a gruff apology to Adaobi. With his bashful smile, he'd coax a grin from his daughter. To make amends, he'd take her for ice cream, pamper her with adoring sentiments. He'd promise her the world; he was putty in his cherished ada's hands.

All would be well in time. And anyway, what if he could see something they all couldn't? What if he was right?

"Yes," Adaobi agreed, "his killer has gone free. They are wasting their time."

For now, she must keep her family whole, shelter them through this tempest. This business would pass. Men, not women, were the ones swayed by hysterical passions. Every war that had passed since the dawn of time, no matter where in the world, was the consequence of the malaise of the masculine spirit. Was it not true? Too much testosterone or not enough, she pronounced. This too shall pass.

She would call upon her chi for defense. She felt a shiver and grasped her bathrobe close, digging her hands into her pockets, finding the dazzling preacher's colorful handbill.

SEVEN

FIDELIS

Never mind that the walleyed father who hunted down his daughter, shotgun in hand, had done so lovingly.

Never mind that when his eyes beheld her, they were wet with tears of relief. Never mind that the Remington 870 was slung over his shoulder, not gripped in his bare hands.

Never mind that over forty years had passed since he had seen combat, and so maybe this was only theatrics, nothing more.

Never mind, because over gin and tonics, stories have a life of their own.

In one rendition, Fidelis savagely broke down the door of the man who had molested his daughter.

In another account, he, a madman gripped by a fugue state, had mistaken someone else's daughter for his own.

EIGHT

CHUK

In another version, the version that reached Chuk's ears, his father was a terrorist, strapped with bombs, who had gone on a rampage. From then on, to the neighborhood boys, Chuk was known as the Underwear Bomber. One rat-faced boy started it all. He was the mayor of the neighborhood. His name was Raphy. He had overheard the story of the Christmas massacre that had almost happened. The adults had mentioned that the terrorist was a boy from Nigeria, and as they say, the rest was history.

It had started on one of those frequent occurrences of late: Chuk's mother had forgotten to pick him up from school. He could have taken the ride offered by Lyle Winchell's mother, but, like a punk, he had insisted that his mother was on her way. Maybe it was best. He didn't want any of his friends to ask to be invited in when they arrived at his doorstep. How would he explain away that, with the exception of a brazen escape of mere hours, his sister remained in her bedroom, imprisoned by his father?

After waiting outside school for an hour in the blistering heat, he'd rolled up his sleeves and ventured home on his own, catching one bus, then another, and then traipsing the rest of the way on foot along the shoulder of Old State Road 50. Damp, exhausted, and fuming, he'd just about reached the Calumet Graveyard's entrance and was within eyeshot of home when the pebbles began to rain on him. He ducked into an old out-of-use bus shelter, waiting and watching as cars whizzed by on the highway, impervious to his torment.

Mama's Boy was what the neighborhood boys had been calling him since the Ewerikes had moved to the development. Then after Chuk's father stood outside in his flowing ishi agu robe, his pride, they called him African Booty Scratcher, ABS for short.

At Lowell Academy High, Chuk was safe from the neighborhood boys' taunts and jeers. There, he roamed the halls with a crew that wore a habit indicative of their rank in the school social hierarchy—slim rolled-up khakis, collared polo shirts, and mohawk fades. They were not the jocks in their letterman jackets or the nerds in their glasses; they were rebels in the guise of clowns. They laughed off the Cs and Ds they accumulated from their noncommittal academic performance, and in the back row of their classes, they leaned back, cracking jokes and fuming about the nonsense lies they were being taught by the Man. Often, they were so high they could only repeat platitudes that they attributed to philosophers like Bob Marley and Young Jeezy. Their reward? Everyone laughed or cheered.

On the first day of the academic year at Lowell Academy

High—Chuk's first year in the upper-levels building, away from his mother's watchful eye—Mr. Kim, the ninth-grade English teacher, had asked for help pronouncing the name listed on the roster: Chukwudiegwu Ewerike. Rather than use the opportunity to explain to Mr. Kim that he answered to Chuk—pronounced *Chuck*, not like his parents said it, *Chook*—he had wanted to let everyone know he wasn't just any freshman. "Do you want my real name or my slave name?" he had quipped. When Mr. Kim had rolled his eyes and lamented, "That's ludicrous," Chuk had responded, "I know that rapper!" to the thunderous applause of his classmates. That had earned him twenty minutes in the "safe seat," a plush chair in the back corner of the classroom, where, unharmed, he might contemplate his options for success. He sat back in the seat, head rested on crisscrossed arms, an unrepentant leer on his face.

In that pose, it was by chance that he discovered that if you slid sideways and scooped your back, the seat would make fart sounds, and so he did it, softly at first, then louder and louder until Mr. Kim, nose scrunched with disgust, sent Chuk to the nurse's office to handle his "obstreperous digestive track." Nurse Newman—a portly Texan whose claim to fame was that Paul Newman was a second cousin twice removed—took his temperature, gave him a Tums, and placed a warm compress on his belly, the one she gave the girls who were "paying their lady toll." Then she told him all about how Paul Newman trained on a ranch near her hometown for his role in *Hud*. Meanwhile, Chuk leaned back and planned his subsequent prank. Next time, a sneezing fit. At school, he was satisfied with being court jester. It was almost as cool as ruling the school; plus, it kept him out of the sightline of bullies.

But the Calumet Graveyard was another story. There, Chuk

was Mama's Boy, ABS, a "whiteboy" who rode to his prissy private school in his mama's air-conditioned chariot. It had never made sense to Chuk. There were white boys among their crew, and boys whose Caribbean parents certainly dressed and sounded African, Latino Mama's Boys who perked when their mothers' tongues rolled to call "mijo, papacito," yet they heckled Chuk's neat clothes and teased him when he protested.

The neighborhood boys weren't exactly hostile. There was no steel in their jeers. He was merely a curiosity, a boy from the other side, who, for a season, was among them. They had never given him a chance to prove that he could be like them. That he might spend every free hour playing *Fortnite*, *Call of Duty*, and *Grand Theft Auto*, as they did; that he might also prefer the *Iron Man* comics over *Superman;* that together they might all cheer for Orlando's Victor Oladipo while jealously scorning and jeering Miami's LeBron James.

No matter how poor his family was—and yes, notwithstanding his mother's assurances, Chuk was certain of their poverty—he didn't belong to the neighborhood. He had grown up in Winter Park, not Econlockhatchee, Chuluota, or in some trailer on the outskirts of Christmas; nor did he take the bus to East River High over in Bithlo, like the others. So, whenever they caught him on his own, the neighborhood boys chased him down, launching rocks and pebbles, laughing, and sneering "Mama's Boy" and "ABS."

No one could know of this, the indignity of being menaced for sport, not Chuk's friends at school and certainly not his parents. His mother would only make matters worse by calling the police or demanding meetings with the kind of parents who would laugh this off as child's play. His father would rebuke him, remarking that Chuk ought to pass his time studying instead of finding trouble. So, like all the other times, there was nothing to do that day but duck under the bench of the bus shelter until the boys grew bored of throwing rocks or were distracted.

By the time everything had gone still, Chuk had caught his breath. All he could hear was the stiff breeze. The coast was clear. He straightened up and dusted off his trousers, flicking away the pebbles and burrs that had become entangled in the cuffs of his khakis. At long last, he slipped his JanSport over his shoulders and started for home, passing the lopsided palm trees at the entrance of the development.

Suddenly, the rabid pack of boys descended. Up ahead was an old ash tree, Chuk's only chance for escape. He bolted to it, but just as he began to scramble up the tree, the hand of one of the boys bit down and yanked at his backpack. He felt himself falling. Before he hit the ground, they were already clubbing him with balled fists. "Underwear Bomber!" Raphy barked.

It was the first time Raphy had said the words. Unused to his breath, they sounded like a command. Someone among the pack seized Chuk's waistband and tugged. He clutched at his slacks, exposing his unprotected face to their blows. As they pawed and pummeled him, all he could think of was concealing the embarrassment of the Fruit of the Loom tighty-whities his mother still insisted on purchasing for him at the start of every school year. In that instance, all his rage was not even for the boys; it was directed at his mother.

A strong pair of hands gripped Chuk, yanking him to his feet. He got his second wind then, striking out blindly, stopping only when he opened his eyes.

The boys had dispersed. It was only Maksym, the handyman's son. He pulled Chuk up by his trousers.

"Get off me," Chuk said. He knew he had just been rescued, but the only thing more humiliating than getting beaten up and pantsed by the neighborhood boys was getting beaten up and pantsed by the neighborhood boys in front of an audience.

"You okay?" Maksym ran the back of his hand across a sweaty brow. His white singlet was yellowed at the pits. Not far away was the lawn mower he had abandoned in his haste.

Chuk forced a chuckle. "You should see the other guy." He wasn't a particularly clever wit, but he had always armed himself with humor, winning nearly every debate or roundhouse with it. Still, humor was a porous shield, so when Maksym didn't join Chuk's laughter, it stung.

"It's cool," he covered. "I've got this."

"Didn't say otherwise."

Now that he was on his feet again, Chuk surveyed the damage—a torn collar, dirt at his knees. "My backpack." He groaned. His final paper for ninth-grade English was strewn across the lawn. Mr. Kim was brutal. He was the sort of teacher who marked off for the wrong font size, and he certainly had it out for Chuk after that initial meeting at the beginning of the school year. What would he say about grass stains? Miserably, Chuk began to reassemble the essay and stuff it in his backpack.

Maksym grabbed a notebook and handed it to him. "You're okay."

"I didn't need your help," Chuk said. "I had them."

"Yeah, sure." Maksym's lips twisted into a smirk. "If it was one-on-one, you could kick the mayor's ass. Raphy, the little shit, he's all talk." A nod. "Piece of advice? Don't fight them all at once. Get them alone, one by one, then, square up and give them the one-two." He pantomimed a jab and cross.

There was a way Maksym twisted his fist at the end of the cross and something he did with his feet. Chuk looked away again, facing the zipper of his backpack. "I didn't ask for your help."

"I'm just saying, that's what I'd do if it was me," he said. "When I was a kid, I was real skinny, so little shits like them thought they could punk me."

"You're still skinny," Chuk interjected.

"Not skinny," he said. "Lean. I'm a junior welterweight."

Chuk thought the distinction over.

"They didn't know my pop taught me how to use these hands," Maksym continued. He bobbed and weaved, nimble and confident. "What I'd do, if I was you, I'd get them real quick." He doubled his jabs before a sudden uppercut. "They wouldn't see it coming. You get me?"

"I guess."

"If you want, I could show you some moves," Maksym said. "They'd never mess with you again."

Chuk licked his lips. He didn't want Maksym to know that he was actually considering it.

"Think about it." Maksym shrugged. "So what's up with your sister?"

What did he want with Amara? Chuk ducked his head and mumbled, "Nothing."

"How come I never see her around?"

"Huh?"

Maksym frowned. "Does this have to do with Ugochi?"

"What are you talking about?"

"She said that name." He frowned. "Something about your dad."

Chuk bristled at the mention of his father. "I have to go."

"Never mind." Maksym stopped him. "Will you send her a message for me?"

"Who?"

"Your sister."

"What?"

"Tell her I'm leaving soon, like I said."

Impishly, Chuk grinned, really seeing Maksym for the first time. "You like my sister?"

Maksym's face covered in a blush. "Just thought I'd tell her," he said. "In case she wants to know. That's all. Tell her, will you?"

"Yeah, sure," Chuk said. "Whatever."

He didn't. That night, Chuk was too preoccupied with a different name to relay the message. There was something too self-satisfied about the way Raphy had conjured his stinging gibe. Chuk googled *Underwear Bomber.* It sounded like a dirty diaper. The first hit was a Wikipedia article. He clicked. The entry said the Underwear Bomber was Nigerian, a young man, twenty-three years of age. He'd tried to blow up a plane for reasons Chuk couldn't understand, but he had only succeeded in burning himself. Chuk winced. How could anyone be stupid enough to nearly blow off his own balls? And what prize did he win? He got four life sentences, plus fifty years! This was the moron for whom the neighborhood boys had nicknamed him? He groaned. Couldn't he go back to being Mama's Boy or ABS?

But then, just before closing the browser, he gazed at the photo, a boy with soft, grim eyes, wearing a clean white T-shirt. He looked familiar, like a fourteen-year-old version of him could have fitted in with Chuk's set: trash-talking ballers, binging DC and Marvel, collecting phone numbers of dimes, bemoaning Algebra I, and earning detention for passing an obnoxious fart in Spanish I.

Somewhere in the eyes and nose he even looked a bit like Chuk. His heartbeat quickened. Why did he do it? What strange, sad set of circumstances could have beset a boy, like him, so that he would one day arrive at a moment, on Christmas Day 2009, when he'd detonate a bomb intended to extinguish 290 lives on Northwest Airlines Flight 253?

That night, for what seemed hours, Chuk sat staring into the boy's face.

For as long as Chuk could remember, it had been a foregone conclusion that his older sister, Amara, was the golden child, which was why her punishment—being locked up in her room, grounded for all eternity—had at first, admittedly, seemed karmic. While his father usually doted on Amara, he would routinely assail Chuk with frowns and glares for the slightest folly—the typical refrain: *Why can't you conduct yourself more like your sister?*

His mother took an opposite approach, extolling the virtues of her cherished okpara. But it was as if this "okpara," the titular firstborn son, was some mighty imaginary figure constructed to entirely oppose Chuk. This okpara was a strong, solid boy who was the high scorer on his soccer team, never complained, ate all his black-eyed peas, asked for extra helpings of homework, and never once failed an exam.

When she looked at his report cards—which really weren't so bad, better than his boys', at least—his mother would always admonish him, saying, "A boy is the answer to his parents' prayers!" She would even note that Amara was the stubborn afterbirth that came spilling out after a succession of miscarriages and stillborns, all boys. Bad luck daughters had names that signaled their parents' reluctant acceptance of things they had little control over—names like Ogechi, "God's time"; Uchechi, "God's will"; or Nkiruka, "the best is yet to come." Still, they had named his sister Amarachi Uzodinma—"God's grace, good way." Meanwhile, his own name, Chukwudiegwu, meant "God is terrible"; his mother assured him that in this one instance "terrible" was a good thing.

That his sister could commit a crime so naughty as to deserve such dire consequences, and that this offense could be so obscene that both his mother and father could not bear to utter it aloud, wasn't altogether implausible. His mother whispered swear words; she practically swooned when she overheard the lyrics to his favorite songs; and she was the sort to write letters to rap music executives, campaigning for music that promoted the betterment of the "fathers of tomorrow." Chuk's father would only gnash his teeth and grumble as if it were all beneath his dignity.

Besides, Amara was a Goody Two-Shoes. Rather than sticking up for him, she smirked when Chuk found himself in straits; she gloated when his teachers failed him; and she insulted and condemned his friends and his music. She had somehow managed to leech on to a new crowd at school, and Chuk suspected that she was grounded because of something to do with them. At the very least, she had hers coming.

On the other hand, strangely, he also felt envious. Despite her defense, his parents behaved as if *they* were the ones being disciplined. They clamored to please her. His mother bowed at his sister's door, chocolates and Popsicles in hand, while his father prepared Amara special dishes from the prized tomatoes, peppers, cucumbers, and cabbages he reaped from his garden. Each afternoon, upon his return home from school, Chuk would stand in the darkened doorway and ask the silent room, *What about me?*

Days and then weeks passed as his parents, stricken and mute, sulked and slouched in the hallways, passing one another like ships at sea. At times, it was as if they couldn't see, eat, touch, smell—could hardly breathe—so Chuk did their breathing for them. He fried eggs for breakfast and then again for the egg sandwiches he made for lunch. He swallowed scabbed-over oatmeal for dinner. Each morning, he would even summon his mother to take him to school. On the days she forgot him, he hiked home, returning after dusk, damp and musky, feet blistered, forgotten. Slowly, Chuk became conscious of a revision that had taken place. It was as if his father's greatest wish had come true; he had canceled his own son.

As a small boy, Chuk's only true job in the Ewerike household had always been to act as an emissary during his parents' spats when communication was absolutely necessary. In this minuscule capacity, he'd idiotically taken pride in his duty and clamored for their praise and adulation. As he relayed their dispatches, he'd exclaim *chai!* or *oh* to accent his mother's frustration or roll his eyes and huff *ngwa* in that deep, guttural way of his father's. Anything to keep him at the center of it, their love.

This was why the night his father had first barred Amara in her bedroom, Chuk had lifted his mother's crumpled body from outside of his sister's door and walked her to his parents' bedroom. His mother had looked as worn as an old boot, and so when he set her on her bed, with her arms out and her eyes wild and full of sorrow, he'd laced her together in his arms as one would shoestring.

Before retiring for the night, she'd wept in his arms with an inconsolable ache that seemed to hollow her out.

He had tried to soothe her, finding himself slipping, unforgivably, into childish appellations. At the start of the current school year, he had determined that he was too old and too cool to refer to his parents as *mommy* and *daddy* anymore, settling on *moms* and *pops*, like in the songs he listened to, but here he was with those soft words betraying his earnestness. "Don't cry, Mommy," he said. "Daddy's trippin'. Don't worry, I'll fix this." He meant it. He had always had a skill, an intuition, that guided his handling of force.

But there was no handling this force. The day after he had led his mother to her bedroom, she emerged from her room, still wounded yet resilient. In the car, she admitted that this was all deserved. "Your sister did something very bad," she had said.

Probably, she had done a *something bad* with a boy. Surely, it was Maksym Kostyk. Why else would he be concerned with her? Not some boy at school, where Chuk bore the weight of his family's secret like an albatross. Each afternoon, as he dutifully extracted homework assignments and exams from teachers on behalf of his sister, he felt so deeply ashamed that he would start to stutter. He couldn't understand this sensation. After all, Amara had misbehaved, not him. His bossy tattletale sister was getting her long-awaited just deserts, wasn't she? Well then, why did he dodge the eyes of her friends and teachers when they asked how she was recovering from her illness?

Always, his face would inadvertently lower, and his lips would quiver. Nothing but air would come out.

"What a sad, brave boy," they would say.

II

NINE

AMARA

What began in the Ewerike household was a kind of hush that filled the house, a slow burn searing bricks at their foundation like rotten loam, leaching rooms of oxygen. Only the ceaseless whir of the ceiling fan cut the air, not movement, not laughter. Each night, Fidelis and Adaobi slept in the same room, pinioned under the weight of their stubborn and watchful love; Chuk lay silently with his back to the wall separating his room from his sister's; meanwhile, Amara grew mad with longing.

Long days, so lonesome, made the nights, open and full of air and stars, fill Amara with a kind of heady rush. Her solitary days in the four brightly lit walls of her bedroom left her utterly bored. Algebraic equations solved, drawings sketched, scattered impressions etched in her journal, none of it was enough. Amara had never known what it was to so wholly crave companionship. At such times, she would peer out the window. Without fail, she'd find

Maksym underneath the awning of his trailer. When he boxed, he was effortless, aquiline and serene. Like the whole world had melted away. Like all opponents became a blur. Like time, gravity, and space were mere nothingness. He could simply exist, his heartbeat as constant as a metronome.

It reminded her of a story her mother had once told her, about Jonah and the Whale. The story was meant to frighten Amara into obeisance; instead, it kept her awake at night. In fascination, she'd imagine Jonah trapped in the belly of the whale, its darkness sudden, like a blown-out candle, the percussive thud of the whale's heartbeat, the damp hot air of the whale's dank, mossy breath, its slippery tongue moving up and down as it swallowed that human crumble caught in its throat, the echo of Jonah's fragile human noises, tinny and vibrating against the whale's fibrous stalactite inner walls, as he attempted to claw his way back toward the light and part the whale's great maw.

But Maksym wasn't Jonah. He was the whale. No, he was a slippery fish gliding underwater, its gills parting and collapsing with each breath, machinery oiled and fine-tuned by unseen forces, devoted to this single magnificent purpose. She thought of it as a kind of nakedness, exposed, his body a weightless, diaphanous thing propelled only by the rhythmic lull of his oceanic breaths. Maksym in the water, Amara in the sky!

While Fidelis paced, while Adaobi fretted, while Chuk and his friends under the canopy of stars smoked weed and dreamed up all the worlds freer than theirs, Amara began to imagine the ground rushing at her. She had a spectacular vision of herself taking flight. What would it be like to have wings? How would the breeze feel through her feathers? It was only then that she realized freedom had always only ever been under the domain of birds—and men—for even angels had to toil for the gods.

Amara sifted through her drawers until she found an old composition notebook. She rocked back into a corner of her bed, a blue pen in her hand, and drew a large, beakless bird spiraling in flight, its neck crooked to the side, away from the viewer. Concentrating on the bird's wings, she gradually thickened the line. She grasped a pencil, added gray, then with colored pencils she added yellow, then purple. She didn't think about composition, proportion, or shading; she only wanted to capture this ephemeral effect before it was beyond her grasp.

That afternoon, the Calumet Rows were calm in the characteristic way of late. Inside the Ewerike household, Amara's father slumped in the hallway, his back to her bedroom door, engrossed in yet another dispatch from Radio Biafra. Perched on his right thigh, his hand was balled into a fist. He sat, the model of a student, as he breathed each syllable of each proclamation. At breakfast the next morning, he would demand action.

All this, Amara knew but hadn't witnessed. She had grown familiar with the rhythms of the household, and she could almost visualize herself as part of the family again. There was the chuckle of the coffeepot, and her mother slurping its dark brew down as she sliced tomatoes. There were the sirens and howls as her brother lost at a video game. There was her father's shuffling step and the snap of the newspaper opening and shutting in front of his monocled countenance.

And there Amara was on the floor, in front of the TV, her earbuds in as she listened to Rihanna, her palms fanned out before her as she painted her fingernails cherry red and mouthed, "Under my um-bre-lla, ey, ey, eey!"

Amara gazed at the nightstand, at her mussed dinner plates. Tonight her father had made a steak glazed with a flavorless rhubarb jam. She ran the edge of her thumb along the serrated tip of her dinner knife, but cutting herself didn't make sense. In eighth grade one girl's arms were perpetually crusted with scratches, welts, and scabs in varying stages of recovery. All the other girls looked on, alternating between awe and disgust. Just like everyone else, Amara had derided the girl, but now she wondered at the secret thrill.

When the ninth-grade class had been initiated into a sisterhood of purged and starved silhouettes, Amara had been too afraid to join. Now, as she gazed in the mirror, she could see that she was growing fat. Just like then. While Sahara and Lois were growing slimmer in anticipation of summers at Cocoa Beach, she had been taking after her mother, growing heavy in the hips. *Do they think of me? Do they even remember me?* Perhaps she could go on a hunger strike like Gandhi. Refuse every one of her father's "special" meals. Day after day, her parents would watch her slowly wither away until nothing was left. They'd be sorry.

A groan. Making herself eat until she puked or starving until she fell over made no more sense than everything else she had tried: urinating on the floor, dousing the walls with chewed-up sweets, or even making a lewd display of soiled sanitary napkins. Her mother only sighed as she tiptoed around the messes while her father heaped her plate with more chocolates and treats.

Why did her brother have such freedom, while she was trapped under her parents' heels? The trouble was being a girl. The problem was this stupid lipstick, the hair, the clothes. A boy, her brother would one day grow into a man. His freedom would only multiply. But Amara was just a girl, would always be a girl, a thing to be watched and worried over, to be fretted, fixed in place, fettered until she was asphyxiated.

Even her mother had eventually deserted her. She was supposed to be Amara's ally, and she had even, for a spell, gone on strike—she pledged she'd give her husband nothing from the kitchen and the *other room*, promising to persist until he released Amara—but she gave in before long. All this vain bottom power amounted to nothing. Her mother abhorred force, yet at the same time, she despised the weak, especially in men, found frail men wanting and unimpressive. And so, in a way, her mother was both her father's greatest foe and admirer.

A whole thirty days had now passed since Amara's father had first turned the key. She had been bleeding then and she was bleeding out again. The spring formal had come and gone, her mother's May Day celebration. Soon, finals would be upon her. Each time her mother returned to the room, she averted her gaze as she emptied Amara's chamber pot, refreshed her basin, delivered her meals, and exchanged her homework assignments. Just once, Amara's mother had studied her face and gently rubbed away at the lipstick on her lips, lightly teasing, "Miss America."

Now, all the blood was flowing from Amara—she was sure of it—and if she didn't find a way to plug it, she might soon be emptied. Her whole body would split at its seams, like a pair of distressed jeans, and her soggy stuffing would spill out and mark the walls so that everyone would know what it meant for a body to wear a wound.

Eyeing her face, Amara shook her head at the prospect that a silly tube of red lipstick had seemed a victory scant weeks ago. She gripped her bottom lip with her teeth so firmly that they left an indentation. She tipped her head back until her eyes were level with their reflection in the mirror. All she saw were irises, dark and unwavering, not the look of menace she hoped for, just fragility. Her face was puffy and loomed large. Long Twiggy lashes clung to her eyelids for dear life, clownish, a mockery. Amara peeled them off. Her hair extensions were clumped together, stiff from weeks of untended new growth and lack of manipulation. Now, if she tried to go anywhere looking like this, she would be laughed at.

Amara riffled through her dresser drawers in search of a seam cutter or at least a pair of scissors; instead, she found her father's old clippers. They must have been there since her mother had last cleaned her nape. In frustration, Amara flung the clippers across the room.

Using her fingernails and a dinner knife, Amara pried the extensions free from the thick strings of thread that twined them to her plaits. When she reached the final row, her hair was too matted and tangled to give up the extension without a battle. It was as if her old life were taking one final stand, enacting one last defense, winner take all. As the single weft dangled from the side of her head like a dead crow, Amara glowered at her reflection. She yanked it. With the extension went a chunk of her own hair. Mortified, she recoiled, letting the clump of hair fall from her hands to the floor. She rubbed at the bald spot. In panic, she loosened the plaits, hoping they would cover the bald spot, but that only exaggerated the vacancy. Enraged, Amara grabbed the clippers. Bits of graying hair still clung to the edges of the blades. She brushed the hair away and gazed at her face in the mirror;

forgetting her brother, forgetting her mother, forgetting her father. The world went empty and dark, except for her.

A fleeting thought: all it would take was a quick, clean slit to each wrist. Then it would go away, the lonesomeness, the sadness, the yearning. She plugged the clippers into the outlet. Buzzing brought them to life. She outlined the joints of her wrists with a light touch.

Push a little harder, she urged.

Her heart raced.

She wanted to be something new, born again, a thing wild.

Seconds later, thick cotton tufts of hair floated around her, covering her dresser; stray strands lined her lashes, cheeks, and shoulders. What would happen if she just kept buzzing until there was nothing left to saw off but bone? Her breaths came out sharply at her reflection in the mirror.

Now I'm ugly, she thought in a panic.

Correction: I look like something new.

You don't know what it is to so suddenly feel free until you've recognized that some loves have a beginning and an end. For Amara, the realization struck as she knelt before the tufts scattered along the tile flooring. Now she wondered if the real reason she had cut her hair was to see if her parents might make some vain attempt to stop her. But her mother had never returned to claim her dinner dishes. Neither had her father.

Now the vile licorice scent of the fennel that accompanied her rhubarb steak ensnared her nostrils and throat, forcing her to gag. In mute fury, Amara snatched the dish and flung the fennel and green beans across the room. The plate clattered without breaking as it struck the wall and floor. The silence of a house at rest swallowed up the noise until the only sound was Amara's ragged, half-damp breath as she struggled to hold back tears that threatened to drown her.

She sank to the floor. Her parents had reached the end of their love for her. In a strange way, she felt unencumbered. If her parents didn't love her, then she was no longer beholden to them. Amara dove straight into no fucks given.

TEN

CHUK

It started as a soft tap, steady like the drip of a leaky faucet.

Tap. Tap. Tap . . .

It was a Sunday, unusually hot for late spring. Maybe this was why everything was so still. Only a fool would chance an outing on such a day. Outside, the air was suffocating; inert, heavy like a thick cotton garb draped over your body. Cars cooked. Even the dogs, left out to roast, were too parched to howl. They lay stretched out on their sides, mute and unimpressed

Everyone in the Ewerike clan was home. That was rare these days. Normally, Chuk's father would be running his letters to the post office. Chuk didn't know what the letters were for, but he suspected that his father was suing everyone who had ever wronged him, his colleagues, the bank, their old homeowner's association. When his father wasn't posting letters, he'd be collecting supplies at his favorite stationery store in Kissimmee. But today, Sunday, he sat inches from his computer, typing.

Tap. Tap. Tap . . .

Of late, Chuk's mother found reasons not to be home. She never said where she was going or when she'd return. Since none of her friends stopped by anymore, Chuk could only speculate that she'd taken a second job somewhere, maybe giving private vocal lessons or playing accompaniment for some Nigerian cultural event or a women's association meeting. In flashes of hopefulness, he'd tell himself that she was out trying to raise extra money for the Christmas season like she had done one year. Or maybe she was in an empty hall somewhere playing piano. He knew how much she missed her old piano. But today, his mother was in the bathroom. Water gushed into the tub, a splash as she planted one foot and then the other into it.

Tap. Tap. Tap . . .

In the living room, remote in hand, Chuk arched his back off the sofa arm, stretching. Scratched his balls. Bored with the selection, he flipped through the channels, settling on USA Network, where a rerun of *Bad Boys* was on. Will Smith and Martin Lawrence were cruising down a sunlit street past a stretch of palm trees, in a black sports car, when Smith suddenly whipped the car to the side of the road. Chuk tossed some Fritos into his mouth and chomped. Dinner tonight. Maybe that's why he didn't notice the noise at first.

Tap. Tap. Tap . . .

"What is that?" he asked the empty living room.

The sound grew.

Dum. Dum Dum . . .

It had hollowed.

Glancing over his shoulder, he called out, "What is that freakin' noise?"

Boom. Boom Boom . . .

Had his mother tossed his sneakers in the wash? Were they in the dryer now, banging away as the machine tossed them with each revolution? Sometimes the force was so powerful that the sneakers would kick the dryer door open. His mother would come rushing down the hallway to slam it shut again. He groaned. How many times did he have to explain to her that sneakers couldn't be cleaned in the washer? Look what she had done to his last pair of Jordans. Soaking them in bleach, then tossing them into the washer, she had said their smell was unbearable. But look how they were now faded, the vibrant edging on the logo stripped away, felt lining ragged and spongy. Those emblems of greatness would never again relive their glory, his boys had never failed to remind him.

Boom. Boom. Boom . . .

He followed the noise out of the living room. It led him directly to his sister's bedroom door. She must have been banging a sneakered foot against the door, probably thrusting, not even kicking. Shadows filled the hallway, so it took him a moment to realize that his father was slumped on the floor in front of Amara's door, eyes staring straight ahead, boring a hole into an invisible spot on the opposite wall. With each kick, his body convulsed.

Chuk turned to his father. "Dad, tell her to stop."

Wordless, his father jerked with another kick.

Chuk pounded the door. "Knock it off," he said. "Dad's right here!"

Boom. Boom. Boom . . .

"Quit it!" He banged. "I'm trying to watch TV!"

Boom. Boom. Boom . . .

"Look what you're doing to Dad! Stop. Kicking. The. Fucking.

Door!" Like he was punting a football, he heaved his leg back and slammed his foot at the door. His father's body jumped from the force of the kick.

Boom. Boom. Boom . . .

"I hate you!" Chuk shouted. "I hate you! I hate you!"

Boom. Boom. Boom . . .

The bathroom door creaked open. Light filled the hallway.

Grateful, he looked toward the light. As fog dissipated, his mother came into view. She was wrapped in a towel, legs and arms damp. Her hair was still covered in a shower turban, but coarse beaded ringlets of baby hair peeked out from under the edge of the terry cloth. He opened his mouth to speak, but his complaint died in his throat. His mother's eyes were red. Was she crying?

Voice small, he said, "Mom, tell Amara to stop. Please. I'm just trying to watch TV."

Boom. Boom. Boom . . .

Without a word, his mother took one sliding step after another until she disappeared into his parents' bedroom. The door clicked shut behind her.

Chuk marched to the living room and raised the volume of the TV louder and louder until his sister's knocking joined the orchestral accompaniment that soundtracked Will Smith as he leaped from a rooftop, tongue wagging, shirt unbuttoned, gun trained on his target. Even as he cranked the volume, Chuk continued to yell, "Quit it! Quit it! Quit it!"

Boom. Boom. Boom . . .

Somewhere, a moan, so low and guttural, shifted the air in the house. It found a way in between his sister's kicking and Martin Lawrence's bleating voice. Words began to form a jeremiad:

Why should I feel discouraged?
Why should the shadows come?
Why should my heart feel lonely?
And long for heaven and home?

His mother's voice. No, she didn't sound like Whitney Houston or even Beyoncé, but her voice was coarse and thick and ambitious. It hooked onto the sound of a feeling. His heart rocked. He hadn't heard her sing in so long. Not since they had moved to the Calumet Graveyard, as Chuk now called it. Even then, preferring soul, pop, jazz, or the insufferable ditties she taught her first graders, his mother rarely sang gospels. She had once said she did not know of sin until she learned the language of God. The one exception to her lapsed faith was prayer. She had always been a firm believer that singing was the only way God could hear the human voice, so she sang her prayers. But he hadn't heard anything like this before. From down inside her, a throaty dirge on her gula, big and wide enough to engulf you.

Chuk could hardly hear Will Smith and Martin Lawrence anymore, but slowly, as if not wanting to disturb a sleeping baby, he knelt on the floor, remote in hand, and silenced the TV. Gradually, the boom of his sister's thrusting foot began to abate; first to the judder of her heel seesawing against the door, until mid-tilt, nothing.

When Jesus is my portion
A constant friend is He
His eye is on the sparrow
And I know He watches me

Wasn't this like when his mother sang to him when he was small? The way her heartbeat would slow when she listened to an aria, how she would curl unto herself, extend an arm to Chuk, who had always been restless, bouncing from one end of the room to the other, but then, *ah*, there he was compact enough to fit into her lap. He would draw his legs in and bundle himself there, caught in the depths of her peace—but only for a spell—before he would spiral away like a Slinky.

I sing because I'm happy
I sing because I'm free
His eye is on the sparrow

His parents' passions had insulated Chuk from their sorrows and hardship. Only he hadn't known until it was gone. His father and his silly affection for his garden, his mother who had wept openly, grieving like a rivaled lover, at the loss of her old upright piano, too large to fit into their new lodgings at the Calumet Rows. *That old thing* that took up space. *That old thing,* a hand-me-down from Full Sail University music department's surplus sale, replaced with a weighted keyboard. *It's not the same*, she had at last lamented, giving in to the ache. *It's not the same.* Unused, the dust-covered keyboard remained, like a forsaken treasure, in a corner of the dining area.

His eye is on the sparrow
And I know He watches me

Except for his father, who had risen, no one could move. As her voice dropped into the final verse, his father stood in the doorway, palms at his sides, the secret swell in his rising chest that Chuk recognized all too well. His father was crying on the inside.

Now silence. Chuk began to understand for the first time that there was something invisible that was hungry inside his mother, and because it hadn't been fed in so long, it was dying. Tears streamed down his face.

With the close of the school year came freedom. As the only son, Chuk had mostly escaped his father's tyranny. There were no padlocks on his bedroom door or window. No one tore through his dresser drawers to destroy contraband. No one hunted him down when he was out with his friends playing basketball or smoking weed behind the Walmart—so long as he kept his grades in the territory of Bs. That first night of freedom, over the spitfire lyrics of Kanye, Chuk and his boys from school lazed in the bed of a pickup truck back of the twenty-four-hour Walmart, sipping from one shared bottle of Hennessy as they congratulated themselves on surviving yet another school year while simultaneously bracing for the report cards that would make the rounds soon.

Bursting with restlessness and reproach for their common lives, Chuk and his friends had made up their minds that the exodus would begin the instant they turned eighteen. Curt and Douglass talked about Vegas, while Juan dreamt of Miami or Chicago. Their parents, upright aspirants of middle-class comfort and respectability, all came from elsewhere—Haiti, Guatemala, Cuba, Cambodia, Down in the Delta. The boys, all freshmen, had banded together, initially as a means of survival, then as a source of camaraderie.

They'd had enough of the side-eyes that accompanied them as they entered the shops and convenience stores in Orlando. They were too cool to admit it, but when they had heard the news about a boy like them who had been killed while visiting his father, they had been afraid. So, they made up their minds that anywhere else was better than punkass Orlando: LA, New York City, Las Vegas, even Albuquerque.

"What about Nigeria?" DeMarcus Whitmore asked that night. Of late, he had developed a curiosity for all things from the Motherland. He wore a dashiki over his school uniform that none of the teachers were brave enough to confiscate, and dark shades rested low on the bridge of his nose, so that when he looked down at Chuk, the Kente-print beret that crowned his head slipped forward as well.

"Naw," Chuk said, chafing at his dismal recollection of the Underwear Bomber. What a relief that his boys didn't know anyone from his new neighborhood. They were the sort who couldn't let a good insult go to waste. In truth, he had never cared for Nigeria. The story of the Underwear Bomber had solidified a reluctant relationship with a place that was so far from the reaches of his imagination that it only evoked distaste. While his sister pestered their parents with questions, he had no interest in learning the secrets held captive by his parents' native tongue.

"Aw, man, how can you say that?" DeMarcus asked. "You of all people. You got a direct line to the Motherland. You been brainwashed by Whitey, or what?"

The others nodded in agreement, even pale, freckle-faced White Mike.

"I'm going to Tokyo," Chuk said. He didn't know where it came from, but it made perfect sense. Tokyo wasn't Las Vegas or New York City, but it had an exotic ring to it. And in addition to the electronics, Aikido, and Judo, Japan had flashy anime, manga, and the newly discovered hentai.

For an instant, DeMarcus considered, but then he nodded his approval. Chuk took a temperate swig of the Henny, mindful of the others awaiting their drop, and passed it on. They did like so until it was too dark to see their hands in front of their faces. Then it was light again, and he dragged himself home, still weary and half hammered.

Then he did it the next night. And the next night. And again.

Until one morning when Chuk found himself face-to-face with his father. As Chuk ascended the steps, it didn't immediately register who it was. Then, buzzed, exhausted, his head listing sideways, Chuk recognized his father's figure as it came into focus. Combined with the tranquil dawn and his father's specterlike hazy outline, this strange meeting had a magical quality. At once, Chuk knew that in some way his fate was beckoning.

"Sit, my son," his father said. "Let us talk as two men."

Not *sit, boy.* An announcement was coming. Knock-kneed and apprehensive, Chuk dropped onto the stoop—not too close to his father, because he might smell the liquor.

His father said nothing. Lost in the brightening sky of oranges and reds, he remained silent.

At first, Chuk squirmed. Cognac soured his breath. Then he felt drained. All the strangeness of the past two months weighed upon his shoulders.

A twitch of anxiety. *He saw my grades!* The imminent threat of his father's disappointment overwhelmed him. Surely it was the C on his English final, a literary analysis theorizing that Romeo Montague was a simp. To Chuk's boys, his thesis was thoroughly convincing, but it was obvious that Mr. Kim had it out for him. Chuk had calculated his score, so he felt confident that he'd be able to slide, just barely, into a B, which his mother would admonish, but his father would accept with resignation and a solemn tale about a boy who had failed to reach his full potential because of his "lackadaisical ways." As always, Chuk would blurt out something nonsensical, hopeful for a laugh or a chuckle, but his mother would cock her head and say, "This boy! Ekwensu!" And his father would raise an eyebrow and ask, "Have you looked at your books today?"

It was funny, Chuk had always complained so long and so lustily about his parents, how he wanted to get far away from them. Now, with the stillness that divided his home, what he desired most was to hear his father's voice thundering on with some proverb about rats and tortoises and crocodiles, which would somehow lead through a forking path to a lesson about a boy studying for his Science 9 exams.

At long last his father spoke. "The sun is rising, my son. You see?" He pointed.

Chuk nodded in solemn relief, wondering if all along his father's sole cause had been to share a sunrise with him.

"A sun is a glorious thing. It's a renewal. It means there was never lost hope." He was looking at the sky, but in that brief moment, Chuk wondered if, in fact, his father was referring to a *son*, and not just any son: that cherished *okpara*, the male heir of a father's lineage. He groaned.

Or maybe his father was referring to his beloved garden, where he spent many hours under the sun, herding seeds and roots into obedience like a jailer, only to fret over all the hazards of the wild just outside of the fence he had constructed. Some seasons, he'd lament the geckos and squirrels and beetles that gorged on the tomatoes, okra, and cucumbers that he spent many an hour describing to Chuk while stroking their flesh like a lover. His father was always in search of a magical organic pesticide. One year he dusted the earth with cayenne pepper, another year it was chili powder mixed with mineral oil, and one year he found great success with uda peppers. He kept these tied together in little sachets, then would grind them under a pestle and douse them in oils before massaging the earth with the concoction.

Until just now, it hadn't even occurred to Chuk to consider the irony in nature's mandate that to love something into survival, you had to kill something else. At the time, he had only grown restless and distracted as his father opined on the textures of spinach leaves. Chuk would twist away to swat at butterflies. He'd scratch at his ear, leap enthusiastically after a gecko—because he'd just learned that if you pressed its belly, its great maw would open, and you could clip it to your ear like an earring. Eventually his father would leave him to his video games. But not today.

His father spoke again.

"Long ago, a prosperous land was invaded by foreigners. Much blood was shed. The indigenes mourned their dead. Then one day, a blazing yellow sun, hot like a flame, rose from the earth, torching an abundant field of green, leaving in its wake an ashy wasteland. The natives saw despair. Until one old man came forward. 'Umu m,' *my children*, he said, 'Lee anya ozo,' *look again*. And they did. Mid-rise, in its ascendancy, the bold yellow sun of eleven rays crowned the singed plain. Behold a kingdom! Biafra!"

A rat was sure to make an appearance, or a crocodile, or a dog. Nearly every one of his father's proverbs featured a half-wit dog that had bitten off its own tail because of his vanity or hubris. But then Chuk began to understand. His father was speaking about Nigeria—well, Biafra.

All at once, Chuk was reeling at the image of that boy of grim eyes extinguished of all hope, the Underwear Bomber. Had the boy's father ever been to Biafra? And if he had, was he a soldier like Chuk's father? Were the two friends or foes? And why, even at war's end, hadn't his father ever returned to a land so darling to him that he refused to forget it?

Sure, Chuk knew about the war. He recognized that his father, a soldier, had endured something unimaginable. He had even been captured by the enemy. But he never spoke of it. Instead, he'd demur, saying, "He who abhors dog meat should not eat dog meat soup." What little Chuk knew of wartime came from his mother, but she spoke vaguely, mentioning that they'd lost countless friends and family during the war, including his father's baby sister, Ugochi. When Chuk had pressed, she'd only say, "They took her." But that was all. Who was they? Enemy soldiers? Where did they take her? Did they kill her? Why not say so? Chuk wasn't a baby. But he would never know because his mother would always sigh in exasperation. "Leave me in peace, Ekwensu!"

"Daddy, what was it like there?" Chuk asked, slipping yet again, forgetting that his father was now *Pops* or *Dad*, not *Daddy*, because *Daddy* and *Mommy* were said by middle schoolers, mama's boys, not high schoolers. It occurred to him just then that in his fourteen years, he had only ever seen old photographs of Nigeria, not his father's beloved Biafra. Surely it was flanked with streets of gold, 3D video games, and women who looked like Ms. Cathy, his childhood pediatric nurse—beautiful, buxom, a buttery voice, and smelling of perfume as she clicked her kitten heels down the hallway—Chuk's first love. Why else should such a place be scored into his father's memory?

As if he hadn't really expected Chuk to be listening, his father started in surprise. "In Nigeria?"

"Yeah," Chuk said.

"In Biafra," he corrected.

"Yeah."

"What do you want to know?"

"What do you remember from when you were my age?"

His father's face softened. "Your age? A boy? Fourteen?"

"Yeah."

"So long ago. *Ah-ah!* Can you believe it?" His eyes narrowed in joyous concentration. "I was just a boy then, like you. Biafra was but a seed."

His face went slack. Voice soft, as if memory were still forming, he said, "I was not yet seventeen, like your sister."

Chuk reflected on that bewildering day when his father had locked his sister in her room after watching the news. He remembered the girls who had been kidnapped, columns of Nigerian girls shrouded from head to toe in robes. Had the girls done something wrong, like his sister? Was Nigeria at war, as it had been when his father was a boy?

Amara would know. She knew about many things, especially concerning females. He would have to ask her. But he hated to ask her anything because she'd call him fetus. He couldn't even ask his friends. They'd mock him. He couldn't ask his mother because she'd be shocked and tell him such matters did not concern well-mannered boys. Better to ask Google.

Blinking, his father continued, "Your sister. She's a good girl, understand? She was confused. Why would she run off with that whiteboy?"

Nostrils flaring. "I never liked their smell. What could one of them know of her world?"

An announcement: "I am the head of this family!"

A sigh, sternness falling away from his features, all the marks of worry having receded: "Your sister."

Each wave of feeling came in a rush. Chuk couldn't keep up.

"Chuks, have you been drinking?" his father suddenly asked.

Smelling liquor on Chuk's breath, his father would return to scolding Chuk about his grades or the opportunities he squandered while playing *Fortnite*. With his habituated disappointment and regret, he'd wish his son had never been born.

"I know what you're going to say," Chuk began without prompting. "Blockhead, goat, anu ohia, ozu, foolish boy, iberibe, nzuzu, akata, ogbanje, Ekwensu!"

His father chuckled. Slurs to some, pet names to another. The Igbo alphabet of insults. His face softened. "Get up now." He reached to stroke Chuk's shoulder and pull him in for a hug, but stopped. "Save that for a time when you have shown bravery," he said.

Chuk drew away.

"My son, I know I have been a little bit more inflexible with you than your sister. I have to be. Soldiers of war are taking daughters, and wives, and sisters to places they might never be seen or heard from again. I am not under some vain illusion that I will live forever. On the contrary, I am an old man and my children came late. My own father, an early convert, married only one wife. There are no uncles or cousins in America. The few relations remaining in Nigeria are not close. One day I won't be around to look after your mother and sister. In my stead, I desire no one else to stand but my son. My mighty Ikenga."

He reached to stroke Chuk's head. They both knew that he'd thwacked it so often it would not be a surprise if a callus had formed. A compromise. A playful tap. "Chai! Ekwensu! Troublemaker!" He cackled. "I was called that when I was a boy."

"You call me that."

He chuckled. "Ekwensu!"

"You're saying I'm bad," Chuk said. "Mom says it means Satan."

His father wheezed with laughter. Then he grew serious. "When the white man brought his church, he brought the devil with him. Before that, Igbos knew of no Satan. Ekwensu is a tricky fellow. He is an instigator. He shakes the world up to beget renewal. You, my son, are a magic maker, a titan." He lifted Chuk's chin. "Chukwudiegwu, save your anger for your father's foes."

Who were his foes? Was he talking about the war again? Chuk blurted out, "Are they the enemies who took Ugochi?"

His father's smile froze.

Chuk swallowed. "Why haven't we, we, met her?" he stuttered.

"Ugochi?"

"Yeah."

Alone with some reverie, his father often would wrinkle his brow, narrow and squint his eyes, and then they would go unsteady. It was his way of subduing a tremor. Chuk would recognize that his father was gone, lost in his private thoughts, providing the perfect opportunity for Chuk's escape from a long-winded lecture or parable. But this time, startled, he realized that his father was flexing with nervousness. It filled Chuk with dread.

He stared intently into Chuk's eyes. "Man's inventions fail each day. Fans stop whirring. Players eat videotapes. Lighters crackle and shit darkness. Gas lines in tanks erupt. Bullets choke at just the moment when they should fire. And sometimes, when a man stands so near to death that he can study its face, death fails too, so miserably that the survivor is caught between life and death, reliving that instant of horror again and again; a nuisance, really; spiraling, stopping, and starting; a plague, a misery with a chokehold impossible to part from when living and in dreams.

"I was not yet seventeen when I became a man. When I was young, I had two duties. I was to protect my nation and protect my family. My mama was gone. My papa was gone. Both died in a car accident when I was too small to remember their voices. When war came, I was just a boy, sef. No one taught me how to be a man. We were a ragtag bunch of recruits to the army. They trained us in weaponry, foot drills, how to ascend walls, and how to clean our wounds. And now I must train you."

Chuk braced for the solemn proverb, not about Ugochi, but about turtles and rats and crocodiles. Instead, his father clapped. Gesturing a briefcase, he said, "My son, I have important business. Your aunt Ugochi is alive. And I am going to find her. I must deliver these envelopes. Much depends on these letters landing in the right hands. But I have been afraid to leave when I shouldn't." His eyes swelled with feeling. "You, my son, my okpara, my mighty Ikenga, you will stand guard in my place. I charge you Keeper of the Abode."

His father kept a key looped to a string wrapped around his waist and dug deep down into his slacks. He bathed infrequently and ate even less, so there was no separating man from key. Just thrice daily the glint of the key would resurface when Chuk's mother or father would deliver Amara her meals and empty her commode. Now, as he reached for the key, Chuk rushed to take it from his father.

"My son," he said, raising a hand to stop him, "the patient dog eats the bone's marrow. Understand?"

Yes, Chuk understood.

His father held out the key. For once, his eyes glinted with pride and hope.

When Chuk's mother called him *okpara*, the word was bloated with self-aggrandizement, like she exaggerated the praise only because she wanted a bit for herself. But when his father said the word, Chuk felt his spine lengthen. His father had always been a mystery to him. He was a shaken bottle of soda, bubbles rising up the neck, fizzing just at the lip, menacing, but also mild and tranquil when undisturbed. In brief bursts of affection, he'd instigate girlish laughter in Chuk's mother and an amused eye roll from his sister.

But his father had always regarded Chuk with marked resignation, his own son an object of contempt to endure. Chuk wasn't certain of when it began, but if there was one act of ineptitude that loomed large in his memory, it was the shaving incident. It was a time meant only for him and his father. His father would lather their faces, and standing alongside one another in the mirror, they would shave together; that is, until the day Chuk decided to surprise his father by doing it on his own. Of course, he did not find out until it was too late that all along his father had been quietly removing the blade from his razor before they shaved. Chuk still bore a mark on his chin from the fiasco. What he remembered most from that day wasn't the pain or the streaks of blood that followed the tracks of the razors, or even his mother's sirening wails; it was the expression that had crossed his father's face, one of failure and liability.

Due to this, Chuk had always spent his days dodging his father, comforted by the company of his boys while shooting hoops at the YMCA, swimming in the leaky pool on Alafaya Trail, lying belly-up on a patch of lawn or in the bed of someone's big brother's pickup truck, blowing whorls of marijuana out like steam. That all changed when he became Keeper of the Abode.

Now, mornings, his father greeted him by shaking his hand, tipping his hat, and calling, "Comrade." At first, Chuk saw himself as Biden to his father's Obama, but when his father chastised President Obama, which he often did more and more these days, that stopped. Now Chuk would nod in agreement, though he wasn't exactly certain what had gone wrong, since his father had once called Obama his junior brother. Chuk thought of himself as his father's Secret Service detail. Standing sentry in the arch of the hallway, back straight, chest ballooned, he imagined himself in dark shades and a dark suit as he surreptitiously shadowed his father's movements, alert to acts of espionage. This imaginary scene concealed the reality: in the absence of his father, the hours Chuk now spent on guard outside his sister's bedroom were relentlessly boring. Just the same, it was a cherished duty placed in his hands.

That morning, from the hallway, Chuk watched as his father rinsed and splashed on aftershave, then slipped into a suit and a smart jacket. He looked like a man off to fire lazy, incompetent workers. This sent shivers of admiration through Chuk. His father no longer looked disheveled. In fact, he looked even more polished and smooth than he had when he used to work at the law firm. Fuck them. His father was off to do something far greater than filing dusty papers. He was off to save the world from Russian spies. His father was Naija James Bond.

Just before his father reached the front door, he stopped and surveyed his son. Chuk waited for the ritual warning, *Only open the door for emergency,* but instead, his father tipped his chin up. Chuk held his breath. He prayed his father wouldn't remember the scar on his chin. He let Chuk's chin fall and returned to their now daily ritual: "Only open the door for emergency, understand?"

"I know," Chuk said.

"What is 'emergency'?" his father asked.

"Life and death, blood and bone."

His father's rejoinder was always an affirmative nod. Then, he'd place the coveted key in Chuk's hand and set out on foot, briefcase in hand.

But this time, just before handing him the key, he smiled.

For the first time, he said, "My man. Commander in chief, I salute you!"

Chuk saluted back.

By midday, his father returned, as always, damp and musky, eager to relieve Chuk of his post and deliver Amara's noontime meal. His father asked for a report of the day's events, and Chuk, with managerial posturing, embellished the facts rather than admit that while he diddled with a video game in the hallway, his sister simply ignored him. He described a querulous litany of curses that echoed from her bedroom. Rather than admit that when he tried to order her to clean her room, she had slipped a note under the door that read *Fuck off, fetus,* he told his father, "I'm afraid I was required to reprimand the ward due to insubordination."

As always, his father listened, his expression grave yet

speculative. With each report, Chuk couldn't shake the feeling of comeuppance. If only his sister had treated him with more respect, then he might have more sympathy for her.

Like always, at the conclusion of the report, Chuk's father patted him on the shoulder. "Well done, comrade." They exchanged an affirmative nod.

It was an education. In this way, Chuk came to learn that the longer his sister remained sequestered in her room, the longer his father would hold him in high regard.

Since that early morning on the porch, Chuk's father had also been entrusting him with errands. Most of the tasks were commonplace—taking out the trash, watering the garden, checking the mail—chores that Chuk would have once bemoaned. Now they filled him with a sense of duty. With each passing day, the tasks increased in significance, so that when his father, from his usual position at the computer—where he spent his evenings laboriously typing, fingers knocking at the keys like an old hen snapping up feed in its beak—handed an empty ink cartridge to Chuk and asked him to fetch a new one from Walmart, Chuk rose to the task like a brave soldier off to battle.

Stuffing the wad of bills in his pocket, Chuk slipped out the front door into a heat so heavy that it hummed in his ears. A mail carrier met him at the stoop. She extended an envelope to him. An address of several lines, in his father's tightly looped script, covered the face of the envelope. The letter had been marked *Insufficient address.* It was addressed to the Fathers of Biafra. Although it had been directed to Ministry of Interior, Garki, Abuja, Nigeria, a place that Chuk had never heard of, much less visited, it had never made it beyond Orlando's central post office.

"Thanks, man," he said to the mail carrier. With the envelope stuffed in his pocket, he cut across the lawn and escaped the complex entrance. Walmart was a short fifteen minutes on foot, a direct shot down Old State Road 50. At such an hour the road was serene and barren.

This was the third such returned letter that Chuk had intercepted, but his father would never know. Every afternoon, right around the time when the mail carrier arrived, Chuk would linger at the window until he heard the sound of the mail truck. Nothing could spoil the good that had come from his father's long days spent at his computer. It reminded Chuk of how his father used to be. The fervor and excitement with which he daily approached his task reminded Chuk of when his father would tune and retune a contract or legal brief like an instrument. Balls of paper would fill the wastebasket as he began again and again, typing and retyping a single verse until it produced the right sound.

In Walmart, Chuk purchased the ink without incident. It was on his way home that he realized he had forgotten to throw away the letter. He had discarded each previous missive somewhere far from home so that its existence could never be detected by his father.

Overgrown scrubs formed a perimeter around Walmart. Adjacent to it, crackling mariachi music floated from a food truck smelling of pinto beans and spices, momentarily distracting Chuk from his task. He contemplated buying a taco with the change in his pocket. He decided against it. Every nickel and dime would land in his father's hand when he returned home. It was a must. This absolute truth would make up for this small deceit. Chuk balled up the envelope and tossed it into a trash can at the rear of the food truck.

A stout lady, dark hair billowing around her beet-red face, bounded from behind the truck, hollering, "You think this your home?"

"Huh?"

"*Huh?*" she mocked. Snatching the crumpled envelope out of the large plastic drum, she asked, "I your mama? I clean for you?"

"No," Chuk mumbled. "I didn't—"

"No more," she said. "Today, I call police." She retrieved a cell phone from an apron pocket.

What would happen when his father received a phone call from the police? How would Chuk explain the letter ending up in the hands of the police? If his father found out, maybe he'd lock Chuk up in his room like his sister? Or look upon his son with scorn. Chuk had to get the letter back. His eyes darted about, landing on a large rock. If he could stun her long enough, he'd have the chance to retrieve the letter and get out of there.

Panic jumbled the lady's words in his ears. As she continued to shout, she began to dial.

Chuk seized the stone.

The door to the food truck swung open. Just under an arc of light stood a boy. At first, with his back to Chuk, he was unrecognizable. Then, Chuk's eyes went crisp and alert as the boy turned. The mayor. Raphy, with his single distinctive feature, the ratlike buckteeth that dug into the meat of his bottom lip. Any other boy would have tried to appear less ratlike, hiding those hideous fangs with a closed mouth, standing tall, flaring those pinched-tip nostrils, or at least appearing less hostile. Not Raphy Gaspar Gutiérrez. Everything about him was a dare. When angered and humiliated, Chuk fought the urge to call him Ratly to his face, but instead, safely at home, he'd beat his mattress, hissing, "Die Ratly. Ratly Die. Die Ratly."

Not even twenty yards separated the two. Only then did it occur to Chuk that what he'd thought was a trash can wasn't one at all. That was what the lady had been squawking about. He was about to speak, but Raphy turned to the still-fuming woman. "Tía, está bien. I know him. He goes to my school. Él es mi amigo, tía. Go inside." His tone was calm and sensible. "He brought it for me." He reached out to her and accepted the balled-up envelope quivering in her hands.

"Matón, no more, entiendo?" she hurled at Chuk. Pointing at a broken patched-over window at the rear of the food truck, she added, "Next time, you bad boy come again, I call police." The door slammed.

It was plain that she didn't believe Chuk was innocent, but at least she had calmed enough to put down the phone and go inside. What an unlikely ally in Raphy. *Amigo*. Maybe they could be friends after all. In fact, Raphy was probably just as embarrassed as Chuk would have been if his mother had behaved that way. Chuk set down the stone.

"Thanks for sticking up for me," he said. "I didn't do that, for real." He pointed at the broken window. "No lie, I thought it was a trash can. I was just throwing away a letter. Okay? Tell her."

Raphy smoothed out the envelope until it was nearly flat. "This?"

"Yeah."

"Fidelis Ewerike?" Raphy read from the envelope. "Who's that?"

"My dad."

"Garki, Abyooo-jah," Raphy read aloud, slaughtering the vowels, laughing at the sound. "Where's that?"

"In Africa." Chuk swallowed. "I guess. Can I have it back?"

"Seeing as you didn't want it and threw it on a Gaspar Gutiérrez establishment, technically it's mine." Raphy spoke in the same sensible tone he had used with his aunt. There was no denying the simple logic. To hand it back would be a favor, and favors were only between friends.

As Raphy pried the envelope open, Chuk stood frozen. They weren't amigos after all. Raphy pulled the typewritten missive out and began, silently, to read to himself. He whistled. His eyes widened. Eyes pitying, he glanced up at Chuk. "I don't blame you for throwing this away. I would, too. Can't even laugh about this. Does your moms know what your pops is up to?" He paused. "Or should I say, *who*?"

Chuk's face burned. For the first time, it occurred to him that he didn't know anything about the content of the letters other than that they had something to do with his aunt Ugochi. And Ugochi had something to do with those girls from that boarding school in Nigeria. But he hadn't really concerned himself with that. It was his sister, not those girls, who was the root of his family's dysfunction. Surely, what had happened to those girls in that boarding school was too far away to impact his own family's quiet daily habits.

Besides, it embarrassed him to think of them as Nigerian in that way. He much preferred the kings and queens that DeMarcus Whitmore boasted of, fondly singling out Chuk and greeting, "My negus." Though Chuk suspected that there were no empires in his family's lineage.

Could his father be having an affair, as Raphy had insinuated?

Only then did it occur to Chuk just how fragile his parents' relationship had become. Yes, they fought from time to time, but their quarrels were never protracted. They always came back to one another sooner, rather than later. They had never been openly affectionate, but he had always attributed it to their being Nigerian and finding it indecent.

Now things were different. Though they inhabited the same home, they never seemed to be in alignment with one another. It was all because of his stupid sister. Whatever she had done had caused a fracture that had grown into a fault line. Their parents were far apart on separate poles. He had to see the letter for himself. Hand out, he reached, but Raphy didn't budge.

"Give it."

Raphy slipped the letter back into the envelope, folded the opening shut, and then balled it up again. Just as he was about to toss it to Chuk, he let it fall into the plastic drum. "My bad."

The way Raphy held the drum, Chuk figured the drum did not contain recycling or garbage as he had initially assumed. If it were full of refried beans and salsa, then Chuk would never know what his father had written.

"Yo, why do you hate me?" Chuk asked. "What'd I ever do to you?"

Annoyance washed over Raphy's face. "You gonna cry like a baby?"

Chuk said nothing.

"Fine," Raphy said. "Whatever." He reached into the drum. When his hand came up again, he tossed the crumpled letter at Chuk.

Time moved slowly. The projectile hung suspended in the air before plopping to the ground a few feet from him. Chuk scrambled toward it, but he stopped just short of retrieving it. Now it was clear that the large drums were filled with laundry. Because Raphy had tossed a pair of white Fruit of the Loom briefs streaked with skid marks.

"Underwear Bomber," Raphy drawled.

A sound like an ocean's waves filled Chuk's ears. His heart hammered. His fingers quaked. He couldn't breathe, he was so angry. His mind shorted and the image that replaced the letter was that of the would-be bomber with the hopeless expression on his face. Chuk picked up the stone again. When he released it, he heard a crack, a shriek, and a moan as Raphy cried out and his tía swung open the door to their food truck.

Static in his ears, Chuk took off in a sprint.

By the time he heard the sirens wailing, he was already in his bedroom, a chair wedged under the knob of the slammed door. Only then did he stop to catch his breath, his heart pulsing in his ears. He laughed first, harder than he had in a long time. Then he was suddenly morose.

Maksym's right, he said to himself. *I have to fight Raphy.*

ELEVEN

FIDELIS

Ugochi Edwina Ewerike.

In the age of the Internet, it should have been simple: contact the American Red Cross and ask them to locate the branch that had handled the Biafra airlift program in the year and region where Ugochi was last seen. They would find Ugochi's name on a roster with information about her foster family. If her name had been changed, they would search through records for girls of her age. They would call every number.

And then it would be like the movies. A voice like a whisper would speak into the mouthpiece. Ugochi's grown-up voice, accented with the lilt of a Gabonese or the chuckle of a Ghanaian. Or maybe she had made it all the way to Canada or France. Fidelis would say, *Nwa nne m nwanyi*, my sister, *do you remember the time . . . ?*

But it hadn't been so simple. Multiple agencies—the American

Red Cross, the French Red Cross, the Salvation Army, and scores of Christian missions—had participated in the airlift and other relief efforts once the infamous *Life* magazine cover of the starving children traversed the globe. To evade detection by Nigerian military forces, agencies contributed under the cover of darkness, often with the pretense that they were delivering goods rather than carting away the orphaned and infirm. Due to the risks associated with the enterprise, records were hastily collected. Only a meticulous reassembly of patchwork documents could possibly begin to form the truth of Ugochi's whereabouts.

Still, Fidelis had persevered. By day he prepared missives. By night, he drank and knocked his hips with laughter. "When happiness is in sight," he had admonished, "why delay the celebration?"

But over the weeks that had followed, postal letters disappeared into the ether. When Fidelis sent out emails, they were almost always returned undeliverable, and on the chance that he should receive a reply, it was only a form letter, impatient and impersonal. Soon, his optimism had become dismay. From dismay, he grew disillusioned and eventually despondent.

Fidelis was versed well enough in Nigerian diplomacy to know that money was the grist of action, but there wasn't enough money these days. And should he become a millionaire overnight, the reality sank in that he wouldn't even know where to begin his search on the ground. Fidelis Chinonso Ewerike hadn't set foot on his native soil since the early hours of a January morning in the year 1970, the day Deputy Effiong, in place of exiled President Ojukwu, had negotiated the surrender of Biafran forces.

TWELVE

ADAOBI

In a split second, some of the schoolgirls had decided to act rashly, unwisely, and be disobedient. Under the cover of night, they jumped and ducked and hid while the uniformed men who had come to take them away pressed on into the dark. Adaobi, hearing their whimpering voices and staggering breaths, had bolted straight up in bed and woken from her dream. Fidelis's side of the bed had remained cold and untouched as he kept vigil in the hallway outside Amara's bedroom.

That was the day, mere weeks ago, when Adaobi had first stumbled into the assembly of the strange preacher. Early in the morning that Sunday, after waking from her dream, she had pulled on her robe, gone to the kitchen window, and peered out at the pitch landscape, but instead of girls, she had seen the back of a boy, pale in the remnants of moonlight, his slim and muscled arms and legs pumping as he sliced through knee-high grass in the direct line of a porch light.

By dawn, well before the rest of the family had risen, she was already in the kitchen. She could not go back to sleep, not with the thundering sounds of those disobedient girls' feet as they escaped their captors. Not with the tinny silence in her home. She'd reached for a coffee mug, but her trembling hands stopped her. She tried again, grasping the mug, only to feel it slipping from her hand and crashing to the tile floor and splitting in two. Holding her breath, she waited a moment, but after a brief stir Fidelis's snores resumed. The children remained in their rooms.

Adaobi knelt to pick up the pieces. Would this be their life? Would the wounds that had been reopened remain open? Her hands began to tremble again, so she jammed them into her robe's pockets, only to find a warped piece of cardboard. It was the handbill the preacher had handed to her. During wartime, after her time with the nuns, Adaobi had turned away from her faith, but now, when everything had failed her, she had just one recourse left. Her family needed a miracle, and she knew of only one place left to turn.

Circling the streets for what seemed hours, Adaobi had finally struck up enough nerve to attend the service. It was held at the Lynx Movie House, an old strip-mall second-run movie theater that boasted three-dollar movies six days per week. On Sundays, it became the Kingdom of the Second Coming of the Marvelous Creator and Holy Redeemer. With its sad flickering marquee featuring *Terminator*, the building looked nothing like the distinguished castlelike Gothic cathedral on the handbill. She sat sweating in her car, muttering to herself, nearly turning around. What cures and miracles could occur in such a place? She even clucked in amusement. Instead of seeking a prayer, she ought to have suggested a family outing. Buttery popcorn in their laps, in unison, the Ewerikes would exhale as Arnold Schwarzenegger punched holes through concrete in pursuit of Sarah Connor.

Adaobi would later learn of the building and its storied past. What the congregation referred to as "The Great Mystery": on a bright sunny day, a mysterious clap of lightning had suddenly pierced the sky. First, a spark, then an explosion, then a fire burned their Gothic cathedral to naught. The senior pastor, a humble, soft-spoken man, was trapped in the fire and charred beyond recognition. Then a tall man, white from head to toe, rose from the rubble. The man took the name of John, and he became their shepherd.

So eager was the congregation to flee the damned site that they had auctioned the land at a loss. The paltry proceeds were spent on simple furnishings and the indefinite Sunday lease of the movie theater. Atop the stage, a cross adorned a pedestal positioned on risers. Dusty plastic flowers were bunched at each end of the stage, and one portrait of a menacing-looking Jesus expressing both anguish and fury hung in front of burgundy curtains.

From the back row, Adaobi listened to three congregants chattering over Pastor John's *appalling* marital status. There were always widows after him, one said, women despondent over the untimely deaths of men they hadn't liked much to begin with, men who had left them nothing but the status of *widow* when they had *chosen* to betray their wives to the infidelity of heart attacks and pulmonary embolisms. Still, these parish women observed marriage as the blue standard for a sister, and if one should have the fortune to attain the beatific title of pastor's wife, she would have direct access to heaven, minus the tolls.

"Chai! It is indignity," one of the women said, wagging her

head, to which one wife replied, "He is a holy vessel, oh. No woman will tempt him."

The third shouted, her hands chopping the air, "He no go put woman before God!"

Clothed in white from top to bottom, but his dark shades, Pastor John was a blond apparition. That first early morning, Adaobi had sat in the back pew, clutching her handbag to her chest. He was the only albino she had ever known to bear the mark immodestly. It astonished her into obeisance. His pearly skin was an anointment directly from God. He was chosen. What else could explain his many escapes from impending misfortune?

Before the service began, one of the gossips had turned to Adaobi. She'd looked her up and down, and then conspiratorially waved her over. Stiffly, Adaobi rose and took the place next to her. "You've come for deliverance," the woman said knowingly. "You've come to the right place. Let me tell you about this man," she said, and then she told his story.

First Pastor John's mother had forsaken him, then his father. Under the lazy guardianship of his grandmother, he was kidnapped by a trader who brought him to a smuggler. When Pastor John hadn't fetched the price they had agreed upon, the trader angrily dumped him along the side of the road—only for him to be rescued by an old itinerant farmer who turned out to be a native doctor.

The doctor had intended to trim each of the boy's appendages, piece by piece, for medicines. He'd calculated all the maladies each aspect of Pastor John's body could heal: malaria, heatstroke, diabetes, impotence, carotid artery, lovesickness, infertility. The doctor started with the pinkie finger on the left hand, what Pastor John called the devil's pistol. Next, he'd planned to work on the pinkie on the right hand.

But on the morning of the severing, a great rumble shook the earth. A bright light slashed the small hut in two. While the light blinded the doctor, Pastor John stood and walked the path God had paved for him. That was why he could no longer look directly at the sun without the aid of his sunglasses. It was why an overcast day filled him with delight.

As if timed, the pastor bellowed, "I *am* Man of the People!"

Applause. Congregants rocking and bucking in time with music that thrummed from the organ in Pastor John's throat. A storm. And he was at the helm of the ship, swaying. Yellow lights blinked behind his stark, trembling figure. He pumped a hat before his face. He was so red from the light, so drenched from the heat, Adaobi felt certain he could sweat salvation.

His organlike voice belted, "Today is a *glor*ious day brought to us by *the* Lord; and the Lord is *good*."

"Amen" was the chorused reply.

"A-men," Adaobi said slowly.

"Our *Father's* love *pours* from the spout of our Savior . . ."

"Amen," said the chorus.

"A-men," Adaobi said.

"A *cool* drink of this goodness enters the soul and *awakens* the spirit, am uh right?"

Adaobi's enthusiastic "A-men!" ahead of the chorus.

"Our Father's *good*ness, our Father's *good* love, is an instrument of *good* grace," he sang. "For we are all *sin*ners!"

Heat swelled at Adaobi's temples. She was brought back to the hospital room, that strange day when she and Gertrude Afolabi had seen the woman's husband, a pitiful sight, bound by tubes and wires. In his place, she imagined Fidelis. She could see it so clearly.

"God's grace is *good*, isn't it?" Pastor John called out, bringing his proclamation to a decrescendo. He shifted the dark shades to his nose. A spotlight shone from the back of the room. Dust motes swirled in the light, casting their shadows. Adaobi squinted at him. In answer, dark nystagmic pupils, so moist they seemed to glitter, gesticulated in the light. "God's *good* grace lifts us out of dark corners."

Adaobi averted her eyes.

His voice grew louder and lustier with each proclamation as he began to crescendo. "All the *sweet*ness I need comes from the *sweet* loving God is giving me." He waved up high. He rocked forward, his lips puckered.

"I'm going to tell you a part of the *story* that I haven't told a soul," he bellowed.

And the crowd leaned.

"When I was a child, my *earthly* father and mother *abandoned* me. I *have* told you this story, no?"

And the crowd breathed their admiration.

"When my *earthly* mother and father *abandoned* me, I felt a stone *growing* in my soul, but I let the sweet *Lord* fill me with light. I let his Word guide me onto the righteous path, and one day I came *home*.

"I cannot say the *same* for my *earthly* mother and father.

"I prayed that the *good Lord* would rake their scattered souls over fire. I prayed that the *good Lord* would tear their weakened flesh bit by bit. I prayed to the *good Lord* that the sparrows would grow fat from their plundered flesh. I prayed to the *good Lord* that what remained would burn."

Pastor John looked proud, smug, satisfied. But how could anyone take such pleasure in calling upon the Lord to retaliate against any mortal, no less one's parents? Adaobi shuddered. Hate of this kind would only eat you from the inside out, leaving nothing but a carcass.

"One *day*," Pastor John rang out, eyes brimming with tears of jubilation, "the *good Lord* answered my prayers."

They're dead, Adaobi thought in alarm. *You killed them.*

Pastor John met her eyes and nodded. "That's right." His words breezed through his body, a triumphant song.

I didn't say that aloud! she thought.

His eyes didn't leave hers. "They caught them thieving, affixed a tire noose about their necks, and drowned them in Hell's fire."

Sweeping his piercing gaze across the room, he stopped at one parishioner after another with each word. "And. Those. *Sinners*. Screamed. And. Wept. Their. Agony. For. Eternity. And. The. Smell. Of. Their. Wicked. Charred. Flesh. The. Particles. Of. Their. Dust. Spread. Through. The. Lands. On. A. Great. Wind.

"I took them inside with each breath!"

He dabbed his face with a handkerchief. "At night, if you listen, if you *listen* hard, you will hear their cries. You will hear the sorrow of the wayward and the damned at the great wrath of my God. And you will hear my God bellow his fury at them." He extended what remained of his left pinkie finger, twirling it about, until, once more, he found Adaobi. He held his pinkie like a pistol, and fired it in her direction, like breaking away the chaff. Adaobi's chest rattled.

"*Sinners*," he continued, "you can surely run, but you can't hide from God. He always finds *sinners*! He always brings them home. Thou who hath smote his *Lord* awaits eternal damnation! Look at God in his glory!"

A madman! Something throbbed at the back of her throat. A

panic swayed within her. To steady herself, she swept her gaze about the room. Drenched in sweat, an old lady moved like a spiral in her seat, her wriggling body pitching forward.

Suddenly, the senior was out of her seat, a flash of red down the aisle to the pulpit.

Pastor John widened his arm, and backed it, meeting the woman's face with a clap.

An *Ah!* and she landed flat on her back, her legs shooting straight in the air.

Adaobi gasped and sat up straight in her seat. Parishioners gathered around the two, breathing hard, clucking, mopping their faces with dewy rags, waiting. A woman was shouting, "This place is boiling with sin!" A man was crying, "Leave some space for Jesus, oh." Someone was suggesting mouth-to-mouth, and someone else was castigating the speaker: "After all, she's only half dead and for just a moment."

Everyone was panicking. Without thinking, Adaobi crawled through an airless gap between a pair of trousers and a gingham skirt. Then she pressed her mouth to the woman's and began to heave air into her lungs and thump her chest. She hoped that she was doing it correctly.

When the crowd parted, it was from her knees that Adaobi looked up into Pastor John's tranquil, expressionless face. With a glare that could shear flesh to expose the muddied soul, his iron eyes calmly roved the scene. She scooted away as he approached the fallen figure. He didn't lift the old lady as Adaobi had expected. He didn't backhand her again. Instead, he surveyed her body as if it were a landscape. He placed a hand across his breast and eased a white cloth from his pocket. Like a blind man, he traced the woman's flesh with a logical methodology—ankles, then calves, then the pits behind the knees—until he had worked his way up her body, all with his lips trembling soundlessly.

A moment later, the old lady rose, like from the dead, teetering on unsteady feet. Spinning, arms open, she beamed as if Pastor John had knocked the devil right out of her.

A round of applause followed as she wobbled back to her seat, her cheek bruised with the print of his palm.

At once Adaobi knew she had been woken from a deep sleep, and this strange, powerful man would soon reveal many more truths to her.

After the service, a caravan had followed Pastor John to his estate for fellowship. Adaobi joined the spiral of vehicles as they inched one behind the other, winding through the palm-tree-lined state roads that wormed to avenues and boulevards and then state roads once more. When the caravan halted, the cars parked in one long queue along a narrow dirt road with an embankment that led to a dense forest. Then, as if rehearsed, the doors began to pop open like umbrellas in rain. And so, too, did Adaobi's.

Though far from luxury, Pastor John's home, a sprawling country house in the colonial style, was large, tiered like a wedding cake, and shingled with a broad veranda wrapped about it. A wall of limestone attempted, with negligible success, to contain the racket of rumbling trains and shrieking tires on Old State Road 50. Planks of rotted railing and curling, chipping paint flaked at the touch. Still, the august home was glorious, so much so that the sisters of the congregation had always believed it was far too great for one man, though Pastor John, having never married, lived alone. So, they found sneaky ways to offer their clamor and liveliness to the austere abode. If their labors were rejected, then they proffered their most cherished possessions, their sons, who came straight from ball practice, damp and musky with sweat, to attend to Pastor John's maintenance.

Out on the lawn, a slim-boned boy of about twelve struggled to rake a push-reel mower along the lawn of the expansive country estate. Sun and heat had conspired to stiffen and blanch much of the lawn, so that the grass looked and moved like hay. From the veranda, where the parishioners had gathered, Adaobi watched as he stopped to scrutinize his work, only moving on to the next row when his inspection confirmed that the blades of weeds were cowed into surrender. On the veranda, most of the men and children straddled the backs of wrought-iron seats, while the ladies who occupied them sat with open fans. Adaobi anxiously twisted and turned in her own seat, gawking at the scene. She felt a great sense of anticipation. They were waiting, holding their breaths. A stark, deafening silence. Even the babes in their mothers' arms soundlessly sucked their pacifiers.

A great force propelled the front door open, and three small boys, eyes downcast and arms weighted with trays of food, made their descent down the narrow pathway. The boys set the trays atop the tables, and all at once Pastor John was among them, towering above the children. He wasn't fat or even paunchy like Fidelis, yet in defiance of his middling size, Pastor John maintained a vastness in his gait. Floorboards and chairs succumbed in gasps and groans as he approached.

With a nod, the parishioners suddenly crowded at the door. In alarm, Adaobi rose to follow, but when she reached the screen door, she was pushed back toward her seat and the door closed, sealing her exit.

Pastor John's head remained bowed, but his lips moved rapidly.

When Adaobi realized he was in prayer, she bowed her head, too. Her overzealous "Amen" at the conclusion of the prayer seemed graceless, and she was suddenly chastened. With downward eyes, she received the dark clot he offered.

Without hesitation, she took a bite, expecting the brittle wafer assigned as the body of Christ at every Communion. Instead, she bit into something chewy, almost rubbery. Backing out of the chair, she spat the morsel out.

"That's flesh and blood!"

Adaobi gathered her handbag, spun around, and headed for the door once more. *Hey-oh! This is Satan!* It was locked. She cursed herself for abandoning her good sense in the name of such tomfoolery. Seeking a second getaway, she found Pastor John blocking her path.

"Look again," he said.

In the middle of the tablecloth lay a half-eaten date.

"What did you do?" Adaobi eyed the morsel from several angles. She probed the date with a finger. It was indeed a date, soft, dark, and wrinkled like an overgrown raisin. What had just happened? Was she losing her mind?

"Do this in remembrance of me," Pastor John said, beckoning for her to finish the date.

She had seen enough.

In two impressive strides, Pastor John closed the distance between them. As he stood hovering over her, Adaobi shrank. She wasn't the sort to scare easily. Why now?

"I know of your turmoil," he said, reaching with two outstretched fingers. "Sister, I have been waiting for you."

The sound that followed was a wet smack and her face stung. Had she been slapped or caressed? When she brought her hand to her hot face, it was no longer her face, but a flood. Injury escaped from every part of her body and erupted in a deluge of tears accompanied by a thrashing moan. The pain of her husband. The pain of her children. The pain of their happy dream turned to dust.

As suddenly as her tears had begun, the cries ceased. At the precise moment when she thought she, this desiccated thing wrung of all its devotion, would lose her balance, Pastor John's arms encircled her.

"I know your turmoil," he said again. "Sister, I swaddle you."

As Pastor John swaddled Adaobi, his lips moving rapidly in silent prayer, memories took hold of her. So many years after the war, and Adaobi could only recall one word from the language of God: *mortem,* the word for death. She had said it for each life lost during the war. First, her father, who had rejected Fidelis when he had offered his hand. Then, her mother, whom Adaobi was told swallowed a bullet when soldiers were at her door. Then, her grandparents. Then, her cousin. Then, her dear friend Dorinda, then Ugochi, her reckless charge; and then one day, she had repeated the word for her Fidelis, believing he, too, had followed the path the others had taken to the other side.

After the war, she had spent three years in a convent, mopping and sweeping floors for the nuns, a small price to pay for food in her belly and a place to lay her head. The nuns had discovered her, after so much loss, a shameless unsheltered girl in the streets, doing what she must to survive, so it was in the priory that she learned Latin, the language of God. The prioress had told her, "His ears are not attuned to the mumbo jumbo of your people."

For her sins, for those were numerous, the prioress assured her, it had been ascertained that Adaobi was sufficiently contrite, as long as she confessed. Adaobi did—but only halfway, because some truths were left only for her heart. She confessed about the sin of wasteful longing for all that she'd lost: gorging on hazelnuts, the tranquility of an evening under the stars, the thrill of children's cheers and shouts as they escaped the mmuo spirits at the Christmastime masquerade festivals; her mother's touch, her father's chuckle, her cousin's incredible whistle, her grandfather's extravagant stories. She confessed about the luxury of longing for the lingering gaze of her beloved. She confessed to longing when she should have only thought about surviving.

Without her speaking a single word aloud, it was as if Pastor John could hear the deepest of her heart's sorrows. She waited for his judgment. While the nuns had condemned her for walking the streets at night to earn money in the name of survival, he did not. Instead, while the world had stripped her bare, Pastor John covered her. At the finish of the prayer, she felt purged of her fears. When she sat up, clammy and damp, she opened her eyes to trays of sautéed meats and vegetables, baked beans, and eggs prepared in various styles—scrambled, sunny-side up, poached. An assortment of pastries, fruit filling protruding from hand-pressed dough, awaited her.

Clothed in white from head to toe, the brothers and sisters of the Kingdom of the Second Coming of the Marvelous Creator and Holy Redeemer encircled her, covering her body with their hands.

Gleefully, they proclaimed, "Sister Agatha, you have returned!"

THIRTEEN

AMARA

The lessons began on a Tuesday—although, when Amara had first peered out her window at them through the security grate her father had newly installed, she had assumed Maksym Kostyk was kicking her brother's ass. It pleased her. In the span of only a couple weeks, her brother had become her father's protégé, an expert at instruments of her torture—goading and insulting her, bossing her around, daily pondering new indignities to unleash upon her—so it was not without pleasure that Amara watched Chuk stumble, flinch, flail, and lunge at Maksym's jabs and drive-line punches.

Of the siblings, Amara had always been the fighter, earning her the mocking moniker *barrister* from her mother; her father said it like a dare. On the contrary, her brother rarely complained or defended himself. Not really. But his impish smile could relax their mother's punishing evil eye into serenity and deflate their father's ire to mild irritation, such that her brother's charm was, in fact, his weapon. Owing to this, their parents had always babied him, asking so little of him, while responding with such exaggerated praise for his hapless efforts.

In the ring, the rules were different.

Underneath a metal tarp next to the Kostyk trailer was a freestanding punching bag. The speedball that Amara had been observing with curiosity all spring was anchored to the side of the trailer. In shorts and sneakers, the boys boxed on earth dead and trampled over. After, they drank from a hose to cool themselves. Throughout their first bout, from her window, Amara had watched, first in awe, then amusement, as Maksym blocked Chuk in with a wall of punches—punches that didn't connect, although, due to Amara's distanced view and Chuk's flinching and flailing, this hadn't been apparent to her at first.

Maybe Maksym meant to humble and humiliate her little brother before teaching him the basics—how to hydrate and stretch properly, how to build strength, agility, and endurance with a jump rope, push-ups, and sit-ups; then, how to shift his weight on the balls of his feet; finally, teaching him how to make a proper fist and punch in various styles and combinations. Hidden from prying eyes, the duo executed drills and labored through a choreographed sequence of moves that Amara mimicked in front of the full-length mirror in her room, alternating between imaginary opponents, her brother some days and her father other days.

She was so concentrated on following along, imitating each movement precisely, that she forgot about her captivity. She had never cared for boxing, certainly never wasted her time watching the pay-per-view events that occasionally caught the attention of her schoolmates, but suddenly she was enthralled to be learning something new, in secret.

Amara marked her days of seclusion by checking Chuk's

progress. Now that summer was upon them, there was little else to do. Two weeks after the lessons had begun, he hadn't much improved—he was still tripped up by foot movements, and Maksym still shook his head and adjusted Chuk's fists, demonstrating and redemonstrating with alarming patience. But the project wasn't entirely hopeless. As the lessons dragged on, Chuk became less self-conscious, and when he stopped playing it cool, he actually seemed to have a chance at improving.

Moreover, he was eager to learn, rushing out the back to meet Maksym by the side of the trailer as soon as the front door slammed behind their father on his way out. While Maksym ran the mower, bagged weeds, or emptied trash barrels, Chuk practiced, silently pantomiming the movements until Maksym appeared behind him, like an apparition, adjusting his positioning.

Her lazy, waggish brother, who, ordinarily, would rather play his video games, who would rather idle by a pool or smoke weed with his shiftless friends, was so faithfully committed to his boxing lessons that Amara realized she finally had a bargaining chip to wager for her freedom.

"You're done," Amara shouted to the powerful odor that engulfed the hallway. Just before their father's return each day, Chuk would bolt home, sweat and funk powerful enough that, even after he changed his clothes, the stink followed him like an aura, so that it wasn't the screech of the screen door or the weight of his footsteps, but rather his scent, that announced his return. Their mother would have ordinarily chided, *You smell like outside*, but both she and their father were too concerned with their own private affairs to take notice when they returned home each day.

That afternoon, Amara had listened at the door. Her senses had been fine-tuned to the routine such that she could perfectly mimic her brother's movements as he flashed past her bedroom door to his own bedroom, where he would change into a freshly laundered pair of shorts and a T-shirt before boomeranging in front of her door with the spray of gunfire or the shrilling tires spinning out in *Grand Theft Auto*. It was the perfect alibi. Amara could already imagine the look of stupor that he would set on his face, so that just as his father walked in, nothing would seem amiss.

But this time was different. She could almost see Chuk, still in his bedroom doorway, one leg in his shorts, one leg out, one arm still tangled in his T-shirt, the other free, as he prepared to launch himself at her door. Half blind from the shirt stretched over his head, he would be stumbling his way back to her door. She knew when his mouth was pressed to the door because she could hear him panting as he tried to catch his breath.

"No, I'm not." He meant to sound nonchalant, but his cracking voice betrayed him.

Faux neediness arched her voice. "You should be here keeping me safe. But you'd rather be somewhere else. I bet Dad would love to hear that."

"You wouldn't," he said. "You'd be a snitch."

"I would," Amara said without a hint of shame.

"He won't believe you."

"You know he will."

"I'll tell him you tried to break out," he said. "I tried to stop you, but you wouldn't listen! I'm Keeper of the Abode. He'll believe *me*."

Keeper of the Abode was some nonsense their father had concocted to keep Chuk in line, but he was so stupid he hadn't picked up on the manipulation. Well, Amara would teach him.

Between the screeching and humming of the city bus out on the main road, and the one hundred seconds it took for her father's long deliberate strides to reach their door, only moments remained. Her window of opportunity to inveigle her brother was fast diminishing. Yet, she hesitated. If she said *it* aloud, would it make it true? Was it true? Had she known it all along, refusing to admit it to herself, pretending?

Knowing it would sting, she wielded the one weapon she had. "He'll believe *me*," she said, her words inflating with her sense of righteousness, "because *I'm* his favorite. *I've* always been his favorite. *You* are the afterbirth."

On the other side of the door, Chuk went still.

So light, so airy, so dizzy, Amara flopped to the floor. She should have felt light like a floating balloon, rising up, up, up, out the window, into the sky, a brilliant, weightless thing. But she only felt like a punctured balloon, its air stinging as it hissed out of her. She felt deflated. She felt ugly. She had gone too far.

One final thrust and Chuk had finished swapping out his shorts and T-shirt. He thudded to the floor. The siblings sat back to back, on opposite sides of the door. Amara could practically feel his heat through the wood. He sighed. Was it a sigh of resignation, irritation, or hurt?

"Fine, you win," he said. "I won't go anymore. Boxing's lame anyway."

It hadn't occurred to her that he might simply give in. But why? For the past two weeks, he had put aside all amusements for this singular obsession. Even at night, she could hear him through their shared wall, grunting and swatting the air. It occurred to her that she hadn't even considered *why* he had started the lessons in the first place.

"Boxing's lame," she said, "so why do it?"

"You wouldn't understand."

She tried another threat. "You leave me no choice, Chuk. I'll have to snitch."

"I don't care."

Maybe their father would lock Chuk up in his room alongside hers. From the hallway, he would guard them both. She had no illusion that he would swap their positions and place her in the role of jailer while her brother became the prisoner. But what would change? She would still remain behind her door, alone.

She felt regret. She had been so consumed by her own woes that she hadn't seen the world at large. Other than his boxing lessons and chores, these days her brother rarely left home, like her. What did it mean to be a guard or inmate? She was suddenly reminded of one of her father's proverbs: Onye ji mmadu n'ala ji onwe ya. *One who holds another to the ground is also holding himself down.*

Voice weary, she said, "All this time I thought you were free, Chuk. I was wrong."

Now it was as if his breath were hers. "You're not any freer than me."

A moment later, the screen door screeched open, then the front door unlatched, as their father returned.

The next morning, Amara was sitting sideways, her eyes blank, turned toward the window, but not seeing. Something had settled deep inside her. It had started overnight as each part of her body was gradually lulled to sleep—first her toes, then her limbs, her center of gravity and all its organs—until her eyelids blinked seven times, not exactly fighting off sleep; still, not inviting it in. She had been in this state all night and into the dawn, eyes loud like sirens, shadows easing in, struggling to remember if she was awake or asleep, or had slept, and if she had, were there dreams, and if there were dreams, were they serene or sinister?

A great gauzy fabric covered the sky. Through it, Amara only saw lights and shadows. She wasn't really thinking about anything or seeing anything—until a slip of paper appeared under her door.

From her bed, she could just make out her brother's handwriting on the letter. But she did not move to retrieve it. She did not even attempt to form words out of his sloppy scrawl.

A moment passed. Another. A bird glided past her window. The lock unlatched.

When she looked up, her brother's eyes met hers.

She blinked at him; he blinked back.

They hadn't seen each other in nearly two months. His gaze lingered like she was someone he had once known, but he could no longer recall her name. He looked at her head. He looked both pitying and shamed. Amara chafed under his scrutiny. It was the pity that embarrassed her. Never mind her uneven clumps of hair. What of the stack of dirty breakfast dishes piled on the dresser? What of the two buckets in the corner of the room, one stinking of her urine and feces, yet to be dumped and replenished upon her father's return? To be living in such squalor!

As if offering her one last sliver of dignity, he turned away. Voice unsteady, he bleated, "Daa-aamn, I wish I could've seen Mom's face when she saw you. 'Chi-*neke!* Chi-*neke!*'" he mimicked. "'You want to em-*barr*-ass me! Are you people trying to kill me today? *Ah-ah!*'" He shook his head like their mother. "'*Hey-oh!* This is Sa-*tan!*'" Chuk was a master impressionist. He had their parents' cadence and grandiose gestures down to a science.

Amara couldn't fight off the snicker that cracked her lips. He wasn't so far off. After their mother had first seen her, she had rocked back and forth on her heels, furiously praying for

Amadioha to *blaster the demon* that had entered her home. After that, Amara had seen little of her mother. Mostly, now it was her father at the door each time the door unlocked.

"So you like girls now?" Chuk gestured at Amara's hair. "Too bad. I know a guy who likes you."

On any other day, Amara would have walloped her brother for making such a cringe joke, or at the very least had a comeback ready. Dweeb, shrimp, fetus—her most cherished insults. But no words came. Without even glimpsing her reflection, she knew what she looked like. She could see it in his expression. It filled her with shame. The crack of smile on her face withered away.

"I was just kidding. It's not bad," he tried. "You just need a line-up." He shot straight up and rummaged through her drawers until he retrieved their father's clippers, the very pair Amara had used to shear her locks.

Is it okay? his eyes queried.

Amara nodded.

At first his hands shook, so he gripped the clippers tighter. He attached the number two guard. Hands steady now, he began to even the length of Amara's hair. After, she cupped her hands in the clean bucket and splashed water on her head. Stray bits and pieces of hair rinsed down her shoulders. Dark smudges bloomed on her T-shirt. It was baptismal. Amara felt resurrected.

Chuk huddled up next to her. They sank to the foot of her bed. He drooped his head on her shoulder. "I'm sorry," he said. "I didn't know it was this bad."

"You're not the afterbirth," Amara conceded.

He sighed. "How long is it going to be like this?"

Would her teen years and graduation roll by? Instead of dances, these walls. Instead of concerts, these walls. It was unfathomable. But then she never could have imagined that any of this was possible, to be trapped in her bedroom for two whole months, or that her father, her greatest ally, could be her jailer.

Chuk retrieved his note from the floor. "What do you know about Ugochi?"

"She's our aunt, Chuk. You should know this. Dad's baby sister."

"I know."

"Where did you hear her name?"

"In one of Dad's letters."

"What did it say?"

"I don't know. I didn't exactly read it."

"What's that supposed to mean?"

"It was stolen, okay? But don't worry. I'm getting it back."

"Who took it?"

"None of your business," he said. "I've got it handled."

"Handled?" she asked. "Is that why you're learning to fight? Don't do anything stupid."

"Don't call me stupid."

"I didn't. Do you remember where the letter was addressed?"

"Somewhere in Nigeria." After a moment, he added, "Fathers of Biafra."

"They must know something about our aunt if Dad is writing them."

"And maybe they can help us."

"Maybe," Amara said.

Then, because she couldn't help it, she asked, "Who likes me?"

They were three now. While Amara's father was off mailing his letters and their mother spent her secret hours away, Amara, Maksym, and Chuk huddled under the weighed-down tarp for lessons. Maksym had dragged out an old lawn chair and Amara watched as he trained Chuk for the battle to come with the letter thief. Though the siblings had reached a truce, there remained a subtle rivalry. Amara had met Maksym first; their lives had intertwined for one surreal moment. For that, they shared a past. Still, she could hardly call him a friend. Not like Chuk. He and Maksym shared cryptic inside jokes and secret confidences, an abbreviated language of snorts and nods, even a nickname that could spark Chuk into a frenzy.

Maksym goaded him now: "Underwear Bomber!"

"Fuck you," Chuk retorted. He swung furiously, some of his punches even landing, until Maksym raised his hands.

"That was good," he said. "Keep that fire, just don't lose your footwork."

Gasping for air, Chuk nodded.

Now that they shared the weekday boxing lessons, the long weekends when the bus didn't run and her father remained in the hallway were unbearable. Before the accident, Maksym passed Saturday and Sunday afternoons driving out to Eustis or Zellwood to clean pools, but with his father's van still out of commission, he spent the weekends picking up his father's slack at the Calumet Rows, going door-to-door for minor repairs and pest control, while his father slouched on the couch with a bottle of gin or Taaka, babbling to himself.

The drinking wasn't what was unusual to Maksym. It was that his father no longer just drank, he also wept, his watery eyes leaking like a faucet as Maksym sidestepped him on his way out of the trailer each day. The meat of his father's thigh was so itchy under his cast that he gasped and moaned and bawled in his sleep. Even a hanger couldn't reach the blistered skin underneath. And he stank.

Of burps and farts, like a rotting corpse. Maksym's fear of his father had been replaced with contempt.

"Recess?"

Chuk nodded and rushed to the trailer. By the routine of it, Amara knew he needed a bathroom break.

"Can I ask you something?" Maksym asked. "Did he do *that* to punish you?" He motioned at her shorn hair.

Amara stiffened. "Who?"

"Everyone says . . ."

"What? What do they say?"

He opened his mouth to speak again and then closed it.

"*I* cut my hair. I cut it because I wanted to."

"It's not bad. Actually, it suits you. You can see your face." His cheeks reddened. "And you have a nice face."

Amara smiled.

"When I first met you, I thought we might be friends. But then you just disappeared. Were you really sick all that time?"

Amara shook her head. "I was . . . grounded."

"Because of me?" he asked. "Because you came with me that night?"

"No, it started long before that. It's something to do with my aunt," she started. "The night of the accident, when I was out there in the street with my dad, for a moment—I know this sounds crazy—I felt like I could see what he was dreaming. He spoke to someone, my aunt. I never met her. She died before I was born. I don't even know what she looked like, but he called me by her name. Ugochi."

"Sounds like a hallucination," Maksym said sagely.

"We hallucinated the same thing at the same time?" she asked, doubtful.

"No," he said. "Then it's a mavka. The spirit of a girl who

died before her time. My mom used to tell me these stories when I was small," he said. "A girl and a boy fell in love. But the gods told them they couldn't be together, so they committed suicide. The guy jumped into a fire and the girl drowned herself. But she became a ghost. From then on, she'd search for her lover along the banks of bodies of water—stalking, seducing, and luring to his death any witless man with the misfortune of crossing her path."

"She's my aunt, not a lover."

"It doesn't have to be literal. It's just something unresolved that won't allow you to rest."

"A mavka," Amara said softly, thoughtfully, remembering her father's eyes as she had followed the light, remembering the voice that had become hers, remembering her father's softness as he had called her Ugochi. "But how do you stop a mavka?"

He wiped his forehead. "The only way to stop her is to appease her."

"But how?"

"Make amends, present her a gift"—his voice dropped—"or make a sacrifice. What do you know about her?"

"Nothing but her name," Amara said. "But Chuk said our dad was writing letters to an organization called Fathers of Biafra. Maybe if I find the organization, I can contact them to figure out what he's writing to them. Could I borrow your phone?"

He handed it to her. Amara turned away from him and moved closer to the trailer, to create some privacy.

Besides her brother and Maksym, it was her one tether to the outside world. For a moment, she thought about trawling her social media sites to see what she had missed out on, to catch up with friends. But she didn't know how to explain where she had been, or that she could only leave the house for these few glorious moments each day. The other part, the part that was hardest to understand, was that they and their world just didn't seem real anymore. Parties, dresses, dates, lashes, hairstyles. What did it matter?

She typed various iterations of *Ugochi Ewerike* in the search bar. And when those queries failed, she tried *Fathers of Biafra*. What followed was a GeoCities website that looked like it hadn't been updated since the nineties. The landing page was dominated by a stretched image of awkwardly posed distinguished-looking men her father's age. Amara could imagine him among them wearing his ishi agu robe, his coral beads, his cap, his cane balanced against a knee. Their mission statement, in a yellow Helvetica shadow-text font, announced their cause: to emancipate the Biafra nation and return it to its former glory. There was a post-office box address, but no physical address. Was this where her father had been sending his letters? Most of the links were dead, although one led to an old Yahoo! Groups page, its most recent posts filled with spam links and block-letter-style diatribes about political pundits of choice.

"What does this have to do with Ugochi?"

She was so lost in her thoughts that she didn't notice Maksym standing in the trailer doorway, his shoulder propping the screen door open. "Do you want something to drink?"

"Th-thanks," she stuttered. And then realizing he had asked her a question, she added, "For letting me borrow your phone. I mean." Why was she suddenly an awkward geek? Had her social skills completely deteriorated in just two months?

"You find what you're looking for?"

"I'm done."

He raised his hands. "I was just asking. You can still use it." But she was already handing it back.

And then because she felt too silly to ask for it back again, she added, "For now."

"Can I help?"

"No, it's okay."

They stood awkwardly, not saying anything, until Amara broke the silence, blurting out, "Sometimes I see you from my window."

"You watch me?"

Now her face burned. "It helps the time pass. That's all. Most of the time you're just boxing." She looked away. "Or you're with your girlfriend."

"I don't have a girlfriend."

She met his eyes. "The one with the tube top and miniskirt."

His eyebrows shot up. "You saw us?"

"Everyone did."

He squinted. "That's over."

"Is that what she would say?"

"It's what I say," he said. "What about you? Do you have a boyfriend?"

She laughed. "Do I look like I do?"

Nodding toward her house, he asked, "When you're in there, what do you do? How do you pass the time?"

"Read, journal, sketch."

"Would you draw me sometime?" he asked.

She laughed again. "Sure."

With that, he beckoned toward the open door. "Let's get those drinks."

Although Amara had been in the trailer before, sitting on the kitchen stool with the sole of her foot in the curve of Maksym's palm, today felt like the first time all over again. Sweat hung heavy in the shadowy room. Blue shadows flickered on the television screen. Mr. Kostyk's leg was propped up on the wobbly coffee table. Flakes from KFC were sprinkled across his chest. He breathed powerfully in his sleep. A bottle of Taaka slept on the floor next to him.

Suddenly, he bolted up. "This man, he will kill us. You see? He will kill us!" His accent was like cursive penmanship. He dropped back to sleep, his head bobbing between snores.

Maksym laughed off her startle as he led her toward the kitchen. "In his dreams, it's always 1989. Come on."

Amara followed Maksym down the slender hall.

Maksym opened a cabinet and retrieved a jug. He began to scoop out a pale, powdered electrolyte mix that looked like Kool-Aid. Amara glanced toward the hallway. One of the three doors was ajar, and she could hear Chuk noisily splashing as he washed his face. If Chuk kept up the noise, he'd wake Mr. Kostyk. She hurried down the hallway to find him, but instead of the bathroom, the door opened to a bedroom. It was spare, antiseptic, almost military-barracks style. A single, narrow cot covered with a thin sheet took up most of the room. A lone light bulb dangled overhead. At first, she thought it was Mr. Kostyk's room. It looked like the room of a soldier. But then she saw a corkboard.

One Polaroid. A slim woman looked directly into the camera, her reedy lips puckered, but not for a kiss. She was plain. Her arched eyebrows were offset by severe bangs. She wore a simple plaid dress. Next to her was a scrawny boy, hair buzzed, his squinting eyes in slits. She reached up and unpinned the Polaroid, to examine it closer. The boy, dressed from head to toe in a camel-colored uniform, was Maksym.

The photo was suddenly snatched from her grip. "Stay out of my shit!"

Maksym was already a flash down the hall, his hands full with spilling glasses of red drinks. She followed him out the door, but she didn't stop to sit on the steps next to Chuk as he did. Instead, she cut across the lawn, giving the speed bag a good hard thump, which just barely eclipsed Maksym's head as he trotted out after her. His footsteps, which had seemed half-hearted at first, grew louder and hastier in her ear as he neared, a rising roar of twigs and grass and dirt. By then she was full-out sprinting, but he was already at her heel, and then because she was out of breath and she knew she couldn't outrun him, she stopped abruptly. He nearly crashed into her.

"I'm sorry. It's the only one I have of my mother. My dad torched the rest."

"I didn't realize . . ."

"It's all right." He laughed. "I'm tripping. You couldn't have known. Come on." They turned to return to Chuk.

"As soon as I raise the money, I'm going to find her. I mean it. I work all sorts of jobs. I can do anything. Whatever these hands touch turns to money." He boxed the air. "I'm hiring a private eye. And once I find her address, I'm gone. We'll go to Mexico City. If you look at least sixteen—I'm seventeen—you can fight anyone underground. Take home cash every night. I can make a good living at it."

After a moment, his voice quieted, and he turned to Amara. "You can come with us if you want. You don't have to stay here. You don't have to be alone."

FOURTEEN

ADAOBI

The shame of all that whooping and hollering and carrying on had at first kept Adaobi from returning to the Kingdom of the Second Coming of the Marvelous Creator and Holy Redeemer. But after a few weeks, the image of the bloodied Eucharist was nothing more than a Raisinet, not even a date, and the tears that had temporarily drained her of sorrow were merely a momentary lapse of judgment. Everything that had taken place that Sunday would have been a mere memory, a bad one at that—the embarrassment of exposing her sorrows to strangers, for carrying on without the decency to hold her head high—had it not been for the news Adaobi received.

Ever since the news of the girls, Fidelis had taken to collecting newspapers. They were piled around his makeshift desk, the names of important dignitaries inked and underscored, men to whom he painstakingly typed his letters addressed Dear Sirs. But one early morning, as Fidelis rested and the children were still in slumber, Adaobi, whose irritation had grown each day as the stacks grew higher, gathered the moldy newspapers in her arms. She hefted them all into a garbage bag and dragged it into the kitchen. Just as she was about to tie and knot the strings together, the overstuffed bag doubled over, spilling on the kitchen floor. Among the many newspapers spread across the kitchen tiles, she saw the face of a man. Although familiar, she could not quite place him, a youngish man with a stern face, scowling eyebrows.

Then she saw his name. Sunday Olusegun Afolabi. Gertrude Afolabi's husband. It was a picture from his youth, from those early days in their friendship when the Afolabis and Ewerikes had first become acquainted, those days when they squabbled and bickered like siblings, yet somehow remained nearly inseparable, ensconced in a friendship of decades that had withered of late.

The obituary listed Sunday's many accomplishments, among them, his crowning achievement, advancing from a beginning as a fledgling adjunct instructor to become full professor at the university where he had taught biochemistry, and then to interim chair of the department. It did not announce the rumored dalliance with a junior colleague that, once soured, resulted in a censure, the one misstep that threatened to sully his impeccable record and forever shifted the dynamics of his marriage in Gertrude's favor. On the page, he was a man of steel, stingy with affection, but he lavished Gertrude with trinkets and was boastful of Gertrude and their three sons' achievements. A line was dedicated to Gertrude and their three sons, Babatunde, Folami, and their cherished Kehinde, the surviving twin. The newspaper was old. The funeral had passed weeks ago.

How the world could shift so completely. A year ago, the Afolabi family had been complete. But now, mere months later, their family was irreparably broken. The Afolabis and Ewerikes had been friends for so many years, attending the same functions, shadowing one another's lives—graduations, promotions, the births of one another's children—that it seemed impossible to imagine that their twilight years wouldn't be shared as well.

Gertrude, alone in that big house. Her sons, all three grown and married to Americans, had adopted American ways. They only visited their mother on alternating holidays. And when the eldest son's first child had been born, Gertrude had arrived with six suitcases, prepared to perform omugwo—cooking, cleaning, washing, and tending to her grandchild for the first months of his life—only to have her in-law complain that Gertrude was "butting in," while her son sat like a woman with his hands in his lap.

Life goes on. Does it not? Adaobi finished restuffing the trash bag. She tied it in a thick knot and hefted it near the back door for Chuk, whose job it was to take the garbage out each afternoon. *Life goes on*, she said to herself, then repeated it. Then she turned on a hot bath. She made the water as hot as she could get it before stepping in, one foot before the other. There were no bubbles or fruity fragrances. Her body stewed and beaded with sweat. She would have to share the news of Sunday's death with Fidelis. Her thoughts spiraled back to that day in the hospital, holding Gertrude's clammy hand while attempting to shield her relief that it was Sunday, not Fidelis, who lay on a hospital bed dying. Had he drawn his last breath that day as Adaobi drove home to her own husband? When the thought came to her, she let out a small sound like a bark. She knew she should cry, but there were no tears left to shed after Pastor John's ceremony, so she lay there like a dead body sinking in a pond.

She did not know how long she had been in the bath, only that the water was cold when she rose, and that the others had woken.

She wrapped herself in her towel and walked to her bedroom. She had not shed a tear, and yet there was an opening in her body, and through it, she began to sing. She didn't know why she sang at all, let alone "His Eye Is on the Sparrow." She hadn't sung it since her days with the nuns, but that opening inside her chest widened.

The following morning, Adaobi intended to drive to Gertrude's home to express her condolences, to apologize for not being at her friend's side. She had concocted an explanation for her absence: a relative in Nigeria had passed and she had been consumed by grief. But as she approached the Afolabi home on Lyman Avenue, she knew she wouldn't be able to open her mouth to say such lies aloud. So she kept driving.

Adaobi drove until she was back on Old State Road 50, dreading her return home. Like when Ugochi went missing, she would have to tell Fidelis that their friend was no longer with them. But then she'd have to explain that she had visited him in the hospital without sharing the news of his stroke with Fidelis. Then she'd have to explain to her husband that her selfishness, not fear, had prevented Fidelis from being with his friend in his final days or even moments. She had been too ashamed for anyone to see her husband in the state he was in. What if seeing his friend in such a crisis would have slapped some sense into his head?

The truth was that, although Adaobi had endured a reluctant friendship with Gertrude all these years, Fidelis and Sunday had been fast friends. No, they didn't call one another to gossip on the phone, or pay one another house calls, but when Adaobi and Gertrude served on the same women's council committee, Fidelis and Sunday's guffawing laughter would fill every room with such clamor that their children would abandon their Barbies and toy trucks and appear in the doorway to investigate the source of such joviality in their otherwise temperate father.

She could not form the proper words to explain. When she reached the turn to her home, Adaobi drove on, the landscape of sheep and cattle corralled behind fencing flickering past her, like channels on a television, as she headed west. She drove until she was on the 408, and eventually I-4. By the time she pulled off the 275 interchange, and looped off the Selmon Expressway, she thought she had reached the ends of the earth; it was only Tampa.

Bayshore Boulevard was cordoned by palm trees that separated palatial mansions from an esplanade, a blur of Spanish- and Mediterranean-style homes of fluorescent colors and cobblestone walkways, the very homes Adaobi and Fidelis had once dreamed of. On a better day, she might have stopped or slowed to admire them, but she kept driving.

Eventually, she reached the end of the Boulevard and pulled over on the shoulder. Dizzy from the heat and the hum of the car's tires, she climbed out, stretching her legs. White clouds made patterns in the blue sky, and in the distance, man-made islands that looked like muddy mounds appeared on the border of the flat, waveless water. Even with the hot sun beating on her brow, the sudden air billowing off the bay was cool.

Cars whirred past. She stood looking at the water, feeling the ground turning. Panic suddenly seized her. Just like that, she was back to the fear of losing Fidelis. Her heart thundered, and her throat swelled until she felt it tightening, and she realized she could not breathe.

Then, suddenly, she was thinking of herself. What if she would take her last breath here in Tampa? How could her family carry on without her?—and at a time when they needed her most? How would her family even know what had become of her? What would happen to her children? How could she allow herself to die among strangers?

In answer, waves slapped stupidly against the loops in the concrete. On this isolated patch of waterfront, chubby speed-walkers in spandex and leather-skinned housewives pushed jogging strollers, reaching the border of palm trees before turning back. Adaobi had always thought these American women silly, wasting their time pumping their arms and sweating in the heat to keep their bottoms flat instead of using the time to prepare their family a proper meal. No matter. At least their families were complete.

An old man, his blackened neck mottled with yellowed tinea, hobbled over, hiked up the legs of his khakis, and squatted over the edge of the bridge. She watched in awe as he hung on the ledge and darted in and out of the water, collecting crabs in a filthy plastic bucket. He worked until his bucket was filled. Adaobi was mesmerized by his slow, steady progress.

After he finished, he collected his booty and went along his way, but as he passed Adaobi, he suddenly stopped in front of her. He eyed her carefully for some time. "It's Sunday," he said.

"Sunday?" Adaobi drew in a sharp breath. Whispering, she switched to his native nickname. "Segun, is it you? Have you returned?"

"Come," the old man said, "let's go." Without waiting, he pressed on, dragging his bucket behind him.

At first, Adaobi started to follow, but then she remembered the tale her grandfather had once told her of a foolish man who had received a knock at his door one night. The stranger announced the name of a man who had recently died. The foolish man followed the stranger until he crossed to the other side and from there he could see his old house, and his old wife, and his old children, and his old life through a shimmering veil. In a flicker, a lifetime had passed him by. Her grandfather didn't have to elaborate on the meaning for Adaobi to understand that the foolish man had been tricked into crossing over into the world of the ancestors, thereby hastening his own death.

But rather than seeing it as an omen as she once might have, it occurred to Adaobi that it wasn't Ekwensu using her friend's Christian name to trick her. It was a sign. No, an instruction. He had told her to come on Sunday. She trembled, first in fear, then admiration. It could only be the handiwork of Pastor John. She climbed into the car and drove home.

That was weeks ago. Now, three, sometimes four days per week, Adaobi rose with the dawn, oiled her hands and her elbows, and drove to the Kingdom of the Second Coming of the Marvelous Creator and Holy Redeemer. At the start of every service, Pastor John prayed for Adaobi as he had during her first visit. She discovered that each Saturday, the day before he performed the laying on of hands, he prepared by fasting. He never asked anything of her. He had only invited her in. On the drive home, a sudden sense of solemnity and indebtedness would rebuke her for doubting his intention. Pastor John's devotion to her stirred up a strange confusion of affection reminiscent of their first acquaintance on her front stoop those weeks ago. Was it the love of a mother for her child, Adaobi wondered yet again, or a girl for her lover, or simply the cherished for her protector? His love enveloped her.

Despite his protests, like the other parishioners, Adaobi found herself offering what payment she could—not her paltry paychecks or even her children. She offered her body, sweeping the aisles and dusting the pews every Sunday before services began, and then collecting dishes and scrubbing them in his kitchen after fellowship, until she was drenched in sweat. Always, he would admonish her for her labors, insisting she was his guest. She went and worked anyway, not out of obligation, but because she felt part of something larger and separate from her own small problems. Each time she did this work, she felt His hands upon her, and they lifted her sorrows from her shoulders, if only briefly. It was a reprieve that gradually replenished her hopes. Although she still nursed some skepticism, one eye raised, the other half closed, during Pastor John's sermons and prayers, she would strain for the sounds of the language of God, certain that keeping the good favor of this strange, powerful man who held the attention of God would surely cure Fidelis of his maladies.

Hearing night sounds—neighbors' laughter, a cascading roar echoing behind her heavy lids—Adaobi dreamed of Ugochi. Before evil had taken her dorm daughter away. When she was just a gangly girl who laughed as she made faces behind her mother's back, squabbled when asked to share, danced an exaggerated step when American pop music played on vinyl. Adaobi preferred brass. She spent her whole life leaning into the melodies of highlife and jazz. Then it was funk, disco. Only by chance, Adaobi and Ugochi discovered soul. When Ugochi began to move with the pulse of that Motown groove, who could resist a two-step? Dearest Ugochi, Adaobi's friend, the silly child of pranks who goaded shy Adaobi to be brave, to dance, to live loudly. Until she was gone and there was only silence.

Isn't it strange that, in the instant when Adaobi felt safe, having hurtled thoughts of Ugochi from her mind, replacing them only with the blare of trumpets and saxophones, she should happen upon an elephant blowing brass from her trunk?

In her dream, the elephant stomped and blew, widening her stance until a bag dropped from inside her, a drawstring snapping open so that out of the elephant's womb fell a human child, all arms and legs. Its mother pounded the earth and roared until a swarm of elephants, a memory, surrounded her, closing ranks. Bodies aligned in formation, they were trumpeting, heralding, celebrating, warding off the wicked.

Under the massive thunder of the undulating earth, the human calf intertwined its limbs around its mother's legs, whimpering, both in terror and awe. Adaobi feared they would trample the poor child. But when she made to rescue the babe, she, looking down, discovered that her own legs had enlarged, scabbed over, and turned the color of ashy dung! Now she, one of them, an enormous elephant, joined their parade.

Just as suddenly as the roars had begun, they abated.

Blinking her eyes open, Adaobi rushed to the window, thrust the drapes apart, and scanned the pitch horizon for elephants. Damp, glistening tops of weeds swayed. Tepid air filled her lungs. She pulled the curtains closed. A temporary relief. Until the anxieties and fears poured back in. She wished desperately for her friend who could ease out laughter—or love because, of course, it was she who had brought Adaobi and Fidelis together, delivering poetry meant, not for Adaobi, but for another! She chuckled. He didn't know that she knew. Adaobi was to believe that all along she had been his intended, loved from afar. Ugochi had sworn Adaobi to secrecy because to reveal such a blunder would embarrass the shy poet. Adaobi agreed. After all, even though the words were meant for someone else's ears, it was still love at first sight. And so, in a way, Ugochi remained an anchor to their long life together.

III

III

FIFTEEN

FIDELIS

Maybe today, right this minute, dearest Ugochi is standing in a kitchen somewhere, her slim fingers expertly peeling an orange, or maybe she is using a large wooden spoon to beat the cassava into fufu. Maybe Ugochi is too absorbed in the task at hand to observe the small child clasped to her leg, frowning up at her in petulance; maybe Ugochi is a mother.

And maybe if Fidelis can keep looking into his daughter's face, he will keep seeing his sister, his beautiful, wholesome sister. His daughter, who Fidelis Ewerike ceased to recognize. She, Amarachi Uzodinma Ewerike, a girl of sixteen, slightly quarrelsome, a skeptical disposition, a sore loser at chess.

He sees his sister.

Is it a tease?

She, Ugochi Edwina Ewerike, the child who would have turned fifteen at war's end if only she had survived, words he once told himself.

But now, ah! What a wonder to inhabit a world of miracles.

SIXTEEN

CHUK

"It's a sign," Chuk's mother pronounced.

"Our Ugochi is coming," his father interjected.

That morning, Chuk had awoken to the shouts of his parents. His mother's shrieks had been unsurprising. His father's wails, however, had been a shock. They stood with their backs to him at the threshold of the front door. His father held the screen door open. But despite their excitement, they remained in the doorway blocking Chuk's view. As he approached, all he could see over his mother's broad back and his father's sagging shoulders was a bit of sunlight. Other than their anxious noises, there were no other sounds.

On his toes, Chuk arched his neck to see over his parents' backs. At first, when the offender came into sight, his eyebrow rose and his lips curled with curiosity. Maybe there was something to his mother's talk of miracles and his father's proverbs.

But then, carefully, he slid one foot forward between the gap parting his parents.

"No! Don't touch," his mother admonished. "Do you want bad juju?"

But it was too late. Using his foot, he shifted the charred bundle that had burned through the night on the porch. His heart sank.

While his mother grasped Chuk and gathered him in her arms to cloak him from the powers of a burning effigy, and while his father, likewise, hissed and sighed, Chuk let out one staggered breath. The insignia on the band was unmistakable: Fruit of the Loom. Wrapped in the bundle of sticks was the charred remains of a pair of underwear.

By ten a.m. that day, the neighborhood swelled with the news of the impending battle between Raphy Gaspar Gutiérrez and Chuk Ewerike. Since Chuk's parents had hurried off twitching with news of their own—his mother with the signs of an omen, and his father with a herald of benediction—Chuk and Amara were free to meet up with Maksym in front of his father's trailer for another round of lessons. When Chuk told Maksym about the pyre his parents had found on their front porch, Maksym announced, "That was an overt act of aggression. It means your time is up."

"But I'm not ready," Chuk groaned. Grasping his face in his hands, he sank onto the lawn chair stretched out in front of the Kostyk trailer. On any other day, they would have already been into a dynamic warm-up drill and a third set of timed jumping ropes, push-ups, and sit-ups.

"You *are* ready," Maksym said.

"No, I'm not."

Amara, who had been silent until that moment, cut in, "He's not."

Both boys lapsed into silence. Despite his improvements, there was no denying that Chuk needed at least three more weeks to get the combinations down. Another week to perfect his footwork, and even still, his conditioning needed another two weeks to build up his endurance. Most of all, he lacked confidence. He was afraid.

Was there a way to walk it all back? Chuk was the clown at school. Could he find a way to coax some laughter out of Raphy and his goons? The thing was, sometimes Chuk wasn't even trying to be funny. He'd say something in earnest, but then everyone would start laughing, so he'd laugh, too, pretending he was in on the joke. He'd play it up. And before you knew it, everyone was circling around him cheering him on. He had developed a reputation for simply taking things in stride. Would it work with Raphy? What if he took the underwear and cracked a joke, faking like he put them on and prancing around? He could just see Raphy, arms crossed, a sneer on his face. No.

If Chuk apologized to Raphy and explained all the stuff going on with his dad, maybe he would understand. Maybe he would see that Chuk's family wasn't rich. Far from it. They'd lost everything in a matter of months. Surely, he would understand what it was like to be a boy whose world had slipped away from him. Chuk's father had become strange and confusing, his mother sad. His sister, with her lopsided buzz cut, was only an inch of herself, the girl who used to be an outspoken goody, who had once seemed to understand the things Chuk didn't.

Chuk felt himself disappearing, too. Boxing with Maksym brought something out in him. It made him feel like if he kept training and working hard, he could be something. It wasn't like working hard on a paper only to get a C on it. Instead of disappearing, he was returning to himself bit by bit, like shading in a drawing. This must be what it was to feel respect. But if Raphy beat him up in front of the whole neighborhood, Chuk would go back to being a nothing.

"Don't worry," Maksym said, grabbing his shoulders, "I've got you."

They followed Maksym into the trailer and Chuk and Amara stood uneasily in the doorway of Mr. Kostyk's bedroom as he snored away on the living room couch, passed out. Kneeling over a crate, Maksym scrolled through a set of videotapes like a Rolodex, searching for a particular fight he wanted Chuk to study. Each tape was meticulously indexed: *Ali v. Patterson, '65*; *Leonard v. Hagler, '86*; *Liston v. Clay '64*; *Patterson v. Bonavena '72*; *Tyson . . .*

While Maksym mumbled to himself, the siblings surveyed the room: an unmade bed, piles of filthy clothes, empty beer cans, and vodka bottles. Empty walls and an open closet. Nothing to see but more foul-smelling clothes in a pile. Boxes and crates up on a shelf. And more bottles. They exchanged an expression of disgust.

"Give me some help, will ya?" he called over his shoulder. The boys heaved another set of crates down from the closet onto the floor. The container hit the floor with a thud. A tape jumped out, startling them. Would Mr. Kostyk catch them? Another snore like a train.

Chuk squatted to grab the tape, but when he was on the floor, he caught a glimpse under the bed. Several impressive cases were smartly lined head to head. Curious, he slid one of the cases out. Just as he began to pry it open, Maksym stopped him. "That's off limits."

"What is it?"

"You want to know?" Maksym sized him up. "Okay, open it."

Chuk lifted the lid and his eyes widened.

"To look at him, you'd never know he used to be a warrior."

In reverence, Maksym fondled the gun's slim barrel. "2B-A-40. Russian design. His favorite, but he's got others. He's a collector." He slid out what turned out to be another arms case, and another, and another, calling off the names of the guns, like a teacher calling roll at the start of a lesson. "Nagant M1895. Tokarev. Makarov. KS-23. AK-74. And this one," he said, opening a smaller case. "This one's my favorite. PSS silent pistol." It fit like a glove in his hand. He cocked it. Then he set it back in the case. "It's the first one my tato taught me to shoot."

"Cool," Chuk said, smirking. Before they could stop him, he grabbed the pistol. "Say hello to my little friend," he exclaimed before pretending to blast a roomful of invisible enemies to smithereens. Then he was Ice Cube: rolling down a street in a gold-rimmed pimped-out hydraulic Cadillac, bass bumping so loud the car gyrated; rolling to a stop, tossing a kiss to an invisible damsel, stepping out, grunting, and then popping off the man who had killed his family. Then, Chuk was secret police, gasping and scowling as he rappelled down the side of a great cliff, dangling above violent waves below, roaring as he pulled the trigger. No sound, except the bodies of his offenders folding one by one as bullets sliced through them.

"Chuk!" Amara barked. He rolled his eyes at her.

Maksym snatched the gun back and steered Chuk away. "It's not a toy."

"Come on," Chuk said. "You're supposed to be my boy."

Maksym held up a videocassette. "Found it. Let's watch some tape. Learn from the masters."

Chuk took one final envious glance at the PSS silent pistol.

Because Mr. Kostyk lay spread across the Kostyk living room couch drowning in snores and blocking their one TV, the trio headed to the Ewerike residence to watch tape. Chuk's father hoarded old appliances, among them, old VHS players. One of the three still worked, and judging by the bus schedule, he wouldn't return for another hour, which gave them time to study tape and put everything back before he returned. Maksym squatted before the TV console rewinding the tape. The three crowded on the floor, eyes pinned to the TV screen yet feeling uneasy, alert to any sounds that might announce their father's early arrival.

Vintage Ali and Liston, young and agile, circled one another in the ring as Maksym narrated. "It was 1965, Lewiston, Maine, the World Heavyweight Championship, and the rematch of the century. Ali was, for all the jabs and the footwork, showmanship." They watched as he hopped from foot to foot as he circled Liston. "But Liston was the Big Bear." Liston had a slow, measured gait with elongated strides. "He was powerful but also precise. He had a target. He wasn't a pretty loudmouth; he was a fighter." Maksym had a no-nonsense way of speaking when it came to fighting. He had inherited it from his father. Ali was midswing with a short right jab. And suddenly Liston was dropping.

"There," Maksym said as Liston struggled to get up.

"I'm going to drop him like that?" Chuk asked.

"No," Maksym said. "You're going to drop like Liston."

"What?" Amara and Chuk replied in unison.

"It's called the Phantom Punch. The most controversial blow in boxing history. Everyone thought Liston threw the fight."

"You want me to throw the fight?" Chuk's voice was small. He understood that he wasn't yet good, but had Maksym lost all faith in him?

"No," Maksym said. "I want you to drop, but then come back around and give him a right cross. It's the one solid punch you've got. And he won't see you coming because he'll be too busy celebrating."

They were too perplexed by the idea to notice the key in the lock, the sound of the door wheezing open, or their father's deep breaths. It was only a sudden shift in the air, an unsteadiness that gave them all, except for Amara, the sense that they were being watched. She was standing, her arms across her chest. "I don't understand why you don't just tell Mom and Dad."

"Tell Mom and Dad what?" their father's voice boomed.

Amara was the last to turn because Maksym and Chuk's eyes were already trained on Fidelis, who stood in the doorway. For a few moments, they were frozen. Then, as if backing away from a rabid animal, Maksym popped the cassette out of the player and hurried past him out the door.

Chuk didn't really know what he had expected of his friend, but his heart sank. Had he expected Maksym to reason with his father or give him a right hook? He did not know, only in that instant, he suddenly felt that everything he had learned all summer about how to be a champion, how to be a man, had been a farce. All the drills, warm-ups, all the talk of being a fighter in Ukraine, of boxing on the amateur circuit in Mexico. All the false talk of standing up to bullies. He felt certain that he had been deceived. Lies. They were not men or soldiers. They were mere boys.

Their father faced Chuk. Amara seemed to disappear. It was as if father and son were the only two people in the world. Chuk swallowed. The secret was out. His father's okpara, his mighty Ikenga, had been sneaking out instead of guarding his sister's door. How could he explain to his father about Raphy? A schoolyard bully? This was his excuse for not following his father's orders? As if he could hear the excuses building in Chuk's mind, his father's face shifted to the familiar scowl, a look not of rage, but of disappointment, regret, and suffering. A look that said, *Oh well, I should have known better. I sent a useless boy to do a man's job.*

I'm not useless! A familiar rush of hot air hit Chuk's face. His hands shook. He felt his fist driving forward. He didn't know his eyes had been closed, or that he had struck his father, until he opened his eyes just in time to see his father's scowl sliding off his face. Chuk's throat closed and then, needing oxygen, he bolted out the door.

SEVENTEEN

AMARA

Amara didn't know where her brother had run to. Only that as the swish of the swinging door rang in her ears, she retreated to her bedroom and closed the door behind her. She felt suffocated, not by her father's presence, not even by the strike her brother had issued their father just before taking off out the door, but by the violence of the silence and its inert blankness. She thought that she would die if she had to breathe another breath of that stillness, and she was afraid. As she ran into her room, she grabbed her notebook, and as if a sudden tempest had taken over her hands, she began to draw. Birds in flight.

Not long after, Amara's bedroom door swung open. It was her father. She gulped, ready for him to announce, "From this day onward, your brother is no longer welcome in my house." She waited for him to shout, to fume, to make threats about her brother. Something.

He said nothing. She watched as he laid out a damp egg salad sandwich, pickled beets, a tangerine already peeled and separated into four huge hunks, and a tall glass of orange Fanta.

He was almost back to the door when he suddenly swiveled around. As if appealing to a judge, he began, "I never knew my own son would conspire with Satan to assassinate his own father! *Ah-ah!* Did I come to America for my own seed to bury my body and dance on my grave?" He raked his fingers across his forehead. "Chai! My enemies have succeeded."

Eyebrow arched, his gaze lingered on Amara's face as if realizing he was speaking to her, not some judge. Then his eyes swept the room, landing, finally, on her sketchpads. With his hand curved under his chin, his head tilting as he studied the drawing, he looked like *The Thinker. Le Penseur*, Amara's literature teacher had called the sculpture, his ebullient southern accent clipping and rounding out the French vowels.

Her father tapped the drawing. "A goddess rising from the waters."

"No, it's a bird." He didn't seem to hear her.

Deep in thought, he traced the drawing with a finger. "But where is her face?" Amara raised her hand. He would smudge it. "Your mother the singer, your father the poet and culinary artist, and you, Amarachi, the painter." With sadness, he asked, "But what of your brother?"

Amara looked at her feet.

His voice softened. Once again he spoke as if reasoning with Amara. "I was not always an old man. I was a boy once, like your brother. As God is my witness, I never challenged my father. A child who looks under his father's wrapper will be blinded. I tell you, I was a foolish boy, too." A sudden chuckle. "So foolish! I fancied myself a poet. I ran this way and that in a beret, like a

French man, carrying a pad and a feather pen in my back pocket. There was no debate; I must compose with a quill to seriously consider myself a true artiste," he said, pantomiming a pretentious poet prancing about, "until one day, my feather pen burst in my pocket and leaked all over my buttocks." He choked with laughter. Through a wheeze, he continued, "All over the trousers of my school uniform. I disgraced myself! After the headmaster finished flogging me, I could not sit for two weeks." He raised his eyebrows. "But I never lifted my hand to strike my master!"

What an odd moment to reminisce. Her father's strange sweep through humor and sadness left her baffled.

"I used to be like your junior brother. I had a lackadaisical manner. I believed words could make peace of war. I ran from my responsibilities. But when the war came, I was forced to stand on my own two feet." He sighed. "You American children with your hard heads and soft buttocks. When I was a boy, even the poets learned to launch a grenade. Like Christopher Okigbo." He shook his head. "Your drawing reminds me so much of his poem *Heavensgate*. He was a soldier like your father." He reached into the pocket of his robe and smoothed his fingers over the cover of a well-worn book. Without opening it, he dramatically recited, "'Before you, mother Idoto, / naked I stand." Gesturing to Amara's drawing, he added, "Like your goddess, you see, Idoto is the great river goddess of a small town in Anambra. The people from the region know her as the guardian and protector in times of war." He waited as if expecting her to ask a question.

Amara said nothing.

With a faltering dramatist's flair, he continued to recite, "Before your watery presence, / A prodigal." Gazing at the cracks in his palm, he finished, "Did young Christopher Okigbo die in vain? His life was but a broken promise."

Silence hung between them. At last Amara asked, "How did he die?"

Her father seemed surprised that she had been listening. With a tinge of irritation in his voice, he said, "He was killed in combat." But then, peering deep into her eyes, he added, "Me, I have outlived a demigod by nearly thirty years. And for what? My own son. I never thought I'd live to see the day my own son would execute me. Chai! My enemies are laughing at me."

Gently, he laid the book on her desk. "I will leave it for you to discover on your own. Perhaps he will inspire you. Perhaps your next drawing will be of Idoto."

He started for the door, but when he reached it, he stopped again. "Amarachi, know that I love you and your brother," he said. "No matter what has happened, know this."

Her scalp tingled and tightened as she held back tears. Chuk was out there in the dark, on his own, angry and afraid. Would he have believed their father's words? Amara hoped he had found solace with Maksym.

As if he had heard her, he continued, "Everything is for you. You were all we could have ever dreamed of," he continued. "When I came to America, all that I asked of God was to provide for me. And He did. More than I could have ever deserved. Others perished. It should have been me, yet here I am with a fat wife and two over-pampered offspring with soft buttocks!

"Ah well, it is I who have offended my Maker. God is punishing me for my foolhardiness. I will not lose my family. Not again. You know my parents died in a car accident before the war. Like your brother, I was my father's only son. I inherited his possessions. When I should have been guarding my kin, I was wearing trousers too large for me." He gathered the dishes. "No, I will not lose this family."

"Your kin," Amara said. "You mean Ugochi?"

For the first time, rather than chiding, *To your head*, as he often did when she or Chuk asked a question he was not compelled to answer, he said, "Yes."

"Dad, what happened to her? I want to know. I need to understand."

"My dear, that is a story for another day."

When Amara heard the music that evening, she was relieved. The percussive and brassy sounds filled the silence that had left her feeling so bare. She hadn't heard her father's highlife music in ages. It reminded her of better times, when he would loop her in his arms and spin her around and around. Tonight the music was obnoxiously loud, as if he intended to cause a disturbance—but at least he was occupied. At least he wouldn't return to cajole her with poetry recitations.

She heard the front door open and leaned into her bedroom door, listening for her brother's clumsy sounds. The steps sounded certain. It was just her mother. Would Amara's father share the events of the day with her mother? Amara doubted it.

And when she heard a knock at her window, Amara thought at last her brother had arrived. Maybe he wanted her to check if the coast was clear.

But when she parted her blinds to peer out, Maksym's face appeared, broken by the checkered pattern of the security grate across her window. He looked jumpy and strange. He yanked at the grate, but there was no give. Although Maksym had been schooled on hammers and hacksaws, her father had fortified her cage against the likes of him. Where there would normally be soldered bolts and locks, there were instead crooked hangers and jagged shards of glass and stone. A deeded lawyer, a passable poet, a garden enthusiast, and a novice chef, Amara's father knew nothing of chains and locks and windows and grates, and yet, fear had made him an apt pupil.

"Is Chuk with you?" Amara asked.

"No," Maksym said, confused. "What happened after I left?"

"You haven't seen him?"

"No. He's not here?"

"Why didn't you do something?" Amara wasn't naive enough to believe that Maksym should have fought their father on their behalf. Still, she was certain that something that didn't happen should have.

"Do what?"

"I don't know." Even though the words sounded false as they left her mouth, she added, "Do what Chuk did." She quieted. "What you taught him."

Maksym let out a whistle. Then, "Did it work?"

"I don't know." She swallowed. "He just left. And my dad is in there drinking and reciting poetry about goddesses. And Chuk's not back yet. I'm scared."

"He's fine." Maksym shrugged. "He can handle himself."

"Maks, he's just a kid," Amara said. "And he's scared."

"Listen, I'll go out looking for him, but I bet I know exactly where he is. I told him if he ever needed to blow off some steam, he could hide in my tato's van. It's where I go when I need space. It's unlocked. There's chips and soda and blankets. No one's driving it off in that condition."

"You're sure?"

He nodded.

"Will you check on him?"

He nodded.

Suddenly, there was a shuffle and thud. Maksym ducked.

After a moment, like a diver, he resurfaced. "What was that?"

"My dad," she said calmly. "He's a sleepwalker. It's a parasomnia. When we were kids, he used to walk now and then, but now it's all the time. He sleeps in the hall outside my door. Since the night of the accident, he's been tying himself to a chair out there. And that? That's probably the sound of him trying to break free."

"So that night, on the road, he was sleepwalking?"

Amara nodded.

"Anyone could have hit him." He whistled. "He's lucky." His eyes softened and looked past her. His voice came out in a soft rush, and he spoke as if to someone else. "You know, my pop, he's lucky, too. Damn lucky. That's what the nurse said. The night we met he could have died. He had too much to drink. He could have killed someone with the alcohol in his system, but he didn't. Instead, he crashed into the tree, crushed his spleen, and broke his femur in two places—and only because he went into shock. Lucky him, if he wasn't diabetic, he would have been sentenced to jail for drunk driving; instead, he was sentenced to the hospital for diabetic shock. Lucky for him, he would have flown out the window if his muscles had tensed up like they do when you have a fright; instead, he went limp and slouched into his seat.

"His face would have been wedged against that tree, instead of the front of his car—because he didn't have on a seat belt. And he's diabetic only because he's sloppy and overweight. And he's overweight because he used to be a soldier, and now, he is only a drunk. He is only lucky because he is a diabetic who numbs his nightmares with alcohol. So, you see," Maksym finished with a weary chuckle, "he's lucky.

"When the KGB cracked down on nationalists, my tato performed his job with efficient brutality. He worked his way up the ranks over a short time. He even helped them to capture Chornovil—he was this Ukrainian folk hero. My tato didn't care. He was just a mercenary, you know. He'd do anything, he'd sell out anyone for a price."

"Even his own family?"

"Yeah." He shrugged. "By the time the Helsinki Group quietly discharged him from service, he had no friends, no family left. No one trusted him. Everyone was gone." He finally met her eyes. "Except my mother. And then one day she was gone, too," he said.

Amara brought her hand to the window and left it there. She wanted to touch his skin, to feel something human.

It was late. Maksym's head rested against the window as sleep overtook his senses, yet he wouldn't go. Everyone else in the world had surrendered to slumber, but not Amarachi Ewerike and Maksym Kostyk. Forget the grated window. The only thing separating them was air. Was it possible to get any better than this? The night was theirs to have and to do with as they pleased. And what a perfect night it was, the sun put away, moonlight to guide you. With Maksym, she decided, she could do anything, be anything. The world was theirs.

When the sky had gone milky, Maksym scrubbed roughly at his eyes as if awakened from a dream. There was a sadness there.

"Maks, are you still going to search for your mom?"

"Yeah."

"Maybe she'll come looking for you. Don't go," she said. "Stay."

If her parents had handpicked an alternative—say a slender, bespectacled Aba-born engineer-in-training who scoffed at his parents' old-fashioned dictates while easily living up to them, or a Lagosian dissident who spoke flattering platitudes about revolution, the Women's War of 1929, and the Eke spirit while burning rubber on his motorcycle—maybe all his allure would have been a passing vagary. He was just some boy, a little on the skinny side, going the way of his deadbeat dad. He cursed too much, made a lot of noise about things he never did anything about, and everyone called him trash. Still, this surge in her chest, of both agony and delight, mounting with each fleeting second, was not, at least to Amara, identifiable as mere mutiny; she had decided on love. Amara sat sweating on the hard tile floor of her bedroom, her damp back pressed to the door, her flicking tongue catching the salty sweat that pooled from her forehead. Even though he had gone, Maksym's presence surrounded her: the sturdy thud of his feet pounding the floor, the arch vibrato of his sigh as he hummed a catchy tune. His scent ballooned around her. She wondered at all the places he had been.

Spring was long gone. It was summertime. Even though the days blurred together, the seasons hadn't. She thought of his pores, suffused with chlorine from the swimming pool, chlorophyll from cutting the grass, a hint of vanilla from the bakery, menthol from that cigarette he shared with his friends, guys like him who slung their shoulders when they walked, but who never moved in packs, all loners in their own way.

Remembering the day they met, so long ago, her foot in his cupped palm, the pulse of his fingertips on her flesh, she traced her thumb along the side of her ankle, his touch, so that it might never vanish.

Amara rushed to her window, looking, not even seeing. She was dreaming. Maksym emerging from a green sea. Concrete sizzling and steaming with each step, vaporized water rising to meet the air. And in the dream, it had just rained. And it was hot, so hot, and the evening so humid and damp. Something about all of it, the leaden sky turning over and hanging thickly, swallowed up the sound when Maksym called her name.

EIGHTEEN

CHUK

You're not supposed to strike your own father. There's some code. Somewhere it is decreed: *if thee boy shall striketh his pater, from this day forward, his britches be too tall to stand under his pater's roof.* Chuk was sure Mr. Kim had assigned it, but was it from *The Comedy of Errors*, *Romeo and Juliet*, or the sonnets?

He had stood face-to-face with his father, looked him directly in the eye as if an equal, and knocked him down. Not only that, but he had also done this terrible deed in front of his sister. Chuk felt aggrieved by his affliction, this unwieldy force within him. He thought about his hands. His hands had grown so large that summer. He could almost palm a basketball. His shoulders were broader, his lats winged out. The little knots on his chest had begun to swell into pecs. Maksym had been training Chuk all summer long to be a fighter. Yet, the one time he had fought, it had been wrong. He had dishonored his father.

How could he strike his own father? What had overcome him? He had done it to protect his sister. That was what he had told himself. But the truth was that he did it for himself. He did it because he was useless or bad, or stupid, or lazy. And when he spoke, he wanted to be listened to. And when he stood before another man, eye to eye, he wanted to be looked upon with respect, not derision. Now he can't remember what it was supposed to resolve for him.

What was wrong with Chuk these days? Everything made him cry. He couldn't understand himself anymore. At sixteen, his father had marched into the swamps of the Delta with munitions strapped to his back. He'd stood toe-to-toe with enemy combatants and fought for beloved Biafra, yet Chuk had been slipping and sliding and hiding all summer from a rat-faced boy.

If you dishonor your father, and in front of a woman, you're supposed to leave his house. You're supposed to make a life for yourself somewhere else. How many times had his father said this to him? But Chuk was afraid. At fourteen, he couldn't imagine living anywhere else but surrounded by the familiarity of home: his father's grunts and bellows, his mother's song, his sister's snide jests.

When his father had enlisted him to be his protégé, his confidant, his Keeper of the Abode, Chuk had lost touch with all his boys. Damian, Lyle, Curt, Douglass, DeMarcus. He wondered if they were still out smoking joints in the back of a pickup truck behind the Walmart, or if they had been bussed to church camp and summer school, or if they had reluctantly taken on summer jobs flipping burgers.

He felt like he was treading water, looking over the glassy surface of a dark lake, but not seeing anything, only feeling his legs weaken the longer he pedaled. All summer, all that training. What had it been for? Running from Raphy? Striking his father. Why had he done it? Because he wanted his father back.

What Chuk did next was for honor. Since the day that Raphy had stolen his father's letter, the one addressed to Fathers of Biafra, everything between the father and son had turned sideways. Before that, Chuk had earned his father's confidence, and Chuk had worked hard to protect his father from disappointment by hiding the letters. He had borne the great responsibility of running errands and protecting his sister with competence and dignity. Until Raphy. Raphy made all Chuk's fears come alive. Because as long as their secrets remained within the family, it was almost like they didn't exist. But if Raphy knew, if everyone knew, then the breakdown of his family was real. And if it was real, then it was forever.

All summer, Chuk had been training for the war to come. Why had he been so afraid that afternoon when he saw the burning underwear? After all, he could jump rope five minutes straight without the rope lashing his ankles anymore; he could do forty push-ups in a row on the tile floor of his bedroom; he could churn out crunches; he could run four miles without a break; he could bob and weave; he could swing at the air in varying combinations; he could double up punches; he could skip from foot to foot—lateral, forward, backward—faster, faster, pivot until the motion was rhythmic and anticipatory rather than reactive. He pivoted, ducked under, came out on top, shot with his right fist, then an uppercut. Above all, he wasn't afraid to receive a blow. The time had arrived.

And so, as the sky darkened with evening's approach, he emerged from his hiding place along the edges of the Hal Buckman Preserve. He had only made it halfway to Raphy's aunt's house when reason edged out his certainty. He could fight Raphy one-on-one. The problem was Raphy's friends.

While Maksym and Amara drew closer to one another at her window, Chuk made his way along Old State Road 50. A stealth breeze switched through the palm trees that obscured the edge of the road, and there was a sound like a baby's rattle shaking. He darted across the road, passed the lopsided sign at the entrance of the Calumet Rows, and then weaved across the green, the overgrown lawn sweeping his ankles, until he reached the Kostyk trailer. He didn't have a plan for how he would obtain the gun. He only knew that it was what he needed to keep the other boys from interfering in his fight with Raphy.

From the looks of the trailer, he suspected that Maksym wasn't home. The lights were dim, and the speedball and punching bag—which seemed always to be warm and alive with the swinging of his fists, the rhythmic pounding like the hurried sounds of an anxious heartbeat and flying flecks of saliva and sweat—were lifeless.

Maksym's bedroom window was open, and he could see through the screen that the room was empty. He removed the screen, edged the window open, and boosted himself up until he reached the windowsill. Then he slid in easily on his belly. Maksym's room was charmless. There were no posters of LeBron or Kobe. There were no *King* posters of scantily clad models spread over elegant

Jaguars and Vipers with fresh tints and shiny rims. There were no posters of Drake or Kanye. Only one bulletin board with the picture of his mother. Chuk stood in front of the bulletin board staring at her picture.

And then he heard a click. Smelling the strong scent of alcohol, he turned slowly, knowing before he had completed the revolution that he would be staring down the barrel of a gun. Although he had never seen him in his full upright position, Mr. Kostyk was taller than he had imagined. He had to be six feet tall, but with the wild, frizzy hair that fanned out behind his balding forehead, he seemed a giant. Even though his arms trembled, his body was thick and firm. A brick chest took up most of his body. Stocky arms and legs made up the remains. Coarse dark hair and deep blue veins climbed up his arms. His elbow was propped on a battered crutch so that it took the place of a cane; so that his hands were free to train the gun on Chuk.

Instantly, Chuk's hands went up, but they were shaking. With Mr. Kostyk blocking the doorway and the window he had slid through just barely open, there was hardly a chance to escape. He searched for some explanation for why he was in Maksym's room. All the training of the past few weeks had taken place while Mr. Kostyk lay sprawled across the living room sofa sleeping off a bender.

"I'm sorry," Chuk said, his hands going up. But he was still nose to nose with the gun. He looked around the room. His eyes fell on the photo. "I'm sorry your wife left," he blurted out.

Mr. Kostyk shifted his feet. His face hardened. His chin trembled. All the features of his face collapsed, first his chin, then his nose, and it seemed the pain was so great that he would burst into tears. Instead, he let out a drunken battle cry, “Ahhhahhahhha!” and pulled the trigger.

Chuk scrunched his eyes closed. He opened one eye. He was still alive. He felt along his arms and chest. He looked over his shoulder. The bullet was lodged in the bulletin board behind him. Right next to his head. Mr. Kostyk had missed. Thank God for alcohol.

“I kill you!” Mr. Kostyk roared, fumbling with the gun again.

With all his might, Chuk barreled, headfirst, into Mr. Kostyk’s bad leg, sending the man crashing to the floor, his crutch going one way, his gun going the other. “Yowwwwww!” Mr. Kostyk yowled in agony.

Chuk was already out the door, down the hallway, through the living room, and out into the night air. His breaths coming in a rush, he kept running without looking back. He knew if he stopped and turned, Mr. Kostyk might have had time to regain his wits and kill him.

He made it out past the property limits of the Kostyk plot, and then, at last, he released a sigh of relief. What had just happened was far worse than anything that could happen with Raphy and his boys. If he could get through that, he could get through anything. He headed home.

From any distance, you’d know this home was enchanted. Bright orange flames from candles echoed through the front room. Mugs of a suspiciously brown ale flowed. Through the window, Chuk’s father swayed in the center of the room to a percussive tune that grew louder as Chuk approached. His mother was in his father’s arms, and he could hear her confused laughter.

"Come now, Miss. Naija!" his father bellowed. Irrespective of her protests, he cajoled her into tasting the concoction and then burst into exhilarated applause when a belch escaped her. Despite her embarrassment, his mother couldn't help but titter. She couldn't help but bellow and *Kayrekaykaygeekaykay* with Fela's "Teacher Don't Teach Me Nonsense."

Never had Chuk seen his parents like this; never before had he heard such music in their laughter; never before had he observed such calamitous movements in a room that was suddenly too small for the figures that jostled as they navigated space, glowing with heat; the thud of their hearts exposed as they leaned into one another's shaky foundations. Once, long ago, they used to be something. He saw it now: a narrow, craggy road, his parents walking hand in hand.

NINETEEN

FIDELIS

"My children, you must understand, we are children of love, who are at war. We must let the wisdom of our ancestors guide us:

"Our own native town, Umuihunanya, was named for the joining of lovers who reunited after a quarrel. You see, Eluigwe, the sky guardian, and Ala, the keeper of the earth, were betrothed to one another. Ala was the most beautiful of the goddesses. Although many desired her, Ala's eye could only see Eluigwe. But he was reckless and thirsty for flattery, so he volunteered himself to the Great Chi for a dangerous mission. After successfully completing his post, he, an unrepentant flirt, grew distracted by the praise of the many undulating mountains. He spread his love around, filling the valleys with rain. He did not return as promised.

"If he had, he would have known that in his absence, Anyanwu, the guardian of the sun, began to woo and tempt Ala. When he learned of this, Eluigwe returned. But it was too late. His adored had fallen in love with her paramour! Scorned, he took back his gift of rain. With only the sun, the earth produced no yam, just a scorched plain. A decades-long famine ensued. Starved children began to perish one by one.

"Anyanwu, having grown potbellied on love, became cocky and indolent, a boring and monotonous lover, so Ala quarreled with him and returned to Eluigwe. Bitter, Anyanwu retrieved his sun. For a short time, the bounty was restored. But then, with only rain, the earth was soon flooded! Again, the children starved. And like Anyanwu, Eluigwe, in his arrogance, once again became a careless lover.

"Realizing what their quarrels had wrought upon the land and its dwellers, Ala went to the Great Chi and Eke for advice. The husband and wife told her if Anyanwu brought his sun and Eluigwe brought his rain, then from the earth would spring forth an abundance of yam. The children would eat and eat until they grew fat. She must choose one swain without displeasing the other. But she loved her inamoratos equally. Chi Ukwu said her admirers were too jealous to share, so she must spend the day with one. Then, while he slept, she must sneak out and spend the night with the other. But Eke, in her womanish wisdom, insisted that the two would willingly share. And she told them how.

"So, Ala summoned her suitors. Calling them lazy lovers, she insulted Eluigwe and Anyanwu. Anything worth having must be fought for, she said, but not by force, through love. Alas, they must compete for her affection. She set aside one day of every week for each beau. On Eke, the first market day, Ala met Eluigwe. He gifted her a glittering sapphire rain. They made love through the night. On Afo, the third market day, she met Anyanwu. He gifted her a bright amber sun. They made love throughout the day.

"Her lovers lavished her with such affection that sometimes she was so carried away that she lost track of the day. Instead of meeting Eluigwe on Eke, she would visit him on Orie, the second market day. Now she must meet Anyanwu on Nkwo, the last market day. Though the sun and rain were fickle, the earth produced a plentiful harvest. Henceforth, the bountiful land of the dwellers became known as Umuihunanya, the children of love.

"My children, don't you see? Our enemies cannot defeat us. Our greatest weapon is our capacity for love."

TWENTY

ADAOBI

Adaobi did not know that Chukwudiegwu had stood toe-to-toe with his father. She did not know of Amarachi's secret rendezvous with her paramour. She only knew that something had shifted in her home. The strange man and his crabs in a bucket with Sunday on his lips, the burning fetish on her front porch, and her dreams of a matriarchy of elephants left her reeling: a reckoning was on the horizon. But nothing prepared her for the music of her youth booming as her husband knocked and swayed his hips at the center of the room as if under a spell.

"Come now, Miss Naija! Miss America," Fidelis sang, "nwanyi oma. Where are you going, beautiful one?"

She shook off his teasing. "I must check on the children." She started for the hallway.

"Chere!"

Without turning, she waited. "Fidé, you dey vex me today."

"Am I your enemy?" he asked. Her hands remained on her hips, so he added, "Come now, is this how you greet your di? Come, drink."

"Nda!" she flung at him.

"Hey!" he exclaimed, as if wounded. "This common greeting? Am I a cockroach?"

Forcefully, she turned to him, warning, "Fidelis, no wahala today."

He laughed. "Adaobi, sit with me." A lamp flickered on, illuminating him. With a damp handkerchief, he mopped beads of sweat from his forehead. A sweating half-drunk mug of Guinness rested on the coffee table. His face looked strange. She couldn't understand if the expression she saw was sadness, remorse, or sweet and soft, but when he handed her the can, she drank.

"What is this?" she asked.

"Nke m," mine, "do you remember how we would meet between the trees when we were young?"

"Fidelis, what is all this?"

As if splashed with hot cooking grease, he recoiled. "Hey! You have killed me. You have changed." He sighed. "Yet in so many ways, you are still the same. For one, you remain as nasty and mean as an old mama goat." In a single movement, he grasped her arm, drawing her to him. They were so close that if he wanted, he could have kissed her. Fidelis stroked Adaobi's face. Her pulse quickened. She felt at sea. Guinness filled her nostrils.

His voice softened. "Nwanyi oma, do you remember?"

In spite of herself, she chuckled, sadly. "Yes."

The person before her was no longer her husband. He was a boy. The lanky poet with soft hands and mournful eyes.

"One day you will spend all your compliments," she teased

back. "Then you will see a beautiful babe wearing red lipstick and cocking her nyash, but the pocket in your throat will be empty. How will you seduce her?"

"I will tell this lady with the red lips and buxom nyash, 'Chere, wait, dear.' Then I will call you. I will hand her fono. You will whisper every sugary lyric I have whispered into your ear, into hers."

"O di egwu!" Adaobi laughed. "You are a fool."

"Yes," he said. "I am *your* fool."

She laughed again.

"Let's dance."

She sighed. "You are trouble!"

"Come now, dance with me," he said again.

And so, she did. Sweat lit up the pores on his face. They began to blur with memory. Marks of age receded to reveal the shiny young face of a teenage boy. The boy's lanky arms hooked around Adaobi's. Her stomach rumbled as he spun her around, a leisurely dance. Sky opened with a hot breath. They were there again. A dirt path led to a clearing in between the trees. Adaobi took a step. Pebbles scratched her shoeless feet. Wind rustled through the leaves. The first notes of a song began: *Isn't it a lovely day*, his boy's voice rang out, *to be caught in the rain?* His voice was terrible.

But just as she thought to protest, Adaobi felt the first pitter-patters of a rainfall. His voice, dampened by the drizzle, was suddenly throaty and melodic. *You were going on your way, now you've got to remain.*

Before she knew it, her face was resting on his shoulder. He spun her.

"I hu n'anya m, my love," he said to her, "you have given me two beautiful children, and a life that I could never have known possible. And I have only taken from you. But today that finishes. We will be whole again. We will stand tall again. I will no longer allow this house to fall."

A loud tumble sounded. Adaobi withdrew from his arms. An aged Fidelis Chinonso Ewerike stood upright before Agatha Adaobi Ewerike. "What are you talking about?"

"I have been going about this all wrong," he said. "I will never find Ugochi from here in the white man's land. I must return home."

"And do what?" Adaobi asked. "Chase your tail like a dog? Where will you go? Where will you look? Fidelis, Ugochi is gone."

"I left before the war finished," he said. "I left my brothers on the battlefield. I have a debt to repay."

"What are you saying? Speak plainly."

"Nwunye m," my wife, he said seriously. "I am not asking for your permission. I am asking for a proper sendoff." He took her hand, kissed it, and walked out the door into the night.

Long after the sun began an abrupt ascent into the cloudless, haze-filled sky, Adaobi awaited Fidelis's return. Up and down the street, clouds of smoke dissipated under sizzling porch lights as night turned to day. A basketball popped and slapped a backboard, car doors slammed, tires whispered on the highway. Then a wino stumbled up the street, change clinking in his pockets. He threw his head back and sang a hoarse shrill, "Teacher, teacher-oh-na, the lecturer be your name!"

When he approached, the strong scent of fish, cigars, and

alcohol preceded him. Under the orange of the porch light, the dirt of his rolled-up slacks and the damp rings of sweat under his arms were exposed. Fingers blackened, eyes yellowed, Fidelis bowed clumsily.

"My lady, may I have the honor of this dance?"

"Mba!" No. He was still drunk. "Where have you been?"

"I am here, nke m," he playfully admonished.

"Don't vex me."

As if speaking to an impudent child, he frowned, but only with his lips. "Relax yourself. You're too young for wrinkles." Beaming, he produced a dripping plastic bag and dangled it before her. It stank of fish. "For my sendoff."

She had hoped that this talk of returning to Nigeria would be forgotten. Instead, while Adaobi had been gripped with worry, Fidelis had been carousing all night, fishing and imbibing. What kind of man had she married? He was nothing but a lush, a scoundrel, a louse. While she had wept, he had been seated on one of the half-lit porches up the street, smoking Black & Milds, drinking gin, and playing cards, wailing with laughter, and moaning with chagrin at Lady Luck's treachery.

"Fidé, I beg," she said, "this has to stop."

Maybe he was right, Adaobi thought as she teetered over the sink the following afternoon. She felt like the ground had shifted beneath her overnight. A wayward husband contained at home was one thing, but one released into the day? Adaobi pressed stockfish in a bowl of water. Whatever Fidelis was looking for, perhaps he would only find it in the land of his ancestors. Surely, he wouldn't find it here, where the Ewerikes remained guests among strangers. She and Fidelis had absconded from Biafra all those years ago—he, an escaped detainee, welcomed first into de Gaulle's France, before eventually making it to America after several years; and she, when he had the means to relieve the nuns of her. That was what the nuns had told her; they hadn't told her about the long letters he had written, pouring out his heart to her and imagining their new life together.

But there was no life for them in Nigeria. Even though Gowon had promised to reintegrate the Biafrans into Nigeria, Fidelis, like so many others, knew that if they stayed, their future was not just uncertain, it was bleak. They would be rebuilding their lives with ashes.

For years, they had kept their passport status up to date. Adaobi had returned just once. During the day, she paraded five-year-old Amara through what was left of the family compound. At night, she lay wide awake, thinking of Ugochi. Wondering what her dear friend's life might have been had there been no war. Fidelis had yet to return to Nigeria. Each time it came up, he found an excuse not to return. But Adaobi knew that he simply couldn't go on seeing what remained of his old life. He preferred for it to live in his memories. So, while there were no fears about retaliatory actions by secret state police, there was a general unease.

But now, Adaobi thought, Fidelis would simply be an old man returning to his homeland. Not a soldier. Perhaps he would rub elbows with the elders who had survived the war and the years after. Perhaps they would sit on their porches and imbibe as they reminisced on their childhood days. Perhaps their memories of Ugochi would be the small pittance Fidelis needed. And then he would return home able to move on.

Back to the kitchen, eyes cast out the window into the distance, Adaobi could see nothing of the palm trees that outlined the border of the Hal Buckman Preserve. Earlier that day, she had gone to the market to cull together the ingredients for the send-off dinner. Water trilled into the sink in sharp metallic pings; she hadn't completely closed the tap. This was the sort of negligence that usually exasperated her. She could nag for hours about her useless, spoiled, akata children who knew nothing of thirst and hunger. They knew nothing of the malnourished belly, taut like a basketball, the telltale sign of kwashiorkor. In wartime, waste was the enemy of survival.

Her blessed, beloved, exasperating offspring knew nothing of suffering. She could lift her blouse, pointing to her belly and embarrassing her children with the droop of her breasts, the languid rolls in her stomach, and the glossy stripes in her sides. They had heard countless tales about the pains she had endured carrying, laboring, and delivering each child, dead or alive. Still, could they know?

When Chuk tapped the faucet shut, Adaobi didn't budge.

When he called, "Mom?" she only blinked.

"My son," she said, speaking to herself, "you know nothing of suffering."

"Am I in trouble?"

Facing him, Adaobi let out a dry laugh.

He cocked his head to the side and furrowed his brow.

Like his father, he had seemed different, almost solemn, foxholed in his bedroom for most of the day, and only emerging now to linger in the doorway, watching her silently.

"Ngwa—" Turning from him, she swept her gaze out of the kitchen and to the living room. She was still too weary to scold him for sitting on the sofa's arm earlier; too worn to run a rag over the dust-covered items exposed by the sunlight. She sighed.

Everything needed to be tidied. Reorganized. Rearranged. Her husband's projects filled the house. While he was indifferent to the clutter, she put things away. Covered them with lids. Closed them tight. He was a collector, a meticulous arranger of junk. He never let go of what belonged in the past: fishbowls brimming with baseball cards he would never trade—he only cared for *football*; a fan with missing blades; a dank un-emptied dehumidifier; stacks of broken VCRs; a dial stereo, dusty from lack of use; a silent telephone, cords beyond use. But today, the makeshift office outside Amara's bedroom would be put away. The door to her room would be unlocked. Once more they would be a family. Indeed this would be a proper sendoff.

"You don't ever want me around," Chuk said. At first, it sounded like a tease, like the start of an ordinary bicker between mother and son, but then his voice grew stern. "Don't lie!"

Adaobi spun around. "Chai! To call someone liar—your mother, sef—that is abomination!"

"But it's true," he said. "You're never around anymore."

"Chukwudiegwu, look at me." She grasped his face. Her son, a mere child with a deepening voice starting to crack, the timid start of a mustache, flared nostrils, eyebrows angled in righteousness! Oh, to see him turning into a man before her eyes! She felt awash with regret. "I am here now. With you. You are my son." She hoped her words would placate him.

"Don't cry," Chuk said. "I was only teasing."

Grasping an unpeeled onion from the basket, Adaobi chuckled. "It's only the onions."

He took one. It slid back and forth in his hands, crinkling, as slivers of dried skin pulled away. "Can I help?"

Sizing him up skeptically, she asked, "You?"

He nodded.

Adaobi chuckled. "Silly boy, men don't belong in the kitchen."

"That's not true," he said. Then, "You're kicking me out?"

"That's what my mother told me."

"But what about Dad?" Chuk asked. "He loves to cook."

"Yes, your father," Adaobi sighed. She chuckled. "Your father is a terrible cook."

"Yes, but sometimes, he gets it just right."

"Perhaps," Adaobi said uncertainly, "the elders get some things wrong."

Chuk took the knife, flexed his brow in concentration, and anchored the onion in his palm, then watched his mother. Adaobi sliced like back home, one hand holding the vegetable, the other hand pressing a knife carefully down into its body. Chuk did the same.

"Hey!" Just before the knife plunged into the onion, she yanked the knife away and flung it into the sink like a venomous snake. "What is this? My son, you are trying to kill me."

Glaring, he looked away. "It's *my* hand, not yours."

"Your hand is my hand," she said.

"I was just trying to help."

"Okay. But, please, do like this." She pulled a cutting board out of the cabinet and showed him how to cut the onion against the block, how to guard his fingers by curling them away from the blade.

"I want to do it like you," he said.

"My son, don't kill me."

He laughed and took the board. At first, his cut was too wide. "Like this," she corrected.

Then it was too narrow. "No-uh." She frowned.

But, at last, it was just right.

And because her silly boy could not help himself, he declared, "I'm a better cook than Amara, right?"

"How's your sister doing?" she asked. "I mean, how is she feeling?"

He shrugged. "She's okay."

There was something he wasn't saying. She opened her mouth to press again, but instead, she examined his jaggedly chopped onions.

"Good."

After the stockfish softened in the water, Adaobi lifted it out and gingerly deboned it. She ground the egusi and crayfish in the blender. She turned to her son.

"You have the most important task, Chukwudiegwu." She handed him a bunch of achara. Peeling and breaking a shoot in her hands, she demonstrated. "Without achara, we cannot call this Ofe Achara."

Chuk mimed his mother's sequence of actions, carefully peeling the achara's husk and breaking the tender innards into smaller pieces. Adaobi nodded in satisfaction. With all the ingredients combined in a large boiling pot, Chuk stood watching the mixture bubble and snap, its fragrance filling the kitchen. All the rap music he played, the music Adaobi often disparaged, came out in an uneven hum when she was cheerful. She sang a few bars of the chorus. *She is not messing with that broke singa!*

Suddenly, he wrapped his arms around her. Everything in Adaobi's heart threatened to spill over. She thought, *Maybe, just maybe, I can put my faith in Ofe Achara.*

Pulling back the lid from the pot, Chuk asked, "Is it done?"

"Leave it," she said with mock sternness.

He twisted a ladle in the pot. "Should I turn it?"

"Do you want to spoil my Ofe Achara?"

Moments later, a bedroom door flung open. Fidelis stood breathing hard in the archway. "What is the meaning of this?" His eyes were dark, but he didn't look angry. He seemed lost. "Where did you find achara?"

Adaobi's voice softened. "My dear, this is for you, for your sendoff."

"Is this some love medicine?" Chuk asked. "What's Ofe Achara?"

"Something your father's mother used to make a long time ago," Adaobi said. "Something she made specially for your father and his sister."

Like a drug, the summer night left everybody's bones heavy and waterlogged from perspiration. Atop their front stoop, the Ewerikes listened for the cries of insects but heard none. Just a short fan overlain with a damp cloth whined each revolution. Up the street, a stereo system's bass hummed. A solo basketball echoed as it slapped the pavement. Two girls called good-byes to one another; a passing boy wolf whistled. By a dim light, the Ewerikes swallowed lusty bites of fish, achara, and egusi.

At the head of the table, Fidelis stood before the family. Glass held high, he proclaimed, "Igbo kwenu!"

"Yaa!" Adaobi answered wearily.

"Igbo kwenu!"

"Yaa," she said with more conviction, turning to the children, who joined in uncertainly.

"We, children of Biafra, celebrate tonight!" Drumming a triumphant tune on the tabletop, Fidelis made a racket of cheers and applause.

In answer, Amara, now freed from her prison, jabbed her fork into the eye of the fish head on her plate, and Chuk stared at his dish soberly.

"Is it too hot, dear?"

"No, Mom."

"Amara, bring water," she said.

"We have a perfectly good pitcher of water right here."

"But is it cold, eh?" she hissed. "Bring ice, foolish girl!"

"I'm fine, Mom," Chuk said.

"Leave him," Fidelis said, grinning. "He is a son of Africa. Pepper is in his blood." To their shock, he poured Chuk a heaping glass of Guinness and raised his glass as if to salute him.

Awkwardly, Chuk gripped the glass, but just as he was about to raise it, Adaobi removed his hand and directed a silent reprimand with her eyes. All evening, her eyes had been telling the children to humor their father. They must not spoil his bliss. Whatever he was celebrating, they would find out soon enough. And while he hadn't yet shared his news with the children, their general uneasiness was a signal that they knew the forthcoming news would leave them in disarray.

"I tell you, this woman was Miss Naija 1965!" Fidelis said, narrowing his shiny gaze on Adaobi. "Every boy wanted to dance with her."

His lovely words, a balm, loosened her scowl, which gradually came apart into laughter as he described her beautiful thick braids, her obscenely curvy silhouette in her school uniform, her catlike walk. She could see herself again, a girl of sixteen in a belted dress, with the sturdy legs her skinny-legged cousins coveted. She could see the girl who had a way of walking and a way of talking that instigated desire in boys and men alike. She, strutting down the red, sandy street of the photographs, backless sandals kicking up dust, while Fidelis looked on in admiration.

"The girl who would become your mother was standing at the gate. She looked up, catching my eye. With such a smile, I had no defense."

Her eyes met his across the table.

"And that walk."

With a chuckle, Adaobi put up her hand to stop him.

Fidelis took a breath. "Tonight, my dear children, I've news," he began. "I am returning to my homeland. A man, not a boy, I return to finish what was started long ago but remains unfinished. With each passing day, Radio Biafra's evening broadcast announces deaths and demonstrations in response to Fulani herdsmen who cross the central plateau into southern lands. These herdsmen are provocateurs whom the federal government has installed to foment instability, a pretense to limit the sovereignty of Igbo-majority local governments. If their plan is successful, they will have our land—and then, come for our wives and daughters!

"Jonathan has done nothing to quell the violence. And so we must look to a competent leader. The head of Fathers of Biafra has raised a call, urging his brothers to return to their homeland and fight for its dignity."

Adaobi's chest tightened. She looked from her children to Fidelis and back to her children again. "What is the meaning of this?"

Fidelis wiped his eyes, which now ran with exhilarated tears. "I have purchased my ticket, nke m. I have packed my bags. I leave in a week's time."

"I thought you were going to see about Ugochi?" Adaobi asked. "Not fight in a silly endless war." She looked to her children for help, but their jaws remained slack with confusion. "These political saboteurs—they are nothing more than migrant herdsmen following their cattle."

As he stuffed his mouth with fufu and Achara soup, Fidelis said, "You people will mark my words. This is only the beginning! The people will not stand for it!"

"You are joking," Adaobi said softly. "There is no Biafra. It simply doesn't exist! And what if it did, what of it? Fighters? Nonsense. They are as useless as the left hand. They know nothing but to throw bombs, to loot, to kill, to defile their daughters. You want to be a hero? Ngwa, go. Enlist."

Fidelis was resolute. "That is what I intend. If they will have me."

"Have *you*? Chai! My husband, sense has chased you, but you are faster."

"People are dying!" Fidelis said.

"And what of it?" Adaobi said. "They died then. They die today, tomorrow. They took Ugochi. And they will take you. And we will all be finished one day."

"Be careful!" he said, his voice rising. "If you repeat her name, I will show you."

Adaobi turned away.

"How can you call yourself ndi Igbo with such a lax attitude for your brethren?" Fidelis implored. "You deserter!"

Adaobi bolted from her seat, still gripping her dish. She stood face-to-face with her husband, the cords in her throat tightening as she spoke. "I stood in the ruins of your foolhardy dream. I, a girl, a mere child, held the hand of your sister. We all played our part, we, the heroes, did we not? And what did that provide us, eh? What would Ugochi say?"

Fidelis looked at her, stunned. The children remained silent. Until Adaobi let the dish in her hand fall, sending fishbones and spatters of clumpy soup in all directions, the slivers of dish to be picked and fretted over for days.

Finding his words, he bellowed, "I was just a boy! I did what they told me! I did what I had to do! I fought for our Biafra!"

"And it wasn't enough," Adaobi said softly.

"Come now, nke m, let us finish this meal in peace." He looked at her, his eyes deep and mournful. "The heroes have died. We are all that remain."

IV

TWENTY-ONE

AMARA

Holding in air starves a fire, but it only builds grief.

Nursing their individual wounds, each of the Ewerikes slouched to their corners of the house. The violence of her mother's words at dinner left Amara tossing and turning at night. How could anyone sleep on such a night? It felt like the Ewerikes' undoing was almost complete. And it had all been because of Ugochi. Dearest Ugochi.

Maybe that was when it all began for Amara. The jealousy.

When she looked at her drawing of a bird in flight, once mistaken for a deity by her father, she began to see a ghost.

I am jealous of a ghost.

The written words, set in fine black ink, stared back at her from her journal. Even they, her own words, did not belong to her—for it suddenly occurred to her that she was Ugochi's ghost.

Each day, the ghost of her aunt had stolen more and more of her father's life from him, and now her mother's. In the process, she had robbed Amara of hers, too. When her father looked at her, when he spoke to her, when he chided her, it was not to her; it was to his sister. Even as his lips formed Amara's name, it was not to her he spoke.

I am Amarachi, she thought. *Who is Amarachi?*

She felt effaced.

The prison had never been the four walls of her bedroom. All along, the prison had been Ugochi. And those girls. All those precious little girls. Amara was their prisoner. Amara was her prisoner. And what was freedom?

Willing herself to erase the words, Amara stared at the page.

Her pencil tilted to the leaf again. Four more words. A proclamation: *Ugochi did not survive.*

From her bedroom out the window, Amara watched Maksym outlined against an orange porch light as he drove his fists into his punching bag. He looked so electric his body might cast sparks. She opened the window. Hot air and the rich charcoal scent of detonated fireworks bathed her in fresh beads of sweat. Firecracker wrappers and casings littered the streets. Black clouds of ash stained the sidewalks. In Econlockhatchee, summer was a season that held on by fireworks.

Drawing her arms to her body, Amara breathed in the smells. She tried the doorknob. It gave easily. Her mother's words had shifted everything in the house. There was no lock. Her father no longer lingered in the hallway. She walked out the door, and past his shadowed figure slumped on the couch. She knew she had to go. If she stayed any longer, she would become like her parents. Had they forgotten what it meant to love?

The next morning, before sunup, Amara went looking for Maksym. She wanted to tell him about everything that had passed. She knew if he wasn't boxing in front of his father's trailer, then he'd be in the van, and if not in one of those two places, then he'd be at the Hal Buckman Preserve. A bluish glow outlined the sloped matchstick trees along the preserve's border. The hot sun had whitened the leaves, now so blank and brittle they offered no promise of shade. When she reached the densest areas of the preserve, where hammocks of sweet gum and cypress trees swallowed up the sun, she listened for his sounds. Bullfrogs hummed. As her eyes adjusted to the darkness, she could see the dark, wavy strip that was the Econlockhatchee River. Maksym stood at its center. Brown water lapped at his neck. Then he was squatting, splashing around, his palms slapping at the beads of sweat that sprayed him.

Flatwoods surrounded the river. Shards of sun-scorched blades of grass swayed at the water's edge. A gray-winged duck sneezed and shivered as it shook out its feathers. Sparkles of water evaporated into a mist. A downy woodpecker, with its ink-red emblem, perched on a tree. An ocher haze surrounded the sun. She rushed through the yellow thickets of grass, calling.

"Maks!"

His eyes met hers; he stood at full height. Water shimmered down glowing cerulean skin, droplets caught in the dark thatch of pubic hair. On the rays of bluish light, his body flickered. Only then did she see the ball of clothes on the bank, damp, as if he had tumbled into the water with them on only to change his mind and slip them off. Amara froze.

Keeping her eyes on the ball of clothes, she backed away. Maksym took one heaving step after another out of the water, advancing as if stalking prey. Without breaking his gaze from her, he slipped on his trousers and began to button his shirt. He took a step toward her.

Her legs couldn't cooperate.

He took another step. Another. Then another.

"Amara," he said. His face was flushed. He seemed swallowed up by air. He tilted his head to the side and squinted at her. She tilted her head to the side, too. They were so close that all she needed was to take the final step that would join him.

Somewhere, far away, a dog was barking, a bird was cawing, and it sounded like laughter. But then, just feet from him, she saw the bruise around his eye.

"What happened?"

"Amara," Maksym said. "I'm going. We got into it last night. He found out that I was in his weapons cache. Somehow he found out that I knew about my mother. He called me a traitor and enemy. He said I could go just like her because he didn't need me just like he didn't need her. So I'm going. I know I told you I'd wait, but I can't. I leave tonight."

"That's what I came to tell you, too," she said breathlessly, the truth of the words taking shape as they formed in her mouth. "I'll go with you."

She hadn't known Maksym long, but she felt he was the only person in the world who cared. He was her refuge. Two people shared so little, but in their fathers, that one object of grief, they were linked. All summer long, without knowing it, Amara had been seeking connection. She didn't know if this powerful feeling was true love; she only knew she didn't want to lose him. Amara reached, her hands closing over Maksym's shirt.

His gasp. "Are you sure?"

A nod. "Yes."

His fast breaths. His tremble. She had never touched someone like this before, but suddenly they were kissing, a terrible kiss, dry and full of force. But because the feel of his tongue didn't exactly gross her out, she didn't pull away.

And then because they had gone so far, and the urge was still there, burning her inside out, their bodies together, they began to rock.

And when her heart quaked, with the backs of her calves, Amara pulled him toward her body.

Maksym lay in the grass, his inert penis on his abdomen. Amara took note of his particulars, the ripe blemish on his right shoulder, the arcs where faded skin had been hidden under singlets and tees. Amara lay trying to remember what it felt like the first moment he was inside her, the moment that was so special it belonged, not only to her, but to her mother, her father, everyone else—a thing to be chronicled—losing her virginity.

She was supposed to feel like a woman. Or a slut. Or sinful. She couldn't decide. Weren't the insides of her thighs supposed to burn from the blasphemy of fornication? That is what her mother would say. She felt different, sore, yes, but it was not exactly the undoing she had expected. She didn't feel unfettered. Or even ashamed. That was the disappointment. At least he had pulled out.

It had all happened so quickly in a spurt of breathy pants and gasps. The whole time, Amara had hidden her nakedness. Not in the usual and trivial ways that girls fret over thigh gaps, stretch marks, and cellulite. There was just a part of her that she kept private, tucked away. She hoped that she had affected an air of aloofness, like she did this all the time.

No, it hadn't exactly hurt. More than anything, it was discomfort, like a bloated tampon blindly bumping her on the insides, causing an ache. This saddened Amara. She knew that it was supposed to feel good when you made love. She had been certain that she loved Maksym, that she had loved him since the first moment she saw him. Now she wondered if she had been wrong. Or maybe she was just broken.

Amara never wanted to be the kind of girl who couldn't find pleasure in sex. She had long suspected her mother was that kind. In this one way, Amara had forever been determined to be unlike her. But now she wasn't so sure. Maybe she had it all backward. Amara was the frigid one, while her mother could love with her body, just as ecstatically as she loved with her heart.

Amara would give anything to do her first time over again.

And again. And again. Until she got it right.

As Mr. Kostyk slept, Amara and Maksym dug a hole and buried his firearms under a tree near the river. They would return later that night. Amara would finish dinner, pack her clothes, and meet him by the tree. Maksym would be waiting. Wet air and the shade sent quills down her arms. She sat up straight, staring at the sky, and wrapped her arms around her knees.

"Cold?" he asked.

"I'm okay," she said. "You?"

He shrugged. She hoped he hadn't registered her disappointment at her first time. There would be plenty more opportunities. Her skin stung from his nearness and farness. Hand dangling in uncertainty, she reached out to him. He stiffened. Stroking him was like petting a feral cat. Eventually, his shoulders relaxed. All he needed was her touch.

Dusk came with ash. With Independence Day nearly upon them and the lighting of bottle rockets each night, it was the perfect time to leave undetected. Her parents hadn't spoken to each other since their big fight at dinner. Even so, tonight they were strangely affixed to one another in their bed, but with their backs to one another. Chuk was locked away in his bedroom, the frantic rush of rap beats thundering through his walls.

The Ewerikes, never a vacationing family, owned one set of luggage they stored in the attic, her father's, for when he traveled for business. It was a sturdy Samsonite ensemble, the same set he'd been using for the last fifteen years. He preferred for his bags to look worn and used. He said it kept the thieves away.

In the attic, she shrugged off the dust and cobwebs. It was a small, angular room filled with what remained of their possessions of their former life. There was one of the four Corinthian columns that had enshrined the entrance to their old home. There was old sheet music, a phonograph player, a dusty evening gown from the annual senior partners' ball. And there were the suitcases stacked in a corner of the attic. Amara lugged one to the center of the room. Finding it heavy, she opened it. Inside was a cache of old photo albums.

Amara and her brother had often peeked at their parents' old photographs, imagining. In her favorite, her mother was posed in a class photo with twenty-six other teenage girls, their thread-tied hair going every which way. All the girls had hard, serious expressions on their faces—except her mother, who wore the whitest, toothiest grin. With such a smile, in such a photograph, her mother's face always drew in the eyes of the viewer. Amara opened another photo album and another, studying photographs marking the milestones of her and her brother's lives: christenings, first days of school, birthdays. She smiled. She wished she knew more about her parents.

She turned to a row of moving boxes saturated with dust. The top of one was labeled with her father's hurried handwriting: *NOTEBOOKS.*

The first few notebooks were filled with her father's poetry and journal entries, juvenile scrawling on matters of love, hope, and morality. As she dug deeper, the journals became darker, filled with grievances, both petty and large: the boy whose best friend had stolen away his love, the instructor who had humiliated him in front of his classmates, and then a list of men's names: Odun, Eric, Charles, Muhammad. And next to each name, the manner of death: stabbed through the heart, slit throat, gunshot to the temple, strangulation. Were these the men her father had killed while escaping capture by enemy soldiers?

All summer long secrets had kept Amara bound in a prison. The secret of her cage. The secret of Chuk's education on force. The secret of her mother's hours away. The secret of her father's madness. One box remained, not as high and out of reach as it had been when she was a little girl, once, pointing and asking, "What's that?," to which her father had replied, "My papers." Gripping the steel-gray tin, she brought it down to her level, pleased to see that, as she remembered, a clasp, not a lock, held it together. She unfastened it and pried the box open.

Amara gathered the pages of a blue airmail envelope in her hands addressed to Mazi Uchendu Kenly Okeke. She ran her fingertips over the colorful stamps. The envelope bore the emblem of the American Red Cross. It was dated August 1968. A memorandum heading declared it a dispatch of Operation Airlift. She read the accompanying text:

Name: Ugochi Edwina Ewerike.
Age: 13.
Place of birth: Umuihunanya, Biafra.
Status, minor: Deceased.
Next of Kin: Fidelis Chinonso Ewerike, brother.
Status, next of kin: Deceased, combat soldier.

A pang caught Amara's chest. The document shook in Amara's hand, but she refocused her eyes, reading the missive again, stopping when she reached her father's name. "Deceased, combat soldier," she read aloud. Impossible. She glanced at the girl's name, and then at her father's. She checked the spelling. Could her father share his name with a dead man? Her heart clenched. Now, she understood his muttered words, heavy with chagrin: *It should have been me.*

Somehow, her father had made it home to the comfort of her mother's arms while a stranger lay in a grave marked with his name. Who had they buried in his stead? And if the officials had mistakenly marked her father for dead, then what if Ugochi were still alive, too? What if this was why she had never returned to him? When they had erroneously declared him dead, perhaps the Red Cross had shuttled Ugochi from one home to another, beginning the ripple that would manifest decades later here in America when her father turned the lock on Amara's bedroom door.

As she smoothed the creases in the envelope, a photograph slipped free. A fragile-looking girl, the resemblance uncanny. A mole, identical to her father's, perfectly small, nestled just above the girl's lip: Ugochi. This girl, this mavka, this shadowy apparition had haunted her father, and in turn, she had haunted Amara. They were a trinity, she, her father, and this little girl. Even in middle age, her father's skin loosened and warped, his hair balding and tightly shaved, there was something familiar about the cherubic cheekbones of the girl. The photograph's matte finish could not disguise the similarities—the dark shiny skin—like Amara's. The hair, eyes, nose, lips, the mole!

Amara outlined the girl's features over her own as if sketching her back to existence. The girl's hair was buzzed low, like Amara's. Her mother had once told her that in Nigeria, the younger girls wore their hair *low*. Only those in their final year at school could thread and braid their locks into stylish patterns in anticipation of courting. Amara traced her own scalp, looked back at the photo: the suggestion of a sneer; a rebel perhaps. Amara traced her own lips. The flick of an eyebrow, deep-set eyes; this girl was a wonderer—no, a wanderer. She was Amara's doppelgänger, both friend and fiend, confidante and competitor. But doubles are bad luck. That's what her mother used to say.

The door creaked open.

"What are you doing?" Light splintered through the cracked attic window. Entombed in the luminosity, Chuk appeared like something holy.

"I've met my mavka."

She sneezed and drew the back of her hand across her face in one sweep, the envelope falling and a dry powder dissipating in the air. Her face itched. Her scalp tingled. She twitched and sneezed again. Her tongue tasted of pepper, uda pepper. She imagined the colors of the world with such saturation, such dazzling brilliance.

Nigeria suffused her senses: its windy rivers, lush forests, and outdoor cooking stoves—all the memories her mother had painted of her childhood, in Umuihunanya, before the war. This was the scent that filled the kitchen when her mother had cooked her large Sunday dinners.

She remembered how her mother had said in the old days uda pepper was used to purge the womb of new mothers, so it must be handled with care. As the scent bathed Amara, she felt a kind of cleansing. Searing tears stung her eyes. Her nostrils overflowed with mucus.

An exhale of hot breath, a burst of flames. Her lungs swelled, threatening to splinter her rib cage. Even her fingertips prickled with the heat. It was then, her body roaring with the sensation of fire, her eyes raw, like an open wound, that she remembered her father's playful childhood cautionary:

—*I will pepper you.* It was an empty threat she had heard more times than she could count, a phrase so silly and foreign to her American ears that she had learned only to punctuate it with laughter.

—*Long throat,* her father would chastise, when she stole away, the spicy suya from his plate still hot and stinging in her mouth, *I will pepper you.*

When Amara would giggle, mocking the strange words, he would playfully condemn, *Akata!*

Amara would sprawl into his lap, giddy with laughter.

How could she have known that to *pepper* someone was literal and to be peppered was the worst pain imaginable?

How could Amara have known that her father's *papers*, the documents hidden away in that old tin up high in the attic, had been booby-trapped, soused along the creases with uda pepper?

How could she have known that these *papers* had something to do with Biafra, a time and place so distant that upon her parents' arrival to America they had chosen to forget?

As she brought her fingers to her eyes—digging at them, this endless pit of pain, its blaze only growing as the pepper seared her flesh—she was deaf to the sounds that filled the room.

A shadow loomed behind Chuk. His mother's footsteps, the sighing weight of each step, the sound of a woman who greeted peril with stubbornness. His father's footsteps, stealthy; it was his breath that you heard, a dense Klaxon that pushed through a barrel chest and out through his nostrils and open mouth, ensnared by childhood asthma and feverish nights in weedy foxholes in wartime.

As Amara howled from the pain, their father's hand sliced through the air, thwacking Chuk upside his head. "What have you done to your sister? I will beat your block head!"

Amara lay writhing and moaning.

And when her father tensed and pulled back, it was not in response to his son's tremendous wail.

No one, certainly not Amara, could know of her father's terrors—crouched in the corner of the room, his arms batting away invisible fiends—no one, apart from her mother.

In the ebbs and waves of roaring pain, the girl in the photograph's deep-set eyes and a voice whispering, "Biko," *please*, "kwushi," *stop*.

Only later would Amara learn that it was her mother, not the girl in the photograph, begging her not to cry.

"You must be strong," her mother said. "Weakness will only make it burn."

TWENTY-TWO

ADAOBI

Like a salve, Adaobi applied prayer. First, she flushed Amara's eyes with milk, irrigated them with water, and wrapped her face in a cool compress. Then, on her knees, at her daughter's bedside, she sang her prayers, begging for mercy. She begged for forgiveness for not teaching Amara right from wrong. If she had been a better mother, her daughter wouldn't have succumbed to the sin of curiosity. That serpent whisper had induced her daughter to forage through her father's *papers*.

A generations-long curse. If Adaobi had been a better child, not a bitter child, maybe she wouldn't have seen and done the things she did so long ago. The things she chose not to remember. All these years later, she couldn't shake the feeling of being unclean. She still bore invisible marks on her body, the touch of strange men she had enticed in order to survive. And if she had been a better wife, perhaps she could have rescued her husband from his walking nightmares.

Adaobi grieved her innocence, those times before the war had sullied her. When boxed up for so long, grief has a way of occupying the spaces once inhabited by love. Adaobi had tried to live by a few simple precepts. First and foremost, she had loved God. Her love for God was only rivaled by her affection for her children. Fidelis occupied the third position of the axis; men, she reasoned, could survive on their own without women. Oh, they never lived as well, but they subsisted nonetheless, chinks in their armor. Matrimony was a luxury. Children, on the other hand, were a half-formed piece that broke off a woman—senseless, defenseless, suckling air until a mother guided its mouth toward sustenance. Passion between a man and woman might peter out from the daily insults of life, but to her children a mother was meant to give everything. She had tried, but she hadn't predicted that the tenderness between a mother and her child could cease as well; this thought alone filled her with terror. *What have I been living all my life for, if not my children?*

She would take her. Take them. Take her girl and boy and get away from this madness. Too much had been broken. She moved from room to room, wardrobe to wardrobe, stripping shirts from hangers, dumping jeans and sneakers into duffel bags. Three bags: one for her, one for Amarachi, and one for her Chukwudiegwu. They would have to leave before Fidelis returned from his long walk.

She kicked the front door open and lunged out into the baking sun. One bag hefted on each shoulder, another at her feet, she made her way to the car, parked perpendicularly on the street. She dumped each duffel bag into the trunk.

Mute and exhausted, her eyes still wrapped in gauze, Amara followed as Adaobi and Chuk led her to the car and lay her on the back seat. Then, Adaobi turned to Chuk, reached for her son.

"Ngwa—"

"We're not going to the hospital, are we?" he asked.

"We're going for help," she said. "Come."

He slowly backed away toward the steps. "What about Dad?"

"What about him?" Adaobi said. "Don't find trouble today. Your sister could have been blinded while he shouted like onye ara. Your own father. Tufia! What if I had not come home at that instant?" She shook her head. "He is finished."

Still, Chuk turned back toward the house. With each step he took, Adaobi took another toward him. When she finally met him on the step, she stroked his baby face. She ran her fingertips over his scalp.

"My okpara," she began, "I made excuses. I ignored it. I didn't want to see your father's sickness. If I had let myself see it, I tell you, I would not have allowed us to stay in this place." She directed her gaze at his eyes. "We will go. We will leave this place today."

"What about Ugochi?" Chuk asked. "If we find out—"

Enraged, Adaobi shouted. "Find Ugochi for what? Eh? She is gone, oh!" She looked around, suddenly aware that they were being watched. That boy, the handyman's son. "What are you looking at?" she demanded. Her voice lowered. She tipped her face to her son's. "Ugochi is gone, dear," she said. "Dead like so many others from that time. My son, the only way you survive this life is to wait out every tempest, salvage what remains, pack it on your back, and go. Lekwala n'azu. Understand? Don't look back. Unless you want to see pepper."

She pursed her lips to speak again. But she could not convey the depths of death to her only son, her silly childish boy. It would be too cruel. The load was too heavy for such a child, a pampered American child, to bear. Death's knell had followed Adaobi all her life. Even on this side of war. The first half of her adulthood she had been barren. When she had finally conceived, there was one miscarriage after another. At long last, expectant with Amarachi, she had succumbed to nearly every imaginable complication, from hyperemesis gravidarum to Rh incompatibility.

When the ancients, interrupted by faulty telephone connections, had instructed Adaobi to return to the ancestral village and take part in a proper cleansing ritual so that bad juju could be scattered, so that Ala, earth goddess, could be appeased, so that the evil Ogbanje growing inside Adaobi could be chased away, she had objected. She had run from her father's home, without his blessing, to marry her silly foppish poet, Fidelis Ewerike, and the ancients had said their offspring would forever be cursed. And because her father had died before she had the chance to receive his absolution, they had told her a spiteful spirit would plague and menace her forever. No, she had decided. She would fight for this one on her own terms. No more prayers. No more potions. No more bound fetishes.

Years later, five-year-old Amarachi in tow, she had returned to her ancestral village to gloat over her victory. Fidelis had forbidden her from going, telling her she had nothing to gain, that the elders would find her actions reckless and insulting. When his refusal had gone unheeded, he had even knelt, begging her not to go, just as he had begged her to marry him those many years ago. But her heart was unabated. She had to reclaim all that was hers. Ultimately, they had settled on a compromise. To guarantee that she would not be careless, she must leave something behind, something she would move Heaven and Earth to return to. That something, at two years old, was her Chukwudiegwu.

Now, as she looked into Chuk's cold eyes, Adaobi wondered if her chickens had come home to roost. Had her son borne resentment against her? Had there been truth to the elders' whispers? A spiteful spirit had taken Ugochi before her life had really begun. Had it come for Amarachi as well? Perhaps Fidelis wasn't mad after all.

All of what was Adaobi's in this, her third life—those few possessions—was slipping away. Her first life: before war, a simple girl with simple tastes, her only excess, a love for hazelnuts. Her second life: wartime and the surrender; a something, not a someone; a thing that did what it must to survive. Her third life: this America, a man, two children. This, her third life, would be her final. She couldn't do it again. She couldn't bear another storm, gather the scattered ruins, pack them on her back, and go.

"Chuks," she said, "our ancestors are powerful. Some of them help us. Some of them menace us. We will find help, understand? I know of a haven. Follow me."

But he wouldn't. Instead, he reached for Amara's hand.

And she took it.

And so it was.

As she sat vigil at her daughter's bedside once more, Adaobi sang. The longer she sang, the more worn her voice sounded, like an old, holey T-shirt rinsed through over and over until it was just rags. She sang in Latin. Then in Igbo. It became one incomprehensible dirge.

Amara's eyes were swollen, but open at last. "Why do you sing if it makes you so sad?" she asked her mother.

Adaobi let out a mirthless chuckle.

"What is that song?"

"It's just a silly song I used to sing when I was a girl."

"What does it mean?"

"Let's see, let me sing it in Igbo, and then I'll try to translate."

Onye mere nwa n'ebe ákwá?
Egbe mere nwa n'ebe ákwá
Weta uziza, weta ose
Weta ngaji nkuru ofe
K'umu nnunu rachaa ya
Egbe oh, egbe oh

In English, she said:

Who made the child cry?
The hawk made the child cry.
Bring uziza leaf, bring pepper.
Bring the spoon for sharing the soup
Let the birds eat it
Oh hawk, oh hawk

Adaobi held back tears. "It's supposed to be a children's song," she said, indignant. "A silly nursery rhyme, for children. A mother is supposed to sing it to comfort her crying child, but in wartime, the children sang it to the mothers, so the mothers would know to lead the maidens into the bush."

"Why?" Amara asked.

"Silly girl," Adaobi said, exasperated. "To hide."

"From what?"

"You shouldn't ask," Adaobi said. "You should only run as fast as you can. And you shouldn't look back. Because if you do, they will *know* you, like they *knew* her."

"Whom?"

"Them."

"No," Amara asked, "whom did they know?"

"They defiled a beautiful thing," Adaobi said.

"What?"

Now Adaobi looked at her daughter, an eyebrow raised in a queer expression as her eyes drifted from Amara's face to her skull. "Amarachi, tell me now, why did you cut your hair?"

Amara shrugged. "I don't know anymore."

Adaobi shook her head and let loose a sigh like it would be her last. "You look so much like her. Yes, you could be sisters." Another sigh rattled her chest. "Sometimes at night, when you're sleeping, I think we're girls again, and I'm looking after her, like I promised your father when he joined the front. You know, they took me in, his people.

"When your father asked to marry me, my mother and father made a list of all the items he must supply for my dowry. *Ah ah!* When the nonsense boy came to my door knocking, his pockets were empty, yet his mouth was full of poetry. My father forbade me from accepting his proposal. If I could not be discerning of a real man, he would pay a diviner to find me one. That day, I ran away to be with your father. Then the war came. I never saw my mother and father again." Her voice broke.

Amara clasped Adaobi's hand in hers, squeezed, drew it to her lips, and kissed.

"I wish you were small again. Everything was so simple. Oh, you were a troublesome child, but if I told you a proverb, you would understand." Adaobi shook her head. "Nne, can you not see? War cost us everything. Your aunt paid the price with her life."

"Ugochi?" Amara said. "My aunt Ugochi?"

"I remember a girl," Adaobi started. "This girl was, shall we call her, 'spirited'—like you. Perhaps that is only a nice way of saying she was willful and disobedient. She talked back to her elders. She did not share. She ran when she was called to the kitchen."

Amara feigned a glare.

"But, in those days, a girl who had spirit was often nicknamed ogbanje, as this girl was. People warned me not to befriend her. But I did not listen. When the girl ran from her auntie in the roads, old ladies sitting on their stoops would curse her, 'A day will come when that girl will find herself trouble, oh.'"

Her face grew dark. "One day, trouble found us all. War came. All the men, young and old, joined. The women were alone, so they left the towns and went back to the villages. Only a few lame men remained. No one was there to guard the women and girls. Enemy soldiers began to take them by force. None of the girls were immune, including my spirited friend. She fought and fought, but when he took her by force, the soldier put a child inside her.

"I took Ugochi to a native doctor to medicine the baby away, and she vomited for six days. But one month later, her monthly blood did not return.

"She thought, *Ah-ah! This baby is here to stay.*

"In six months' time the baby began to show. She tried her best to hide her belly under wrappers and gowns, but eventually, the villagers began to take note. I pleaded with my friend to visit the native doctor again. The girl knew what would happen if she were to have the child. She refused. She was too stubborn, a disobedient, willful girl. She said that the child had chosen to stay—it was much more stubborn, willful, and disobedient than her.

"As she grew larger, people began to chant, 'Akwuna! Ashawo! O kwara iko! Prostitute.' They treated her like osu. No one spoke to her. They turned away when she was near. If she tried to eat from their pot, they spilled the porridge and ran away. In those days, there was so little food that waste was immoral, yet they would rather starve than eat from the same pot as this unruly child."

"It wasn't her fault," Amara interjected.

"At night when the others were asleep, I would deliver her food. And books."

Amara shook her head.

"In times of desperation, even the most cynical will revert to the old ways. The villagers believed that any child born of rape was bad luck. And surely any child born of the enemy was evil. The evil child growing inside her was an omen. She had two choices: she could return to the man who had raped her, so he could claim her as one of his concubines, or she could give birth to the child on her own and return it to the Mother of the Earth.

"Once she had placated Ala, the girl would return a virgin. She could move forward with her life as if nothing had happened. But to do this, she must make a journey into the evil forest, give birth, set the screaming infant on the ground, and leave it there to be reclaimed."

"To die," Amara said. "You mean to die."

"Yes," Adaobi said mournfully. "Babies who showed signs of evil or bad luck were taken there." She shook her head. "It was the ancient way.

"By the ninth month, she was ready to birth the child. We stayed up all night talking, laughing, and crying about the old days. I kissed her and watched her disappear into the bush. Then I slipped back into my room just as the sun was coming up.

"When she did not emerge the next morning, I returned the next day. And when, once again, she did not emerge, I spat and cursed the earth, but I faithfully returned. I returned every day for two months before I realized she would never return." Adaobi paused, gazing at her daughter. "You see, my friend had given birth, but she could not bear to abandon the child in the frightening forest. She stayed by its side."

In and out of the clapping breeze, a blur sharpened to reveal leaves shivering. Heat thrummed against Adaobi's temples. From where she stood, surrounded by vegetation, she could see a bent figure in the distance.

It was a girl's face, a girl whose hair was plaited. She drew her wrapper close to her body and soundlessly wailed. Her body was heavy. Her back throbbed. Her limbs hurt. She ached between her legs. Adaobi reached out to the girl until it was as if she had become the girl.

"You are but a virgin, Amarachi," Adaobi began, but something in her daughter's expression told her otherwise. "Right?"

Amara shook her head.

Mschww, she sucked her teeth and shuddered in disdain. "Amadioha, blaster this miscreant who has trespassed my haven!"

And for the first time in a long time, Amara chuckled.

"Well, he is at least tall?" Adaobi asked. "An upright, studious boy from Umuihunanya, Umuahia, Aba, or Ikwuano, no? Someone who wears spectacles, listens to Tchaikovsky and Femi, who recites the fabled origins of Ndi Igbo and a Shakespearean sonnet in the same breath."

"Like Dad," they said in unison and then they began to laugh.

"I hope you used something," Adaobi said, raising an eyebrow. "Remember your aunt's story."

"We did," Amara said.

"And you won't do it again?" Adaobi pleaded. "Until you are married."

Amara said nothing.

After a moment, her mother started again, more seriously. "Amarachi, I've been fighting for you since before the beginning, before you were born, before you were the seed of a thought—so, please, do what I say. Promise me. Tomorrow is Sunday. Tomorrow, Pastor John will exorcise you. I have seen him cleanse the defiled. To behold such a miracle! Tomorrow, he will wash away our sins in the name of the Holy Spirit. Promise me you won't look back, like she did." Her eyes alerted, like she had heard a sound. She turned to the window. All Amara could see were the whites of her mother's eyes. She spoke again. "Amarachi, promise me you won't ask, you will only follow."

"I will," Amara said, "but only under one condition."

"What?"

"That he exorcise the whole family. Not just me. Everyone, including Dad." Something wet fell upon Amara's cheek.

"Why are you crying, my child?" her mother asked. "Who made you cry?"

Amara wiped her eyes.

"Why are you crying?" her mother asked again. "Was it the hawk?"

Amara sniffled.

"Tomorrow is today," her mother said.

Amara looked down at her hands.

"Listen!" her mother said.

Together, they peered out the window at the turning sun, at the lengthening sky. Tires hit pavement, wind battered clouds, a bird's caw. Leaves. The crack of a tree branch. It wasn't so quiet out when you were listening. And they were.

Fireworks had burned into the early hours of the morning, and now the sky was husky with the smoke that hovered above the trees. Its charred scent was mixed in with the strong odor of perspiration. When they found Fidelis, it was through the help of the handyman's son, who had been up early cutting the grass. He'd tipped Chuk off, motioning in the direction of Fidelis, fast asleep, curled like a milk-fed baby under a sweet gum tree that bordered the Kostyk trailer. And so the two, mother and son, arrived to retrieve their patriarch.

Cocooned in the brush, Fidelis was shirtless, his slack skin and the hard gray knots of hair on his chest bared. Sounds began to swirl around them. A crowd had formed: children of their neighbors hurled abuse at him, their cracking voices sweaty with laughter. Adaobi anguished at the affront to his dignity.

Drawing her lips into a sneer, she waved them off. This was a mere annoyance, not the start of a scandal. Plenty of men absorbed defeat through drink. Others used the bottle to celebrate. A family man had too much to drink and lost his way home. What of it?

"Ashy man!" one child called.

"Pervert!" another said.

"Classy man," yet another bellowed in derision, turning his fingers out as if he were posh, drinking from a teacup. Settling on the proper slight, the others followed suit.

"Classy man! Ashy man! Classy man! Assy man!"

Perhaps their neighbors in their hand-me-downs, soaked and splotched with grime, reeking of sweat and Axe body spray, had never forgiven Fidelis for his haughtiness, for the British-sounding accent that rang of contempt, for the flowing ishi agu robes and starched suits that dressed them down.

Gesturing at Fidelis's holey pajama bottoms, a bucktoothed boy bellowed, "Underwear Bomber's daddy!" He threw a pebble. It struck Fidelis in the forehead. The boy tossed another. And then another. Before long, the others followed.

"Go away!" Chuk shouted, spinning around and around, trying his best to flick away all the boys and their stones at once. Cowlicks, flattops, bowl cuts, braids, and rattails scattered in every direction. The variegated shade of nations retreated, waiting until they were just beyond the border of the trees to resume their jeers. Then, gradually, they began to close in again.

Adaobi shrugged Fidelis out of his daze. Wide-eyed and frightened, he mumbled, a trail of words that made no sense at first until, as he repeated them again and again, they began to form: "I found her, nwunye m," my wife, "I have found her."

"No, Fidé, you were sleepwalking."

"I held her like this," he insisted. "I saw their faces, the rows and rows of girls, blanketed in sheets, bracketed by their grief, widowed by their agony."

"This is no time for poetry," Adaobi said.

"I squeezed her. How could I allow her to slip from me? They have taken her."

"Stop this, Chinonso. Ekwukwala! Don't speak." With each word, she shook him.

They were being laughed at. If not by these street rats, then their parents; if not by them, then the landlords and bosses, and moneylenders who had all turned their backs on the Ewerikes. Everyone was watching her family crumble before her very eyes, and they were laughing. "I said, stop this nonsense. Ekwukwala!

You are well, oh. You are pretending. Stop this sly business," she said, shaking him. "You are polluting the air with lies! Speak the gospel and shame Satan."

She sank to her knees in defeat. Her breath slowed. "God will punish the wicked man who has made medicine on my husband."

With reddened eyes, Fidelis probed Adaobi. "I have failed Ugochi, nwunye m," he said. "I have failed Amarachi. I have failed our daughters."

And then, Chuk stepped forward. He took his father's hand. The father looked up at the son. And the boy led his father home.

TWENTY-THREE

FIDELIS

Calm yourself, Fidelis told himself.

But he could not, even when standing upright, still the itch in his leg. Few men can endure the nightmare of being chased in and out of regret. Few men can forgive themselves for a failed promise, let alone two. Even a lifetime of atonement could not rearrange the depths of his disillusion, the uselessness of his battle-worn body still filled with its holes.

Fidelis felt the urge to look into the faces of 276 schoolgirls—delicate girls who played with baby dolls, plaited their hair, shook to pop music, devoured dime-store novels, laughed behind their hands—girls whom the world was fast forgetting.

Girls whom the world did not bring back. Girls who were and would be and had been his sister, Ugochi; his daughter, Amarachi; his wife, Adaobi; and the countless others whom he, a schoolboy, had cherished.

Long ago, Fidelis was a soldier. That is a lie. You never stop being a soldier. Wars never end, only battles do.

Fidelis *is* a soldier. A soldier must detect, calculate, attack. A soldier must reclaim what is his, and then he must protect it. He must close ranks. He must create a border. He must. He must. He must.

All night, Fidelis Chinonso Ewerike had walked.

He had started on Old State Road 50, his palms flat at his sides, his eyes occupied and private. He did not notice the glare of headlights, the blare of horns, the hurled insults as he brushed hands with death again and again through the night.

He did notice the reminder of a burn, a scorched scent that filled his lungs and made him think of ash.

Remember that you are dust, he thought, *and to dust you shall return.*

TWENTY-FOUR

AMARA

Only a few hours had passed, yet the abrasions had already begun to recede, her swollen, bulging orbs had retreated, and a sclera, flush with cracks and seams, had calmed. All the physical signs of healing were there. But when Amara looked at herself in the mirror, she was met with large, foreign, unseeing eyes. Did she blind herself? Or worse, could she be touched in the head, like her father? Had her worst injuries been inflicted by her own hand?

Stumbling out of her bedroom, Amara found the living room empty, and while the sky had darkened, a bright light guided her to the front porch. Only then could she see it, a blaze. All fires are instigated by a source of desire—lightning's strike, an incendiary torch, or something as blameless as a lapsed sparkler. In its greed, a flame laps and swallows whole leaves, shrubs, woods, without even pausing to chew; into its maw, glass, plastic, metal—all man's inventions—then, at last, man himself.

From where she stood, it was handsome. She marveled at its grandeur. How striking, how arresting! It was the season of fires, yet here was a fire of their very own. Neighbors crowded their doorways looking on in awe at what was, in fact, a bonfire. A stark white figure stooped before the flames. Amara's heart swerved. Could that be her father knee-deep in flames amid a dream? She ran.

Before she reached the tall albino man dressed in white but with dark shades, she realized it wasn't her father. This stranger looked like he belonged to another time. Just as she was upon him, the man swiveled around, meeting her with a rare combination of scorn and glee that started from his eyes and settled into a smirk on his reddened lips, and flung an item into the fire. Flames spat and popped in answer.

Amara's eyes smarted and her insides filled with smoke. Cheeks burning, she pulled back from the flames. "Who are you?" she asked the man.

He tilted his head, and orange shadows spread across his profile. "I am Pastor John. I have been called upon by your mother to exorcise your demons," he said. "This fire is a receptacle for all that ails you. Whatever touches the fire and burns is released from you." He held a box in front of him. Even in the dark, her father's labeling was prominent on the box.

"No, you can't," she said, snatching a piece of paper she recognized as her father's *papers*, the blue carrier envelope embossed with Ugochi's photo. "That's my father's!"

"Amarachi!" her father called. "Leave him."

Amara spun around, finding him in the street, he and her brother supporting her mother, who looked like she might split in half. Amara wanted nothing more than to hold those damaged pieces together.

"I gave it to him," her father said. "My dear, it is time."

Pastor John put out his hand.

Reluctantly, Amara placed the paper back in it. Each flare attacked the likeness of Amara's aunt as a child; Ugochi's eyes were serrated by the teeth of each flame, and she was blind, so she couldn't see; and she was silent, so silent that Amara felt she'd never recover. She felt a cry rising in her throat, and she held her hands over her mouth, suppressing its sound. This was her whole summer. The root of her father's despair. How could they just throw it away, like it was nothing?

As if he'd read her mind, Pastor John said, "An uncluttered mind has room for new memories."

When the last of Ugochi's visage had been consumed by the flames, he strolled down the steps and sidewalk to the street. As if on cue, Chuk and Amara's father released her mother. Pastor John hooked his arm around her mother's. She rose with him. Her knees buckled again, but he pulled her up and led her to the porch. The others joined them, and they sat in a line together on the porch. They sat with their chins upturned to the sky as the sky burst with light. Somehow, they had all missed it. It was Independence Day.

Still, Amara stood apart from them. It had been too easy. How could he just give up like that?

"Amara!" It was Maksym, fire extinguisher high in his arms. Worry etched his face as he regarded the miniature bonfire still burning in front of their unit.

Looking from Maksym to her family, she lingered, remembering her promise to him. He had waited for her. But he wouldn't wait another night. But she couldn't go now. There was too much left to fight for. Amara shook her head slowly. Maksym's face fell.

Then, she held up her hand. He held up his, too.

"So long," she said.

The following day, all dressed from head to toe in white, in the style of the cherubim and seraphim, the Ewerike family, led by Pastor John, stood in a line along the crest of the rise where Amara had once rescued her father, a day so long ago. They were to retrace the steps they had taken all summer and replant the seeds so that something new could form.

As Pastor John prayed and poured libations, the Ewerike family watched somberly. And then it was Amara's father's turn to speak. He was not exactly somber, as one would expect of a man mourning the loss of his baby sister. On the contrary, he bore a genial smile. He offered an affectionate apology for the simplicity of the burial, for the lack of the ritual cleansing and purifying of the mislaid body, for the absent palm wine and kola nut, for the deficient pomp. "She is only a girl, sef," he bellowed, "not some high-handed chief, and she died in a lowly, suspicious manner, so we will offer her the dignity of simplicity."

At the close of his prayer, the ground seemed to tilt, like the Earth was askew. Having lost his balance, her father staggered. Amara was certain he would fall. But it was then, as he balanced precariously, that she caught sight in the distance of a something lurking. She scanned the horizon. For a brief moment, she thought it was the winged seraph that Pastor John had spoken of moments ago in prayer. She blinked; it was gone.

"Did you see that?" her father asked.

Amara's heart thundered. She had. She felt unsteady.

But when she looked again, all that remained was a hot white breeze, a gust that whipped through the crowd, lifting their loose, blanched garb, caressing, cradling, rocking them, until finally, with her hands clapping, feet stomping, head shaking, and eyes tearing, Amara's mother exclaimed, "She is with us, oh!"

Her mother could see it, too.

Like that, Earth righted itself.

And Amara turned to find Pastor John silent and smug as he gathered his things to leave them, for he had summoned an angel.

Every year on the Fourth of July, the Calumet Rows hosted a block party. That evening, neighbors spilled onto the streets with foil-covered bowls and platters of tamales, empanadas, curries, and wats that they carefully arranged on picnic tables as they greeted one another through accented tongues. Everyone was there; that is, everyone but the Kostyks.

From their porch, the Ewerikes watched, Fidelis with one arm around Adaobi's shoulders, Chuk and Amara gathered at their sides. Under the evening sky, their neighbors began to dance, bodies dripping and swaying. Picnic tables and chairs were pushed away. The lawn filled with laughing Haitians, Ghanaians, and Cambodians. The Puerto Rican and Dominican wives joined the crowd, furiously beckoning their sheepish husbands, who hesitantly strummed their hips as they inched toward the center of the dance floor.

Its first notes lilting and melodic, Bob Marley's "No Woman, No Cry" began to waft through the night air. While the revelers danced, Chuk played it cool from the sidelines, shuffling and reshuffling a deck of cards in anticipation of a round of Spades that would never begin, and his parents sat sedate on the opposite side of the porch waiting. Only Amara remained distracted, sick with loneliness. All around her, everyone was laughing, but all she could think of was Maksym. She wondered if he was safe.

The first clicks and notes of "Stir It Up" commenced, and Amara's mother stood. She gyrated and bucked her hips slowly and rhythmically. Her body undulated with such ease that Amara wanted to grow large and heavy, like her mother. She imagined herself swallowing heaps and heaps of boiled yam and fried plantains, slick with grease, her palms lined with the sticky remnants of fufu, her mouth stinky from peppers, their scent lingering on her body. Amara wanted desperately to have her mother's heavy breasts and hips. She wanted all the heavy parts to fill out the space of a breezy gown. She wanted a large body that moved with the heft of a woman aware fully of its grace. She wanted to be *wise*, what her mother said when she meant a girl was womanish beyond reproach.

Her father's eyes were suddenly alert, and he stood as if asking a question. Her mother looked away and then she focused her eyes on him, and there wasn't any magic to it, but the crowd gradually parted, allowing them to reclaim one another. And that they did. Their bodies curled into one another, their limbs twisting and locking, every movement in conversation.

At once they were the bold young couple they had been so long ago, folded into each other. Hair styled in girlish plaits around her skull, cowrie shells shining like jewels, Amara's mother glowed. Slim and long-necked, a mischievous hand finding the sliver of exposed flesh on her lower back where her blouse had risen, Amara's father puffed his chest in pride. It was as if at any moment, a schoolmaster or guardian could descend on the youthful lovers to scold them for impropriety.

You should have seen them, Fidelis Chinonso Ewerike and

Agatha Adaobi Ewerike. That summer night, the season someone's boys stole everybody's schoolgirls. At fifteen, Amara once thought she knew of love and its crooks and valleys, its dangers and rewards, but at sixteen, she knew she had been a fool. She knew now that what she and Maksym did wasn't making love. This was it. Even though their clothes were still on, even though their bodies were standing upright, no one could convince her that her mother and father were only dancing.

Her father had his arm looped around her mother. He gently kneaded her back. Pressing her face into his throat, she leaned against him as she lifted her lips to his ear to whisper a secret. He squeezed her shoulder in response. For the first time, she thought of her parents as lovers, not just those who loved. Seeing them together, she imagined them walking hand in hand along the sandy red streets of broken stone in Port Harcourt, the city her mother had often described to Amara.

In her imaginings, her mother, wearing a belted linen shift and sandals, kicked up red dust with each step. Her movements—her hippy gait, her lips that curled with girlish laughter—guided Amara's father. Wearing his slim-legged blue jeans and long kaftan, his voice beckoned and teased her. As Amara watched them, she tried to imagine the forlorn face of her mother when she met Amara's father, the year before the Biafra War.

Gazing at the two, Amara could see the narrow concrete houses set in a row, high wrought-iron gates topped by shards of glass encircling them; the concrete walkways, goats and hens trotting in the streets; the blare of megaphones from church services every day of the week. She could imagine the cacophony of their sounds and Fidelis panting in the heat as he wiped away the dust on his grimy okada.

She could visualize her father rolling up his jeans and wiping down the parts of his motorcycle. Her mother had always said he was a motoboy, the kind of boy who flew down the streets, weaving in and out of cars and street vendors on his okada, so gracefully it looked like each pedal was a wing on his feet. This motoboy made her mother blush and preen.

When Amara's mother recounted these memories, she'd often stare through the ceiling with a look of ache. She would say, "You'll never know what it's like to lose everything."

If only she had been wrong.

Those summer days in her childhood as her mother lay in bed next to her regaling her with stories of her youth, Amara was always too tired, and too sweaty, and too itchy from mosquitoes to try to figure out what her mother meant or even to pay attention to the lesson that would follow. At the time, she'd tell herself that her mother was talking about losing keys. Though she knew it wasn't so, she didn't bother with finding the truth. Now, she was parched, but the bottled Fanta was warm, and it was dark out, and so she'd have to wait until light came before fetching another bottle from the corner store. She'd look for the truth. But first, she would wait.

Her parents' story was a true love story. Her father, still a schoolboy, went to war. He was captured and imprisoned. He fought for his life. He killed a man to escape. Her mother remained in the village with Ugochi, other children, oldsters. The village was raided. They were bloodless and alone. Except at night, two hearts were beating for one another. The surrender. A few years after the war's end, her parents reunited in London. They hadn't separated since.

Amara marveled at what it meant to come over, under, and through the pain they had endured. Seeing her mother as she was then, Amara thought of how the soldiers had violated her aunt Ugochi. The war had defiled not only their innocent nursery rhyme but also her innocent aunt, a girl of just thirteen.

Now Amara wondered if the soldiers had *known* her mother the way they had *known* her aunt. Had they raped her mother, the gainly girl who had walked down that dusty road in the linen dress, a girl, just on the cusp of womanhood, still shiny and new to the pleasures of love, not yet sullied by the caprice of heartbreak?

When rain began to fall in light whispers, the party continued. Smashing their heels in puddles, some even giggled from its tickle. Laughing raspily, Chuk and a couple of neighborhood boys, huddled under a tree, shared a bottle of beer. And just like that, the Underwear Bomber was no more.

The spinning world had stopped, leaving Earth at a fragile angle on its axis. Amara felt topsy-turvy with it.

Bottle rockets, punctuated by powerful booms, broke the night sky, splintering it with diffuse light. Soot rained upon the earth. Even palm fronds exhaled in admiration. When her father heard the blasts, he dropped to his knees, and Amara witnessed the flash of panic on his face. But then her mother folded her arms around him, pulling him closer. They were no longer at war.

Amara watched in confusion as her mother leaned into her father, who was chuckling. "What is it?" her mother asked.

He shrugged.

"Tell me now," she said, mildly irritated.

Amara saw it all in her mother's chest, like that deep sigh she had exhaled before telling Amara about her aunt. How could her mother convey the sense of loss for all the things she had once dreamed would be? In the time of that wasteful years-long fight, when she, just a girl, saw her future so vividly, didn't she imagine herself in her ichafu headscarf and embroidered blouse and wrapper, her beloved balanced alongside her, festooned in a lion-emblazoned ishi agu robe, grasping a hand-carved cane, wearing that red cap signifying his many accomplishments, as dancers danced, as mmuo masqueraders prowled, taunting and terrifying their children: Amarachi, Chukwudiegwu, and the others who had come first?

"Here we celebrate America's independence," he said, "instead of our own dear Biafra."

With lit sparklers leaving glittering trails in their wake, Chuk and the neighborhood boys weaved in and out of idling cars.

Her father sat with a puzzled expression on his face, as if trying to remember something curious about that 30th day of May in the year 1967.

"Then today, we celebrate Biafra," she offered.

He didn't reply at first. He looked out past her. Gradually, his eyes focused on Amara, sitting there on the edge of the lawn watching them. She shrank at his gaze. When he spoke again, voice soft, yet sharp, his eyes didn't leave her.

"Nke m, do not joke today," he said. "I am a man who has grown old overnight. I am a man who is fat with regret."

Rain thudded against the bent backs of palm trees. It was dark outside, the fireworks were over and the partygoers had now dispersed. Thirsty, Amara made her way to the kitchen. When her father turned from the counter and offered her a mug of warm Fanta, she molded her fingers around it without protest. The harsh fluorescent light stung her eyes as she warily eyed him. His face was stern. He sipped from his own mug.

His hands rattled against the sink as he returned the mug to the stack of dishes. He had always been potbellied, but there was also something waifish about him that she had never noticed. Was that a shuffle or a drag in his step? It dawned on her that her father had grown old overnight, or had she only ever seen him through the eyes of the little girl she once was?

He flung the window open, and she was awash with hot, damp air.

Suddenly she felt a fury. She didn't understand why. What could possibly be worse than those long days of internment in her bedroom? What could possibly be worse than the burn in her eyes? She blurted out, "How could you do it—?"

"—A man has the right to protect his belongings!" her father said.

"—To me?" she finished.

He groped the lapels of his bathrobe at his chest. His face clenched, a look both tired and angry. "If you had not scattered my belongings."

"How could I have known?"

"Don't spare the rod," he said reasonably. "This is what the Bible says. This is what I should have done, oh! I have never blamed you for your tomfoolery."

He blamed her. "Is that what helps you sleep at night?" she asked. "If you'd spanked me, I would have known better? This is what you tell yourself?"

"I never meant to harm you." Adam's apple bulging, he nodded and swallowed.

"But you did!" she said. "And then you left."

"Amarachi, I wanted to take you to the hospital. But how could I touch you, eh? How could I bring you to a bad place, oh? They would take you, like Ugochi, and never bring you back. What kind of father would that make me? You are too much like her, in spirit and demeanor. I could not allow that bad thing to happen again."

She didn't answer.

In exasperation, he hurled, "What is this trouble between us, eh? Should a daughter look at her father with such disdain? What have I done to deserve such dishonor?" He shuddered, speaking to himself. "How can a seed that was once inside my body regard me with such foreboding?"

Still, she didn't answer. He lifted a frying pan out of the sink and handed it to her. "Hit me," he said impatiently. "Hit me as hard as you must."

Stunned, Amara put the pan down. For nearly the whole summer he had kept her prisoner in her room. Her eyes had burned because of his booby-trapped documents. What could a frying pan do anyway? All that pain. All that darkness. The terror. A pan would leave a lump if she thrust with her full might, but that was it. Maybe the lump would diminish into a knot. Before long it would be a fading bruise. One day it would be no more, all but forgotten. Not like these, her memories.

Opening and slamming cabinets and drawers, she flung out salt, narrowly missing him, seeking the uda pepper.

"I threw it away." When she still hadn't stopped searching, he added, "I forgive you, ada. Now you must do what you must to forgive me."

With a sudden flick of her wrist, Amara had a knife in her hand. "If you want to even the score, if you're serious about it," she said, "then stop playing games."

"If you cut me," he said, "will the pain go?"

"Yes."

"Do what you must, oh." He turned his back to her. He slipped his bathrobe over his shoulders. It landed in a puddle on the floor, leaving his sad, skinny shoulders exposed through a ratty T-shirt. A baggy pair of boxer shorts rested sideways on his hips. With his back to her, she could see lumps on the backs of his thighs, wounds from the war, lumps she'd forever run her fingers over as they snuggled on the couch and listened to King Sunny Adé and Kenny Rogers when she was a little girl.

She looked him over. Where to cut? Where would it hurt the most, without being fatal? Where would the possibility of permanent maiming reside, without the probability? She could slice him, a perfect line along his kneecaps. For months he would stand straight because it would hurt to bend at the knees. Or should she slice his buttocks as his headmaster had once? Instead of sitting smugly in front of the *Nightly News*, he'd be forced to lie on his belly like a beached whale. How humiliating for a man of her father's disposition.

His death wasn't what she wanted. No, she wanted him to feel as she had. She wanted the world to slip away from him, to surround him with its depth and darkness. She wanted him to be both frail and afraid. And she wanted it to be at her own hands. As she ran through the options, she was silently pleased with how easily she could separate empathy and compassion from the task at hand.

She ran a finger over the serrated edge of the blade.

Back tilted sideways, her father waited. He let loose a sigh, a perfect exhale of breath indicative of tedium.

In outrage, she faced him. "Am I boring you?"

"As a matter of fact, you are," he said. "Do what you must, oh."

This wouldn't do. She dropped the knife.

He picked it up and handed it back to her. "Do this now."

"How is this fair?" she asked. "You're looking."

"I will turn my back if you worry about seeing your father's face in pain."

"Your pain?" she asked. "For you, I have no pity."

He frowned.

Flustered, she added, "You should be surprised, like I was." The room slipped. She sank to the floor. Her arms enfolded her body. Too staggered to cry, she sat in stunned silence.

Once more she ran through the options, striking the frying pan from the list; striking a butcher knife, because the only way she could do it right—to beat him, but not kill him; to leave him terrified; to launch the attack in surprise, so that at every turn he sensed danger; to set him up so that he stumbled unawares—was beyond her comprehension. He had splintered her faith in him so thoroughly.

His voice softened as he joined her on the floor. "My daughter, my ada, i mara mma."

"What does that mean?" she asked without turning.

"You don't know?" he tsked.

Amara wasn't amused.

"It means, You. Are. Beautiful," he said. "Like Ugochi."

Amara wasn't ready to forgive him for those long, lonely nights, but she was astonished at the unearthing of her hunger, like she had been starved, waiting her whole life for the sustenance of his warmth. She held fast.

"Tell me about Ugochi."

"Your aunt?"

"Yes."

"My baby sister. I shouldn't have said her name. Forget I said it."

"You know I can't. Not now."

His voice shook with anguish. "It's bad luck."

"What?"

"Looking the past in its face."

"But you can't turn away from the past either," she said.

"Very well." They rose together. He positioned her face toward their mirrored reflection in the window. Together they looked the past in its face. Glaring into the reflection of her eyes, Amara imagined it snowing in summer and out of a clump of snow, a dandelion emerged. She imagined that the light that was summer washed over the sky.

"Your aunt, my sister," he said. "You have her face. Her hair was low like yours. She had your eggplant color, your nose, your eyes."

Amara widened her gaze so that she could see the contours of her face, the sharp jut of each cheekbone, the uneven tilt of her ears as she angled her head from one side to the next. Now that the swelling from the uda pepper had diminished, she could see that these were the eyes of Aunt Ugochi.

"What does her name mean?" Amara asked.

"Ugochi is 'God's eagle,' the one who is meant to soar. She is His glory, His crown," he said. "When our parents died, I became her guardian. I was still a boy, sef. Fifteen years. She was my everything.

"When war came, when Biafra became a nation, I went to fight. Ugochi stayed with the women and children in the village. She was just a girl.

"'Starvation is a legitimate weapon of war,' they said. After the blockade, there was no food. Everyone was starving." He struggled with the words, held his breath, let it out full of air.

As Amara listened, her mind drifted to a faded image she remembered from years ago. It was spring break, meaning spring cleaning. She and her mother were sorting items collecting dust. In the attic closet, Amara had come across an old cardboard box, in it a faded *Life* magazine. A white-haired child in a white dress looked up with big, sad eyes. The little girl held the hand of a smaller child whose grim expression said more than any words could. Amara remembered asking her mother if the miserable-looking children were her and her brother.

Underneath the magazine was a faded blue carrier envelope. Her mother snatched it, admonishing Amara about her father's *papers*, shoving the box and all its rumples of paper back in the closet, high and out of reach.

His voice drifting into her reverie, Amara's father continued, "They didn't just starve. They were raped, they were mutilated, they were tortured. They left my sister, a child sef, with a child. And then they left them for dead. When the orphans, the injured, and the infirm were flown away by relief agencies, they took my Ugochi."

Amara blinked. "To where?"

"They were scattered every which way of the world. It was an act of charity. But they never brought her back."

Where had they taken the children? How many had been airlifted out into the world? How frightened her aunt must have been, surrounded by skinny, potbellied children, like her; sick and hungry, like her, with no one left to care for them. How scary to feel the air churn below as the helicopter lifted them high into the night sky. Imagine the panic in their hearts at the deafening roar of the propellers.

"I promised I would come for her when Biafra proved to be victorious," he continued. "I have broken many promises. And because of that, I never allowed the war to end, so I could tell myself the losses were not in vain. So I could keep fighting. So victory could find me. I didn't know my life is already victorious. I became the very thing I protected against. Dear, don't ever blame yourself as we have blamed ourselves. It is our undoing.

"Ada m, I saw. Finally, I saw. Don't you see? She brought us together. She has gone now. To join ndiiche. I know now. And I feel such peace."

There is a door in every abode behind which secrets are contained. In the Kostyk home, it was a small metal chest Maksym's father kept under his bed, alongside the collection of guns. When Maksym first stumbled onto the chest, he had expected it to be a trophy case full of the medallions and trinkets his father had stolen, believing them due to him, the unsung hero. Instead, there were copies of rambling letters he had sent to the Soviet consulate pertaining to his arrest and release, petitioning for his records to be expunged, for a statue to be erected in his honor so that anyone who heard his name would remember him as the patriot he had once been.

In the Ewerike home, it was a small box stored in the attic. A box filled with ramblings, poetry, and photographs.

Later that day, pen in her hand, Amara's fingers guide ink across a page in her composition notebook.

Ugochi's spirit is within her, woven into the fabric of her

constitution, like an extra set of spiritual DNA, a chimeric twin vested with Ugochi's unfulfilled dreams, longing, fears, aches, and memories. They not only look alike—there is that—it also explains Amara's restlessness and obstinance, and the inexplicable rage she so often feels these days. Knowing this, feeling it, believing it with all her might, a crack opens inside Amara and light filters in. All along it has been present.

Amara thickens the line.

Amarachi Uzodinma Ewerike. Amara always believed her parents named her "God's grace" and "good way" in commemoration of their migration to America; their young immigrant hearts and hopes had rested on her fulfillment of their America. Hands linked, her parents would have stood in the window of LaGuardia Airport. Hands linked, they would have marveled at the gray landscape, the great distance of concrete between home and here.

Amara flattens the line. She shades.

But now she understands. Her name is a joining of two outcomes—a moment of grace for the escaped prisoner of war and the women and girls whose lives were momentarily fragmented by a violation.

At the same time, Amara is the hopeful path for her aunt who had only begun the first leg of a long journey, an aunt who is nowhere and everywhere all at once.

She looks at the image. She smiles. It is her first self-portrait.

TWENTY-FIVE

FIDELIS

Long before the Biafra War, Fidelis Chinonso Ewerike was a boy, a schoolboy whose eyes remained awake at night. His faultless stare, even during his dreams, was a source of bemusement for his father, awe for his mother, and humor for his junior sister. She had only just discovered Mary Shelley and Bram Stoker, Fidelis's blunder, so that she both thrilled and recoiled at the mere suggestion of fright.

Arms straight ahead, she would sway from heel to heel as he studied under lamplight throughout term recess, meticulously scribing his English exercises. Later, while he'd doze on the veranda, she'd flick her fingers in front of his open eyelids, snap at his ears, push twigs up his nostrils, belting the refrain, "Fid-Dracu-lis!"

His grandmother called it an omen. *Night is for darkness*, she'd warn. "A small child should not insist on seeing what is not meant to be seen, knowing what is not meant to be known!"

He was born breech, and his top teeth came in first. It was an omen. So his grandmother took him to see the native doctor. Many times, his parents had narrated the story of his mother rushing home from her secretarial post for midday break, finding her son's void crib, the house girl wild and frightened, everyone a flurry of worry until the old in-law traipsed home late that night, bearing a burden on her back: Baby Fidelis, naked but a blanket, trembling, drooling, mucus caked on his upper lip, arms dotted with mosquito bites, and the crust of leaves and a smoky sodden clay the dibia had soused him in to make amends with Ala, doyenne of earth and cradle.

Tonight, his reveries are of his sister's elfin jests, his grandmother's warm back pulsing from her heartbeat, and the fragrant attar of the earth as the ground shook beneath her footfalls. Soil soaks inside him, filling his pores, and stuffing the gaps in his mouth, his nose, and then his ears.

No thunders shrilled that night; still, sleep was his enemy. Fidelis struggled to comprehend how the world had turned from his grasp so fast. A fire started inside him that night, but should it be no surprise? A slow ember that had been ignited the night that someone stole everybody's girls: schoolgirls, and his Ugochi, and his daughter, just a baby, sef, his Amarachi.

He saw these girls sitting at a broad table eating a gourmet dinner of several courses, beginning with the spicy suya he so hungered for as a child, and ending with a bubbling pot of his mother's Ofe Achara. They were dipping their tongues in the hot soup, biting off hunks of yam, sucking their fingers, swallowing big, hearty gulps, wincing at its spice and heat, a spasm that turned to laughter.

Fidelis reached out to touch them, these girls, realizing only after his fingers met glass that he stood behind a window on the outside. And they were sealed in. And there was laughter, but also a twitch of fear in their eyes, because a glass house can be felled by a pebble. And Fidelis wondered if he was the stone or the thing defending them.

He began to cry, a sweet foolish sigh. It was a wicked thing, this desire, like a hunger in him, for these girls to yield to his arms and hands and fingers, from all the world's rage, including his own, for he had once hated for them, and longed for them, and he felt perturbed in their presence, and at the same time so in love, because girls were a dear thing to him.

For a brief moment, every girl is his sister, and his daughter, and so he loves them with all his heart, even as they expose the broken bits that escaped him on his journey from a house called War. But now he is home. But not his Ugochi.

Who is a vision: Who is the mother of those beautiful girls. Mothers wearing red. Mothers baring their breasts. Mothers baring backsides. Mothers who are warriors; mothers who slay their enemies. Mothers who keep vigil while everyone sleeps. Surrounded by their husbands and their brood, holding up their banners, reminding all creation that even if the world forgets, they will never stop remembering Aisha, Hauwa, Falta, Hajara Isa, Kabu, Maryam, Hannatu, Laraba, Deborah, Saratu, Asabe, Margret, Yana, Saraya, Jinkal, Eli, Rifkatu, Maryamu, Hamsatu, Rhoda, Christiana, Raklya, Halima, Hassana, Ruth, Safiya, Serah, Aishatu, Mary, Victoria, Bilkisu, Rebecca, Zainab, Awa, Sarah, Godiya, Glory, Ladi, Rahila, Ihyi, Lydia, Zara, Rejoice, Sikta, Esther, Rose, Miriam, Kuma, Agnes, Patience, Tabi, Jummal,

Elizabeth, Suzana, Yayi, Kwamta, Grace, Nguba, Monica, Dorcas, Solomon . . .

"I bid you farewell."

At night, that night, Fidelis and Adaobi are rejoicing.

Fidelis and Adaobi are in love, and they are making love, clinging to the thing in them small like a fire, burning off all the bad, buoying it up and out into the open, leaving a crawl space that will stretch its shape into the system called hope, a complex arrangement of equations to be navigated with a fine, steady hand.

Fidelis and Adaobi are a forest purged of its darkness, clandestine petitions and prayers intertwined like locks of leaves and branches and duff, at long last released. A prescribed burn.

See this palm? There, open, porous.

ACKNOWLEDGMENTS

Much gratitude to the countless friends and family who have encouraged my writing from the start, and my colleagues and friends DeMisty Bellinger, Meredith Doench, Chielozona Eze, Lisa Kopel, Johanna Skibsrud, Rachel DeWoskin, and Sarah Newman, who shined a light on the glimmers of possibility.

I have been fortunate enough to develop this project in settings around the world that have broadened my perspectives on the human experience. Thank you, Sewanee Writers Conference, my workshop and its leaders, Margot Livesey and the late Randall Kenan; Vermont Studio Center, Madison Smartt Bell and Major Jackson; MacDowell Colony; Bread Loaf, Bakeless family, and Camargo Foundation; Ragdale Foundation; Brown Foundation at the Dora Maar House; Sangam House and Bronwen Bledsoe; Villa Lena Foundation; Jan Michalski Foundation; and Villa Ruffieux.

Even in these perilous times, many institutions continue to support the arts; I am grateful. Thank you to the George A. and Eliza Gardner Howard Foundation; Northeastern Illinois University and the Office of the Provost; the University of Arizona College of Social and Behavioral Sciences and Office of Global Initiatives; the University of Chicago Division of the Humanities, Department of

English, and Program in Creative Writing; the Nigerian National Museum; the National War Museum and the Ojukwu Bunker.

A special thank-you to Jill Grinberg Literary Management; my agent, Larissa Melo Pienkowski; and my editor, Kathy Pories, whose support has been immense.

Thanks to my sitter, Sydni Shavers, and the members of the meal train.

For my family, who have always championed my writing and my little blessing. I cherish you.